I0742811

Clocks & Boxes

Clocks and Boxes

The South Hertling Chronicles Book 2

BG Hilton

BGHilton.com

© BG Hilton 2018-2023 The moral rights of the author have been asserted. All rights reserved. Except as permitted under the Australian Copyright Act 1968 (for example, a fair dealing for the purposes of study, research, criticism or review), no part of this book may be reproduced, stored in a retrieval system, communicated or transmitted in any form or by any means without prior written permission. All inquiries should be made to the author.

ISBN (print) – 978-0-6454919-2-0
ISBN (ebook) - 978-0-6454919-3-7

Cover illustrations by Joel Tarling - www.joeltarling.com

Editing by Pamela Wildon at the Picky Bookworm - thepickybookworm.com

A catalogue record for this book is available from the National Library of Australia

Dedication

To my father.

Also by BG Hilton:

Champagne Charlie and the Amazing Gladys
Mysterious Aisles

About the Author

Australian SFF author BG Hilton spent most of his life doing jobs so tedious that his only escape was entertaining himself with crazy fantasy stories, and now he writes them down in the hope of entertaining others. He specialises in Speculative Fiction, Humour and Non-Fiction. He works in the education sector these days, which would probably surprise any of his teachers. His debut novel -- the Steampunk adventure 'Champagne Charlie and the Amazing Gladys' was published by Odyssey Books in early 2020. He lives with his family in Sydney, and consequently spends a lot of time in traffic. You can find him online at bghilton.com.

Contents

The Story So Far

Let's go back to part 1 of the South Hertling Chronicles, *Mysterious Aisles*. In the suburb of South Hertling stood two hardware stores, both alike in dignity. One, the fair Handy Pavilion (yay), standing in the South Hertling SuperCentre. The Pavilion was nothing special in itself – just a link in a corporate chain. But the people who worked there liked the place, and they looked out for one another. The other store was the DIY Barn (boo), which was an intrusion into this dimension as a force for evil with a really difficult to remember backstory.

For those who haven't read it or can't remember the many loose plot threads, here's how it ended:

1. The DIY Barn was blown up, costing the lives of supernatural sisters Angela and Sadie McGregor. Where the Barn used to be now stands a huge, creepy pyramid.

2. The shopkeepers of the SuperCentre approached Handy Pavilion General Manager Jasu Shan, asking her to be their leader.

3. Some Pavilionites escaped justice, but many more were arrested for their role in the carnage in Wellington Road.

4. Amongst those Pavilionites at large are: Sadie McGregor's protégé, Donna; time-lost scientist Fanaka; killer cyborg Nalda; ape-man Zorbar Ofthechimps; dryad and former baddie Gwen Harper; Gwen's lover/former accomplice Christian.

5. A crystal skull with phenomenal powers is missing. The rogue brownie who attempted to use the skull to destroy the world is likewise missing.

6. A time disturbance caused Axel Platzoff to die young, causing no end of problems for the middle-aged Axel who is somehow still alive.

7. Karl Wintergreen, a stationary shop proprietor and inveterate conspiracy theorist was told the secrets of the universe by the mysterious cowboy Buck Dusty. Buck is now dead, and Karl is quite mad.

8. Bruce (a robot truck possessed by a ghost) and Norman (a demigod) were trapped inside the Pyramid.

9. Fiona (a water witch) vanished in the confusion.

Characters

Alfred J. Pilbrook – The owner of a watch and clock shop in the South Hertling Super Centre. Short, middle-aged, balding, divorced.

Axel Platzoff – Reformed supervillain who used to work for the Handy Pavilion. Former arch enemy of Vincent Pizarro (they made up). A time travel accident resulted in the death of Axel as a young man, but somehow middle-aged Axel is still alive. C'est la vie.

Buck Dusty (deceased) – A mysterious cowboy and former Handy Pavilion employee. Agent of the equally mysterious Grey Barn. Betrayed Christian to the DIY Barn. Before being killed by Jasu Shan, Buck passed on his understanding of the universe to Karl, who went spectacularly mad as a result.

Brains, The – Artificial intelligences from the future. Control the Earth. Okay at drawing, if you don't mind extra fingers.

Bruce – An electrician who was murdered by a rival in love, then buried under the floor of the Handy Pavilion. The murderer was a concreter, so the burial spot looked great.

Bruce's ghost later possessed the body of a killer robot, and can change itself into a truck. Currently trapped in the Pyramid.

Captain Pete –Captain Pete has one arm and a mysterious past. He works as an aquariumist at Place O'Pets, he has some sort of past connection with Emma and nobody seems to like him much. Surprisingly, he was actually a sea-captain at one point.

Carol – Owner of a coffee shop in the Super Centre. Kind of hipster-y. In her twenties or thirties; it's kind of hard to tell. Tattoos. Piercings. Makes great coffee. Wife of Zorbar.

Cats – They're cats. Probably. In a way. Okay, they're not *not* cats.

Christian – A mildly disreputable former Handy Pavilion employee. Boyfriend of Gwen. Late teens/early twenties, kind of douchey-looking. Not a great guy, but at least he's trying. That's worth something, maybe?

Dark Brownie – A brownie, who turned to the dark side after being given a pulley (a far more serious deal than giving him an item of clothing). Very short. Dresses like Sam Gamgee in a Goth nightclub. Goatee.

Donna Coseco – An employee of Emma's. Formerly worked in the defunct Handy Pavilion, where she was the protégé of the late Sadie MacGregor, an eternal servant of the Light. Twenty-ish, medium height, kind of intense.

Emma Crispin – The owner of a shop in the South Hertling Super Centre that sells storage products. Short, middle aged, slightly terrifying. Looked upon with awe and admiration by her employees.

Erik Coseco – Donna's great-grandfather. World's greatest escape artist.

Fanaka – A temporal scientist from an alternate universe Kenya, who stranded himself in our world when an experiment went wrong. Late twenties, tall, handsome, intelligent. He is largely unaware that he is tall or handsome, but he will *not* let you forget about the intelligence. Boyfriend of Nalda.

Fiona – A water witch. Friend of Norman's. Former lackey of Axel's. Missing.

Gwen – Right, Gwen. (deep breath) Gwen is a dryad who lost her ears to an alchemist in an attempt to win the love of Norman, but then she got injured by an exploding deathray of Axel's and became the Phantasm of the Pavilion, with Christian as her minion, but then Ms Shan got her ears back and she kind of chilled out again. (exhale)

Jasu Shan – Former manager of the Handy Pavilion, now leader of the anti-Pyramid resistance. Lives in a secret bunker in Emma's shop. Partner of Mrs Liselle.

Jimmy Harrison – Owner of the Super Centre's music

shop. Formerly a moderately successful musician in the 1980s. Nepo baby.

Lena – Counsellor for the time-lost of South Hertling.

Mrs Liselle – Manager of the Super Centre. Girlfriend of Ms Shan. She hasn't had a lot of character development so far, and kind of resents it.

Mildred Po – Mildred runs a shop that sells telescopes and microscopes. She is also working on a rocket ship. The reason for this is not made clear in the text, but it involves her husband and it involves the moon. Maybe he is the prisoner of the Moon Men? Or maybe he ran off to the Sea of Tranquillity to avoid paying child support? Your guess is as good as anyone's, frankly.

McKinley – A fat, cynical cat who is overly fond of catchphrases.

Nalda Teheintausand – A killer cyborg. Hailing from an AI-dominated future, Nalda was sent back in time to kill the parents of the leader of an anti-robot revolutionary. Unable to find a sufficiently huge gun for the job, she settled for preventing the parents from meeting. She is now waiting for the Age of Machines to roll round, but worried that the future might be mutable. Girlfriend of Fanaka.

Norman – A knockabout lad in his twenties. Much to his annoyance, Norman is the son of Zeus and therefore technically a demigod.

Ron (aka Ronald Teerexbane) – A time-lost man from an alternate universe known as Nazi Dinosaur Earth. Not fond of Nazis. Ambivalent to dinosaurs.

Stavros Theopoulos – owner/manager of a kebab shop. My solicitor asks me to remind the reader that there is no evidence that this shop is a front for an evil secret society, and any suggestion otherwise is purely malicious speculation.

Vincent Pizano – A lawyer. Formerly the superhero known as Captain Stellar, Vincent suffered a mental breakdown and walked away from heroing. Works for an LGBTQ+ advocacy group, but has a side hustle for keeping the former Handy Pavilion workers out of jail.

Voyager - An otherwise unremarkable young woman who accidentally gained superpowers in the same accident that disfigured Gwen. Has saved the world at least once, despite not really enjoying being a superhero.

Woman in Laplander Hat – A mysterious woman who wears a Laplander hat. The source of the Watch and the Measure. Possible time-traveller, definite plot device.

Zorbar Ofthechimps – Son of a well-to-do East Sydney family who, for reasons that need not concern us here, was raised by apes. Tall, muscular, handsome, extremely poor syntax. Married to Carol.

1 Time

Alfred could tell it was almost midday, because the shadow of the Pyramid was pointing directly at the door of his shop. For a brief moment, he looked up into the burning eye in the golden capstone of the cyclopean structure and shook his head. He found that the best way to deal with the presence of a massive limestone Pyramid in a sleepy Australian suburb was to avoid thinking about it too much. Consequently, he sighed and looked down at the carpark.

It had been weeks since the Battle of Wellington Road and the rise of the Great Pyramid. When the gargantuan monument had risen from the ruins of the Mega Centre, it had initially been goof for business. But after the initial round of news crews, scientists and general gawpers had dissipated, people had joined Alfred in simply pretending the thing wasn't there and going about their lives as best they could.

They said there were people trapped inside, too. Alfred found this the hardest thing to think about.

A clock chimed – the only clock in Alfred's shop that was set to the correct time; more importantly, it was the only one which had the ringer turned on. Twelve o'clock. Usually, Alfred hurried to be by the door by the third ring, but that day he had the good fortune to be at the right place at the right time to see Emma Crispin leave Storage Universe to go to Carol's Café.

The same time ever day. Precisely.

"Morning, Alfred," she said, her grey bun bobbing as she nodded at him.

"Afternoon, Emma," he replied. It took everything he had to keep his knees from trembling as he said it. She passed him without so much as a second glance, and he returned to his store and the gentle ticking of the clocks to sit behind his counter and sigh.

"I've finished the repairs, Alfred," said Alfred's new employee.

"That was very fast, Fanaka," Alfred said.

"Oh, did I do wrong?" Fanaka frowned.

"Well, my previous repairman generally took eight hours a day to earn his eight hours pay."

"Ah, I see," Fanaka said, with a look that said that he did not. "I'll try to dawdle over my work in future."

"By which you mean, you'll take more care and double check all your work," Alfred hinted.

"Yes?" Fanaka said, literally scratching his head.

Alfred sighed deeply. He was a short, stout, pale man – sunken chested, and balding. When he'd met Fanaka, he'd resented the tall, broad-shouldered and extraordinarily handsome Black man. But it hadn't taken Alfred long to realise that underneath it all, Fanaka was even more awkward than he was. He'd warmed to the fellow after that.

"Just try to make your work fill the time available, Fanaka," Alfred said. "Isn't that how they did things…"

Alfred realised — too late! — that his words were leading to the phrase 'where you came from'. He had an intuition that words should not lead *there*, if at all possible, though he was a little uncertain why.

Fanaka didn't seem to notice. "We practiced a more cooperative form of economics in my timeline," he said.

Relieved, Alfred moved on. He went to the door, hoping to catch Emma on her way back from the café, but his way was blocked by the bane of his working life – a customer.

This customer was a tall woman with wild grey hair that poked out from under a crocheted Laplander hat. She wore an ankle-length patchwork coat over a baggy old tweed jacket and jeans and glared at him through the most intense grey eyes that Alfred had ever seen. Unconsciously, Alfred took a step back.

"Clock?" she said.

Clocks and watches were Alfred's business. The mere

mention of them should not have confused him quite as much as it did. He hesitated, and the strange woman's eyes grew even more intense. He became aware of his hesitation, which just increased his uncertainty. He swallowed, but his throat seemed very dry.

"Clock?" she repeated.

With enormous effort of will, Alfred answered: "Clocks, watches, timepieces. What are you looking for?"

"I'm looking for Mr Clock, the proprietor of this establishment."

"Ah, I see," Alfred said. "I am the proprietor of Arthur C. Clock's Timepiece World but, alas, my name is not Clock. I am Alfred J. Pilbrook. The name of my shop is… ah… it is more whimsical than accurate, I suppose."

"I see," the woman said, with a look that said that she really didn't care. "That is by-the-by. I have a watch in need of repair."

"There I can help you," Alfred said, and smiled as winningly as he was able. "May I see it?"

Alfred hoped to move the conversation from his threshold to the counter, yet the woman remained in the doorway. She reached into her pocket and withdrew an enormous hunter pocket watch with an elaborate design on its silver case. It was a thing of beauty. Real craftsmanship, not the usual Japanese tat that Alfred usually sold and repaired. It took an effort of will to hand it back.

"That's an antique, madam," Alfred gasped, shaking his head. "I'd recommend a specialist repair service."

"No, no, that won't do," the woman said. "No, hm, won't do. I need it fixed immediately."

"I'm not doing anything right now, Alfred," Fanaka said.

"There, you see?" the woman said.

Alfred tried to argue. He had a million reasons to say no. Insurance issues alone meant that he shouldn't handle a watch like that, to say nothing of the question of sourcing parts. But his resolve had never been great, and the woman's insistence and Fanaka's enthusiasm wore it down very quickly.

"Oh, come on, man, take a chance," the old woman said.

Behind her, Alfred saw Emma, her hair in a grey bun that seemed immune to the afternoon breeze.

Take a chance.

"Very well," he said. "If you'd come over to my counter, I'll get your details."

"Excellent," the woman said, turning to go. "I shall return yest… tomorrow. I shall return, yes, tomorrow. Yes, tomorrow I shall return."

"Thursday would be better," Fanaka said.

"Thursday. Indeed."

The woman left, the pompoms of her Laplander sweeping behind her.

"Strange person," Alfred said, handing Fanaka the watch.

Fanaka whistled. "What a beauty! If I didn't know better, I'd say finest Malawi craftsperson-ship. But given it's from your timeline, I suspect it probably has a French mechanism."

Alfred watched Fanaka, as Fanaka watched a watch. The simple joy on the repairman's face was a thing to behold. Alfred wished he were as fascinated by clocks and watches as his employee.

People always assumed that Alfred was a horology nut. They saw a fussy little man who owned a watch shop and just leapt to the conclusion that he was the sort of person who valued mechanical precision above all things. In fact, he'd inherited some money in his early twenties and decided to buy a shop. A local watch repair shop came up for sale at just the right time, so he sort of lucked into the business. That had been three shops ago. Three shops, two daughters... One wife.

Alfred sighed as he looked out into the carpark again. It was filling up, Pyramid be damned. After all, it was lunchtime and that was a busy time for people dropping in for minor repairs. "Put that watch aside, Fanaka, I'm going to need both of us on battery changing duty."

The big man put the watch away, with one last look

glance – a glance so longing that it bordered on the adulterous.

"Are you married, Fanaka?" Alfred asked.

"I have a girlfriend," Fanaka said with a shy grin. "Well, I say *girl*friend. She's about fifty percent machine, so…"

"That's good," Alfred said, hurriedly. He did like Fanaka, but sometimes he found it necessary to pointedly ignore his nonsense. "It's good to have someone. You know. Someone in your life."

Alfred half hoped Fanaka would ask him what he meant. But Fanaka simply nodded in a half-listening sort of way and said, "It's good to have people in your life… Oh, that reminds me: I need the morning off, Friday. I want to visit Axel in the hospital."

"Axel, the one in the coma?" Alfred said. "He's one of your Handy Pavilion friends, isn't he? A werewolf or something?"

"He's an ex-supervillain, not a werewolf," Fanaka said. "Jane was the werewolf."

"Much of a muchness," Alfred said, without much conviction. "Friday mornings aren't very busy, feel free to go."

The conversation seemed to end there. Alfred returned to his own uncomfortable thoughts.

2 Space

Emma loved untidiness. That would have surprised most people that met her. She wore immaculately fitted suits and kept her hair back in the tightest bun you could imagine. The jewellery she wore was restrained and tasteful. Her car was ten years old, but as clean and well-maintained as the day she bought it. Her staff at Storage Universe in the South Hertling Super Centre all looked at her with a mix of utmost respect and abject terror. She looked like the sort of person who said the phrase "a place for everything and everything in its place" more often than she said "good morning."

But she loved untidiness, sure enough. Mess, unruliness, chaos… she loved them all, like valued enemies, like worthy foes. She loved untidiness like a hunter might love a wily jaguar, like a master detective might love a criminal mastermind, like a knight might love a dragon. Oh, she'd fight her foe. Destroy it if she could. But that didn't, for one moment, make her love it any less.

The day she found the Measure, Emma arrived at work as she did every morning – an hour before opening. She fed her guest in the cellar, then cleaned her little shop from top to bottom. She had already cleaned it before leaving the night before, but that made no difference. When her staff arrived, she would make them clean it again, for chaos is a tricky foe.

The first of her employees to arrive was her newest hire, Donna Coseco. Donna was one of the refugees from the Handy Pavilion. After the Battle of Wellington Road, the shopkeepers of the Super Centre had committed themselves to hire as many of the surviving Pavilionites as they could. Those Pavilionites who remained out of hospital or prison, anyway.

"Good morning, Emma," Donna said, before commencing with the unnecessary dusting.

"Good morning, Donna. How are you this morning?"

"Tired. I've was up late trying to exorcise the fallen Brownie from the Centre. Unfortunately..."

"'Fine,' Donna," Emma said, though not unkindly. "When I ask how you are, you just answer 'fine.' If you're not fine, call in sick."

Donna looked guilty, which pleased Emma. Her job – her vocation – was all about guilt. For every person who purchased Storage Universe items to genuinely organise their lives and reduce clutter, there were perhaps another ten who were motivated purely by guilt. They looked at the chaos of their lives and felt that something should be done, so they bought drawers, hangers, organisers, bins… and then they left them some corner of their homes, still in their original boxes.

Chaos was a cunning foe indeed. Emma sold the weapons that might fight it, only for Chaos to take those very weapons and use them as its own.

After cleaning, the morning's business went well. In the afternoon, Alfred from the clock shop came by to purchase a little plastic cabinet with dozens of tiny drawers. He seemed to dawdle in selecting his purchase, scratching his moustache as he opened and close drawers. This lasted until such time as Emma was behind the counter, at which point he hurried over and put down his prize.

He opened his mouth to speak, but Emma cut him off: "A cabinet full of tiny drawers. I would have thought you had one of these."

Alfred blushed, as if he'd been caught out in a deception. "Several," he said. "But a watch repair shop can't have too many tiny plastic drawers. C-can it?"

Emma gave a brittle smile which seemed to wither the fellow even more. Alfred paid by card and slunk out of the shop.

"Well?" Emma said to Donna, who was hovering suspiciously nearby. "Are you going to tell me that I am cruel to him? That he is clearly keen on me?"

"No, Emma," Donna said. "I think if you really wanted to discourage him, he'd be so discouraged you'd never see him again."

Emma had not been expecting that answer. She turned to her young protégé with renewed interest. "You're perceptive, for someone so young."

"I learned a lot from… from my old boss at the Handy Pavilion," Donna said. "She understood people, in a way… Look, I think that there is a lot about Alfred that you like. His kindness, his competence, his perseverance…"

Emma rewarded Donna with her brittle smile. It seemed to encourage the girl, just as much as it had discouraged Alfred.

"But you know who you are, and what you want," Donna said. "Alfred has a good heart, sure, and he means well. But he lacks purpose. You don't want him to go away. You want him to find his purpose."

"My purpose is to fight chaos," Emma said. "Do you think I will win?"

"Of course not. But that's not the point, is it?" Donna said. "Look, Alfred is good at what he does. The trouble is, he only does it because he can't think of anything better to do."

"I wish he had purpose, you know," Emma said quietly. "I would think about it… If not for that… I only wish he had purpose."

Donna smiled broadly and went back to dusting immaculate shelves. "Oh," she said.

"What is it?"

Donna held up a small brass object. "Looks like a tape measure," she said. "I think that odd woman must have left it. You know, the one in the Laplander. She was measuring up these shelves when… ah… I think it was while you were at lunch."

"Put it in lost property," Emma said. The words came out of her mouth as if she were swearing. Lost. Property. In her view, people who couldn't keep an eye on their property didn't deserve to have any.

And that might have been the end of the story, had the afternoon been a busy one. As it was, it had gone quiet after lunch and Emma was at a bit of a loose end.

"It looks old," she said. The brass had that glossy patina of long use. There had once been a pattern engraved in the side, but it had worn smooth from long use. "I wonder if it's even metric."

Emma pulled the tape out a way. The yellow paint was cracked here and there, but she could still see that it was divided into neither centimetres or inches. The increments were longer than either measure – almost as wide as her hand. Out of curiosity, she measured her palm on the tape. Her hand was exactly one unit wide.

"How odd," she said.

"Let me try," Donna said. She measured her own hand. "Same here. Now that's a coincidence."

Emma pursed her lips. She took Donna's unresisting hand and held it up. She pressed her own hand against it, like a slow-motion high-five. She lined her index finger up with Donna's, and found that her hand was narrower by half a finger-width.

"Huh," Donna said. "So how…"

"I don't know," Emma said. "But with all that has been going on around here lately, I think it might be wise to find out."

Donna looked at Emma expectantly. After about a minute, Emma took an apple from her desk drawer. She munched on an apple as she read a catalogue about desk organisers.

Donna coughed. "So, aren't you going to investigate, or something?"

"I didn't mean *now*."

"Oh," Donna said.

3 Hope

On the first Thursday of every month, the Time Lost Support Group met at the old Scout Hut at South Hertling Reserve. In the draughty, echoing space, a ragged circle of folding chairs was set up. Everyone was seated, except for a thickset, olive-skinned man in a grubby military uniform.

"Hello, I'm Ronnie," the man said.

"Hi, Ronnie," chorused the group.

"I fell through a portal from Nazi Dinosaur Earth," Ronnie drawled in a Texan accent. "It's… It's better here in some ways. Not *quite* so many Nazis, you know? But you're not allowed to shoot the Nazis that *are* here, for some reason." He paused and shook his head. "I do miss the dinosaurs, though."

"I don't quite follow," Fanaka said. "I suppose there are dinosaurs and Nazis on Dinosaur Nazi Earth, but are the dinosaurs Nazis?"

"Some of 'em, I guess," Ronnie said. "I'm probably stereotyping here, but mostly the therapods. But most of the dinosaurs are just dinosaurs, you know? They're usually pretty apolitical."

Fanaka wrote this down carefully in his notebook. Besides Ronnie and himself, the group that night included a little white man with an enormous head who wore a tight-fitting jumpsuit, a blonde woman in seventeenth century buccaneer regalia, a Japanese man built like a sumo but dressed as a Roman gladiator, an Aboriginal woman who wore a 1960s spacesuit and Lena, the counsellor. A smaller turnout than usual.

"That's great Ronnie," Lena said. "Great. How is the job search coming?"

"Things are moving a little slowly," Ronnie said. "Turns out my degree in lemur husbandry doesn't open a lot of doors around here. I was thinking of maybe making and selling... uh... we call it 'bronto powder,' but I think you guys call it methamphet..."

"Aaaand we're putting that idea on the backburner," Lena said, hurriedly. "Who else has something to share? How about you Fanaka? How's Nalda?"

Fanaka was from an alternate past and his girlfriend, Nalda, was from some sort of apocalyptic future – but they made it work, somehow. Nalda didn't like coming to these meetings and only made the effort when Fanaka looked like he might sulk if she didn't.

"She's fine, thanks," he said. "She's working at the Disposals store now. It doesn't suit her. I think she'd have preferred something at the arts store, but they hired Belinda for some reason. Anyway, yes. I do have something to share. Look at this!"

Fanaka held up a huge silver pocket watch. "Observe. It is currently set at the correct time, 7.47, yes? Now I set it to… say… 5.23. I close the watch. I open it and look! It is back to 7.47."

Ronnie applauded, but his clapping slowed to a stop when he realised that the others were silent.

"Fanaka be no stage magician!" the buccaneer said. "He do be an engineer and physicist from… What was it? The Pan African Institute of Steampunk Technology and Wonderment. He be saying there's something up with that thar watch, says I."

All eyes were on Fanaka, almost hungrily. Time is a one-way street for most people, and like a lot of one-way systems, it is not uncommon for people to become lost in it. South Hertling had an abnormally high concentration of people from different eras and alternate worlds. The support group was there to help these time-lost people make the most of their new situation. Every other week they came to the Scout Hut to share stories and help each other find their way. Some had ties to

South Hertling—jobs, friends, lovers. And yet, there were very few among them who wouldn't go back to their own times and places if they only could. A magical watch in the hands of a temporal engineer… it gave them hope.

"At the present, I don't know what this watch can do," Fanaka said. "It is not my watch, anyway. Soon I will have to give it back to its owner. In the meantime, I can do some experiments…"

A groan rippled around the circle. "You've been experimenting since before the Pyramid went up, Cuz," the woman in the spacesuit said. "And what's that got us?"

"No firm results, ye swab!" the buccaneer bellowed. "Every time ye believe ye have nailed down the true nature of causality, ye be finding a whole tray-sure trove of conflicting data!"

"Well, that's true," Fanaka said, defensively. "Time's a difficult thing. Even if I established a working theoretical basis of time, there's no guarantee I could get you home. There's only one power source I know of that would be sufficient, and that's the Crystal Skull that was lost…"

"When raise our hopes?" the astronaut said. "Look, I'm sick of this bloody dimension. I want to get back to Awakabal Moonbase. But hope… hope *hurts*."

"Look, Fanaka is doing his best," Lena said. "Although

they do have a point, Fanaka. The purpose of these meetings is to come to *terms* with being lost in time, not necessarily to find a solution. Yes, I know you're an engineer, and engineering is about solutions. But maybe do that on your own time?"

Grumpily, Fanaka pocketed the watch. "I was only trying to help."

"When ye can help, then help," the buccaneer said. "Until then, still yer tongue, ye lubber."

"And no lubber-shaming!" Lena snapped.

For the rest of the meeting, Fanaka remained quiet – borderline sulking. When the discussion ended and everyone helped themselves to instant coffee in Styrofoam cups, he sighed deeply and slunk off to the door.

"Can I have a word before you go?" Ronnie said.

Fanaka regarded him wearily. "Yes?"

"You were there, right? I mean, when the Pyramid went up."

"Yes," Fanaka shuddered. "I saw the whole thing. I still don't know exactly what it was that happened. I'm told a man named Buck Dusty knew what was going on, but he's dead. And there are some people trapped inside – Norman and Bruce and possibly Fiona. They probably know something, but of course they can't tell us."

"But it's connected, isn't it?" Ronnie demanded. "The

Pyramid is connected to the weak temporal boundaries in this place. To this power source you mentioned. This Pyramid is at the heart of it all."

Fanaka shrugged. "Perhaps. I'm a scientist. I like to control variables – examine one element of a problem at a time. When the Pyramid went up, everything was happening all at once."

"But your gut feeling?"

Fanaka's gut said 'yes.' It said the Pyramid, the Skull, the Battle – perhaps even the mysterious Watch – were all connected. Obviously. How could it be any clearer?

But he said: "I am a trained scientist. My gut feeling is no more meaningful than your own."

"Well, *I* think it's all connected," Ronnie said. "I think that all the weirdness that's happened in this neighbourhood recently was like… like you know when a t-rex is coming because you see ripples in your glass of water?"

"Uh…"

"Or the local equivalent of what I just said!" Ron snapped. "I think all the strangeness lately was just the wobbles that preceded the arrival of the Pyramid. Perhaps if we…"

"Well, there you're wrong," Fanaka said. "I've been examining time around the Pyramid and it's no different from background time. Whatever caused you to come here, whatever is holding you here, it's not the Pyramid. But I'm sorry, I cut you off. You were saying: 'perhaps if we…?'"

"Nothing," Ronnie said, suddenly defensive. "Just thinking out loud."

4 Food

Alfred's usual lunch was a roast beef sandwich with horseradish. Most of his life, he'd eaten it on white bread with the crusts cut off, but his doctor had all but twisted his arm over his diet, so now he ate it on multigrain with crusts *and* alfalfa sprouts.

Today, though, he was doing a thing he rarely did, and that was eat out. He did this perhaps once a year, and never happily. The great comfort of a regular lunch is never having to decide what to eat – but he had left his sandwich at home in the fridge, so it was eat out or go hungry.

Alfred leaned on the counter of his shop and chewed his lip. There was a food court in the South Hertling Mall, but it was far enough away that he felt justified in ruling it out. And both of the food outlets at the Mega Centre had been destroyed at the coming of the Pyramid. That left just two choices: Carol's or the kebab shop.

The nice thing about Carol's was that he could easily order a roast beef sandwich on multigrain bread with alfalfa sprouts, which would certainly please him no end. On the other hand, he felt, in a disgruntled sort of way, that if he was going out, he ought to eat something different from his usual. He sighed the weary sigh of the tortured everyman, ground down by the mundane horrors of existence and trudged from his shop to have a meal that was slightly too greasy for his tastes.

As he left, he noticed Fanaka's girlfriend Nalda, and hurried on, happy to not have to talk to her. Nalda caused mixed emotions in Alfred. On one hand, when she turned up to share lunch with Fanaka, he found himself jealous that Fanaka had someone to eat with. But on the other hand, she frightened the ever-loving bejeesus out of him. He gave a friendly nod in her direction and hurried on without waiting for a response.

He took the long way around to the kebab shop, past the Gulf of Carpet-Aria and through the little gap between Hoonworld Auto and the health food shop. Going that way, he avoided going past the music store, for fear of a running into the proprietor Jimmy and ending up on the receiving end of some interminable anecdote about Being in a Band in the Old Days.

At last, Alfred found himself in front of the grim, foreboding façade of the kebab place. The shop had always bothered Alfred. It offended him as a small businessman that such a large building had been rented for such a small shop. The actual kebab sales area was just a little hole-in-the wall place, while the free-standing building it was embedded in was a square, two-storey structure made of cyclopean stone blocks. It was showy, expensive, and probably a violation of zoning laws.

The shop's owner, Stavros, was out front, chalking up some specials on a blackboard that was bordered with pictures of craftsmen's tools. He was a tall, thin, thoughtful looking man, of about forty. His hair was thick, but greying, and he had an intense look in his brown eyes that Alfred found disquieting. His employees, to a man, wore polo shirts with all the buttons open, showing off chest hair and usually a medallion, but Stavros wore a white business shirt and neatly ironed grey slacks that somehow never got grease on them.

"Alfred," Stavros said. "Don't often see you here! What can I get you?"

Stavros was right, Alfred seldom came by this way even for a chat. And now he was expected to make conversation... What about... Weather? Family? Did Stavros have kids? Was he even married? The man wore a ring, but it had a weird device on it that made it look unlike a wedding band.

"Hello, Stavros. Going to the Centre meeting next Friday?" Alfred hazarded.

"No, I think not," Stavros said, with a shake of his well-groomed head. "It's all gotten a little strange since... you know." He gestured slightly in the direction of the Pyramid. "Besides, I'm having some friends around that night."

"Do you mean here? Because sometimes if I'm driving past, I see lights —"

"What are you having?" Stavros smiled. "No don't tell me, I think I remember. Chicken yeeros with barbeque sauce, yes?"

The lunch rush was over, and there were two workers behind the counter, but still Stavros made a point of donning his leather apron and serving Alfred himself. Sighing, Alfred took a seat on the stool furthest from the other customers.

"How are the Centre meetings going?" Stavros said.

"Oh, they're going," Alfred said. "Fund raising for the Handy Pavilion people who are still behind bars, and pep talks from... you know who."

"She is a good woman," Stavros said, laying out sliced tomatoes with mathematical precision. "But misguided."

"How do you mean?"

"What if... now hear me out... what if the Pyramid is not our enemy? Your kebab, sir."

Alfred unwrapped the foil around the delicacy and took a bite of the soft, salty meat. It needed horseradish.

"But it's a huge, evil-looking Pyramid with an eye in the top," Alfred said. "That makes it a *bad* mysterious Pyramid, right? Almost by definition. I mean, that's pretty certain."

"Looks can be deceiving."

"Not *that* deceiving."

Stavros leaned in close. "Ditch the Centre meeting this week. Come by here. There's a few of us who aren't happy with the way things are going. Come and listen; maybe have a chat."

Alfred squirmed. He was not the sort of person who liked going behind the backs of others, but on the other hand he was a sucker for peer pressure. Perhaps that was why he chose not to have many friends.

"I don't know…"

"Look, we're not opposed to… you know who, and the others. We just think we should, you know, think things through a little more carefully. We don't want to do anything drastic."

Alfred sighed again as he felt his resolve crumble. "We don't want do anything drastic." Could there have been a slogan that better captured Alfred's soul?

"All right, I'll come," he said.

Stavros smiled and put a can of soft drink next to the kebab. "No charge," he said, and there was something in the way he said it that made Alfred want to go and eat his lunch outside.

As he stood up to go, Alfred noticed a homeless guy outside the door, shuffling along, hunched over in the remains of an old grey suit. No, not grey. That suit was probably white when it was new…

A shock ran through Alfred as he recognised the vagrant. Karl Wintergreen!

Karl had run a stationary shop and turned the SuperCentre newsletter into a platform for his various conspiracy theories. He had been missing, presumed dead, since the Battle and the rise of the Pyramid. Alfred waved to get Karl's attention, but the move seemed to spook him. A look of horror flashed across Karl's bearded face, and he turned and ran.

Alfred tried to follow, but a large man was entering the shop just as he tried to leave. By the time the doorway two-step had been accomplished, Karl was long gone.

5 Maths

It is a truth, universally acknowledged, that a single man in possession of a shovel may dig a hole in half an hour, but two men with shovels can take up wards of four times as long to perform the same task.

First comes the need to closely examine the area to be dug out. This takes fifteen minutes to half an hour. Following this, there must be a rambling, expletive-filled discussion on hole digging in theory and practice, possibly including a short lecture on the history of hole-digging. This takes a further half an hour. After that, a thirty-minute cigarette break is a must. Finally, the men commence the actual digging which – to the horror of maths teachers all around the world – takes almost exactly the same amount of time as if one man did all the work.

Donna sat on a sunny bench outside of the Barbeque Imperium, watching two men digging a hole in a garden area next to the carpark. She wasn't watching them in a sexy diet-soft-drink-ad sort of way. She wasn't particularly interested in either of the workmen. It was just that the men leaning on their shovels was the only feature of interest in the carpark.

Her attention was momentarily redirected upwards as a superhero flew overhead. After a moment's hope, Donna realised it was not her friend and former workmate, the superhero Voyager. She sighed and went back to looking at the workmen.

"Hey, Donna."

Donna recognised the voice but didn't look at the speaker. "Hey, Christian."

"Mind if I join you?"

Donna shrugged and gestured at the bench seat. Christian sat. "How's Storage Universe?" he said.

"Pretty good, actually," Donna said. "How's Barbeque Imperium?"

"Good. It's like, I get to spend all day helping people to have fun and enjoy their lives, you know? It's…"

"And how's *Gwen*?" The words came from Donna's mouth as cold as a mountain stream.

Christian fell silent for a minute. A workman picked up a shovel and for a moment it looked as if digging would commence. But her merely pointed the shovel at the ground for a moment before returning to leaning on it.

"Look, I know you don't like Gwen…"

"She tried to sabotage the Handy Pavilion."

"Yeah, but…"

"And you helped her."

"Look, she's…"

"And you remember what she tried to do to Norman."

Christian stopped talking, but Donna could hear his laboured breathing as he tried to control his emotions.

"Yes," he said. "I remember. I know what she tried to do. And I'm still with her. Okay? I'm still with her, Miss Judgemental."

Donna sipped her apple juice. "Judgement is what sets us apart from the beasts."

"I defend you, you know?" Christian said. "I defend you. You know why the others don't talk to you? They think that *you* think you're better than everyone. And it's gotten worse since…"

Christian trailed off.

"Since Sadie died?" Donna said. "You can say it."

"I'm sorry, I…"

"Sadie died, and now she's dead," Donna said. "She was the most moral person I ever met, and she tried to shed that light on others. I try to live my life the way she would have wanted me to, and if that makes me unpopular, well…"

The workmen were now deep in argument about something or other. Nothing is simple, Donna thought. Nothing is easy. Even the most straightforward things are just nexuses of complication and confusion.

Christian sighed deeply. "No one wants to talk about any of it," he said. "The battle, the Pyramid… The fact half our former co-workers are in prison and others still trapped… Everyone just avoids the subject. It's weird, I'd rather hear you tell me how many wrong choices Gwen and I made, than talk to the people who just pretend nothing happened."

Donna turned, and for the first time looked directly at Christian. She'd never really thought much about him, she realised. When first she'd met him, she'd seen him as nothing but a determined sales whizz. After his relationship to Gwen had been revealed, she'd seen him as nothing but her catspaw.

But he was a person. Sadie had tried so many ways to tell her that. That even the worst people are still people.

"Yes, Gwen did – or tried to do – some terrible things," Christian said. "And I helped her with some of them. There was no harm done. True, that's because we were trying to do harm and failing. But still… it's over now. We're all in this together. If you don't like me or trust me, that's fine. But we're all in this together so… Ah, I don't even know where I'm going with this," he concluded, literally throwing his hands in the air.

For a while, Donna said nothing. "Do you see those workers?" she said at last.

"Yeah. What are they digging? Didn't there used to be a

flower bed there?"

"When they go on break, I'll need your help."

Christian smiled. "Really? Okay."

Five minutes later, the two men shuffled off towards the kebab shop. Donna produced the brass tape measure from her pocket. "Here. I'll hold the end. Help me measure the distance over to the flower bed."

Christian took the brass case and walked over to the abandoned shovels, unspooling the tape as he went. When he got to the bed, he called out, "One brownielength… What? What's a brownielength?'

"Grab a shovel and start digging, right at the point you measured to."

Christian only hesitated for a moment before starting to dig. Donna walked over to join him. This time the maths teachers were right, and together they dug faster than one person digging alone.

"This is weird," Christian said.

"We do a lot of weird, here."

"True."

Soon, there was a small hole, perhaps deep enough to plant a sapling. Donna measured to the bottom.

"Half a browniedepth," she said. "Keep digging."

After a few more shovelfuls of earth, Christian gasped as

he hit something made of black cloth.

"Keep digging."

A few shovelfuls later, and the hole started shouting. "Stop shovelling! It hurts! Look, you got me. I'm coming out."

Something squirmed underground, and the cloth-covered object rose in the hole. Donna and Christian stood back as it broke the surface, revealing itself to be a small head clad in a black hat. Some more struggling, and the head was joined by black-clad arms, which struggled to pull a torso and legs to the surface. The little man brushed himself off. He stood a little over a metre tall, and he wore a black coat, waistcoat, knee-breeches and hat, and his tiny face was adorned by a wee little goatee:

"So, you found me. Clever. Clever!"

"What the Hell is this thing?" Christian asked.

"A Dark Brownie," Donna said.

"Sounds delicious. Like it would go nice with a cup of coffee."

Donna frowned at him. "No, he's a brownie. They're helpful household spirits – usually. They help with chores around the home in return for food. If you give them an item of clothing, they leave forever. And if you give them a pulley, they turn completely evil."

"Quite so, Miss Saheco, quite so." The brownie stroked

his moustache. "You know, we are not so different, you and I."

"Oh, shut the fuck up. Christian, use that shovel. Knock him out."

"Really? Didn't you just now tell me off for being too evil?"

"NOW."

Christian shrugged and whacked the Brownie on the head. The Brownie's little buckled hat crumpled under the blow, and the little man fell over.

"How did you know the Brownie was hiding underground?" Christian said.

"That's where evil brownies hide," Donna said, "But their presence kills flowers, so that's how I knew he was here."

"And how come his eyes turned into little 'X's when he fell unconscious?"

"Now that *is* a mystery," Donna shrugged. "Come on, help me get him back to Storage Universe. You-know-who will have some questions for him."

6 Cat

As she did every Tuesday, Emma stopped by the Place O'Pets to pick up supplies. She bustled in, studiously avoiding Captain Pete, the one-handed aquariumist. She made her way past displays full of flea collars, chew toys and lizard dentures, to the food section. There she filled her trolley and took it directly to the counter.

At the till stood the imposing, muscular figure of Zorbar Ofthechimps, husband of Carol from the coffee shop and semi-domesticated ape-man. He scratched at his lime green Place O'Pets polo shirt, as if he wanted to tear it apart, but managed a genuine smile for Emma.

"Zorbar have question, Miss Crispin," he said. "You buy dog food. Zorbar smell dog. You buy cat food. Zorbar no smell cat. Why that?"

Emma's eyebrows shot up towards her severe hairline. "You can smell the pets of individual customers on them? Even in the middle of a petshop?"

Zorbar's scarred brow crinkled. "Miss Crispin *not* smell like that?"

"Oh, Zorbar!" Emma chuckled. "This cat is a very rare breed."

"Zorbar see. Also, Zorbar visit prison tomorrow. See Pavilion friends. Have to tell them Norman and Bruce still trapped in Pyramid. Bad news. If Miss Crispin have happy message…"

Emma shook her head and Zorbar's face fell. Emma waved and headed back out of the shop. "Captain Pete," she said icily on her way out.

"Emma," Pete said, with just as much frost.

She loaded the dog food in her car. Carrying the cat food, she made her way to a little alley between Carpets! Carpets! Carpets! And the Perforated Eardrum Hi-Fi. She peeled the lid off a can of cat food, placed it on the ground and took a step backwards.

A little later, something came out of a crevice in the wall. It looked a little like a cat – a little. It had four legs, a tail and a head with triangular ears. There the resemblance ended. The creature was a solid lemon-yellow colour, with a thick, round body. Its eyes were enormous, perhaps a quarter of the size of its round head, and half closed in a disdainful squint. It walked up to the food on all fours, then it stood on its hind legs and picked up the can with its front paws. It opened its mouth unfathomably wide, tipped the contents of the can right in and swallowed.

"Well, good afternoon," Emma said.

"It is now," said the thing that might have been a cat, before licking the inside of the can.

"Zorbar was wondering why he couldn't smell cat on me," Emma said.

"Yeah, well, I don't sit in laps, lady," the cat said. It extended one of the claws on its right paw and began picking its teeth.

Emma gave her brittlest smile. "So, do you have something for me? Or are you just going to spit out catchphrases that stopped being funny years ago?"

The cat sighed. "I dislike weekdays – and quite deeply, at that," he muttered. "Okay, I managed to sneak into the meeting at the kebab shop. It was pretty low-key. I think they're trying to recruit some new people, so they toned down the invocations of elder gods and so on."

"New people? Such as?"

"Rick from the sports shop. Gloria from the hobby store. Oh, and Alfred."

A pang of pain struck Emma in her perfectly organised heart. Alfred. He was sweet in his unfocused way... Too unfocused at the moment, but perhaps... Perhaps he had potential...

"Internal monologues on your own time, lady," the cat said.

Emma glared at the creature, which at least had the decency to look embarrassed.

"What do you think the chances are we could get one of our people in there?"

The cat rolled its enormous eyes. "Your people. I just work here. But yeah, I know what you mean. You won't get any of the Handy Pavilion people into those secret meetings, no way. Stavros is picking his marks carefully. On the edge of your little resistance operation… slightly dithery… A little slow, no offence to your cardigan-clad, would-be beau. Stavros won't try to recruit someone committed like you or Donna."

Emma pursed her lips. Much as she hated to admit it, the cat had a point. Anyone who was loyal enough to be trusted as an informant probably wouldn't get through the door of the kebab shop.

"I'll have to ask a friend."

"You mean Jasu Shan, the former manager of the Handy Pavilion, who's hiding in a secret basement under your store?" the cat smirked.

"Yes, McKinley," Emma said, raising an eyebrow. "I know that you know. You'll have to try harder than that to shock me."

McKinley the 'cat' glared at her and put its paw on what would have been its hip, if its body hadn't been a boneless, ovoid shape. For the hundredth time, Emma wondered at the thing's anatomy. It seemed to be male, and yet it had no trace of visible external genitalia. Even more disturbing was the fact that, even though it was constantly eating, it appeared to have no anus.

"Okay, I have stuff to do," McKinley said, turning to leave. "Cat stuff. You wouldn't get it."

"Yeah, hang in there," Emma said.

The cat looked back once, did a double take, then vanished around a corner with a look of pure contempt. Emma walked back towards Storage Universe. A dread was building in her heart. She was still not sure what Stavros Theopoulos was up to. Was he working for the Pyramid, or did he have some other agenda? Unfortunately, there would be no way to get a double agent into his group.

The only chance would be to turn someone who was already there.

And that, like it or not, meant talking to Alfred. Worse, it meant manipulating Alfred. Emma didn't like the idea, but there was really no way for her *not* to manipulate him. Alfred was so besotted with her that anything she asked him to do would probably be tainted by that. She might go to him as a friend and a colleague, but there was little chance he'd see it in those terms.

There was one other option. She could get someone else to recruit him. Who was the one person least likely to make Alfred's heart race? Across the carpark, the door to the Disposals store opened. Emma smiled as she saw her answer.

7 Help

The day was bright, so Fanaka had to press his face against the front window of Karl Wintergreen's stationary shop to see inside. No much had changed from the last time he looked. Perhaps that the film of dust that covered the shelves had grown deeper? Otherwise, no change.

Fanaka had never been a particular friend of Karl's, but his mind troubled him whenever he thought about the man's disappearance. And now, Alfred said he'd seen Karl around...

It meant something. Fanaka was a scientist. Discrepancies and anomalies were, to him, like a pea beneath a mattress to a princess. He grimaced at the empty shop, shook his head, and carried on his way to his destination – Stars in Their Eyes Optics next door.

The proprietor, Mildred Po, was with a customer, so Fanaka passed the time examining a reflecting telescope by the door. The fellow finished his business, turned for the door, and saw Fanaka standing there. He hesitated for a second. Fanaka smiled politely, the man gave an unfriendly smile in return and hurried out, clutching his purchase a little tightly to his body.

"Odd people in your timeline, Mildred," Fanaka shrugged.

"The world is as it is," Mildred shrugged. "Like it or not. What can I do for you, Fanaka?"

Mildred was a short woman in her mid-fifties. Her shop was a gleaming white room full of telescopes and microscopes, but she dressed in black velvet clothes and heavy eye makeup that made her look as if she ran an occult bookstore.

"Are you busy? I have something slightly unusual that I am studying, and I wondered if I might make use of your best microscope."

There was one other person in the shop; a young woman of perhaps eighteen who sat on a stool, playing with her phone. Mildred shouted at the woman in Cantonese. The young woman shrugged and did not look up.

"Follow me," Mildred said, leading Fanaka into the back room. The storage area was bigger than the showroom itself, though it wasn't overly full of telescopes. It was a cool, concrete-walled room lit by buzzing fly-specked fluorescent tubes. One wall was lined with telescope boxes and a small optical workbench. The rest of the area was a large workshop, in the middle of which was a conical shape under a tarpaulin.

"Use that one," Mildred said, pointing to a large device on a shelf above the optical bench. "I've stronger ones if you need them, but they'll take some setting up."

Fanaka took the microscope down, placed the watch on the scanner and played with the controls. It had been over a week and the watch's strange owner had still not been back to collect her gleaming treasure.

"I've been working on those calculations you made," Mildred said, as Fanaka adjusted the lenses.

"Helpful?"

"Somewhat, yes. But imprecise."

"There are too many variables involved. Precision can't be conjured from thin air…"

"Precision is more important than ever, Fanaka," Mildred said, with a wave of the finger. "That's what you never understand. It is in rough seas that the hand on the tiller must be firmest."

Fanaka rolled his eyes. "If you say so. I'm just glad I could help with your… Oh! Goodness me! Would you look at that?"

Mildred pulled her hair into a ponytail and looked into the eyepiece. "My word. That is extraordinary. I've never seen metal milled so smooth. It's almost…"

She stopped mid-sentence and picked up the watch. "How old is this?" she said. "It's silver, so it's soft. It can't possibly have remained this unscratched through any significant use. Yet it doesn't look new. How old is it?"

Fanaka gently took the watch from Mildred and returned it to the velvet bag he'd been keeping it in. "I'm not quite sure. I'm still trying to identify the maker's mark here. The style of the watch inside and out suggests early-nineteenth century. French manufacture."

"A reproduction?"

"In my experience, reproductions tend to have modern clockwork or an electronic mechanism. This is authentic inside and out."

Mildred hunched her shoulders and half closed one eye. "'Well, I tell ya, dat's a conundrum,'" she said.

Fanaka stared at her blankly.

"My Columbo impression is wasted on you, isn't it?" she said.

"I'm sure it's quite good," Fanaka said. "This watch… I tell you, it's baffling. I just don't know what I'm going to say to my boss."

"That's quite a good Colombo impression yourself."

"Is it?" Fanaka sighed. "That's nice. Look, the watch just *feels* wrong. That's no help, is it? We're scientists, we don't rely on feelings."

"Feelings are electrochemical impulses in the brain," Mildred said. "That means that they are part of the objective universe, and we should observe predictable patterns in them in case they are of use in our studies. Or in other words," she added before Fanaka could object, "have you felt anything like this before?"

Fanaka furrowed his brow. Had he? Yes. Yes, when he was handling…

"The glass Skull!" he said.

The Skull was an artifact that had lain under the Handy Pavilion. Christian's girlfriend, Gwen, had somehow tapped into the power of the Skull and used it to create a pocket dimension. After the dimension collapsed, the Skull had been found under the bathroom floor by a couple of plumbers. Christian had taken possession of the Skull, hoping to rescue Gwen. Unaware of this, Fanaka had borrowed the Skull to use as the power source for a super-weapon. The Skull had not been seen since the Battle.

"It feels just like the Skull," Fanaka continued. "Only the Skull was an intrusion into our universe as a polydimensional object of unfathomable…"

Fanaka looked down at the velvet bag that he held in his hand. The Skull had been a source of unfathomable power. Misused, the thing had almost cracked open the universe. If this watch was remotely similar… But no, that made no sense. Why would someone simply *give* such a powerful artifact to a humble watch shop? The Skull had been discovered accidentally, but the planting of the Watch had to be deliberate.

Perhaps he should ask Axel Platzoff?

No! No. The mere thought of talking to Axel after everything that had happened… Just thinking about Axel made his head hurt. No, there had to be another way to find out what was going on.

Fanaka noticed Mildred was looking at him with concern, and realised that he'd been staring into space for the past few minutes.

"How's your husband?" he said, desperate to change the subject.

"I'll know when I finish building that rocket," Mildred said, gesturing at the tarpaulin. "If it works, I can build a scaled-up version of it suitable to get me to the moon…"

"Ah, yes, yes, of course," Fanaka said. "I'll see myself out."

8 Ghosts

Past

"Is Fanaka here?"

Alfred looked up from his laptop. Ostensibly, he was balancing his shop's books, but actually, he was worrying very hard about things he had heard at the kebab shop the night before. He pulled his thoughts to the present and took in the customer – a thirty-ish white man, in a camouflage jacket over a t-shirt, who spoke in an accent Alfred couldn't place. "Today's Fanaka's day off," he said. "If you need a watch repaired, you can leave it with me. I'll give it to him tomorrow."

The man scratched his head. This gesture caused his jacket to fall open, so Alfred could see his t-shirt more clearly. It showed what looked like a feathered velociraptor in a pickelhaube helmet, one tiny arm held up in a Roman salute. This image was framed by a circle and featured a line through the middle.

"No... no... I just need a clock," the man said. "Thought I'd say hi while I'm here."

"A clock? Well, you've certainly come to the right place, ha ha. What sort of clock?"

The stranger's brow furrowed in concentration. "Certainly not for a time bomb," he said.

"I should hope not," Alfred replied.

"Ha ha."

"Ha ha."

"Nothing untoward at all, in fact."

Alfred rubbed his moustache. "So, what *is* it for?"

"I have an employment job," the man said. "For work. I need an inexpensive battery powered alarm clock. It should run on a minimum of five milliamps. Oh, and the alarm needs to be worked by a green wire and a red wire. Very important."

Alfred squinted. "Are you sure you don't need this for a time bomb?"

"Oh, most definitely."

"Because I can't help but notice the smell of diesel fuel and fertiliser that…"

"I am on trial, here!" the customer said. "I have no time for these wild accusations. Hearsay! Prejudicial! Good day, sir!"

With that, the stranger swept out of the shop. Alfred considered calling the police, but he remembered what Stavros had said. Keep your head down, Alfred. Alfred hadn't been sure about a lot of things that had been discussed at the kebab store, but that had made the most sense. Keep your head down.

Present

Around lunchtime, another stranger came by. He was a pale young man of medium height in a BBQ Imperium apron. Alfred had seen him around the Super Centre before, and had always been stung by a pang of jealously, when he'd seen the handsome young fellow strutting about. These days, however, the fellow walked with the more cautious step of a man in a long-term relationship – which honestly didn't make Alfred much less jealous.

"Hey, mate," the young man said. "I'm looking for a…"

The man took a crumpled piece of paper from his pocket and smoothed it out. "An orichalcum clock?"

Alfred scratched at the little wisp of hair at the top of his bald head. "Don't believe I know that brand."

"It's not a brand, I guess," the BBQ man said. "It's more like a mineral. It's like how a quartz clock keeps time off the natural vibration frequency of quartz. Only this one runs off an occult mineral that vibrates at the speed of magic. We need it to correctly time an exorcism. "

Alfred ran his tongue over his teeth, while he tried to decide just how much of what he'd just heard should be allowed to penetrate his brain.

"I see," he said. "Well, as I say, I don't think I have one of those."

The young man examined his paper. "A mithril or unobtanium clock will do in a pinch," he said.

"Well, I don't know what to say…" Alfred began. "I don't think I have… Wait, did you say an *uno*btanium clock?"

"That's right."

"Oh, I think I might have one of those."

Alfred unlocked a drawer behind his counter and took out a cardboard box. "Got this as part of a job lot from an importer that closed down."

As Alfred opened the box and the shop's fluorescent lights buzzed and dimmed. From outside in the SuperCentre, he could hear the howling of dogs.

"I don't display this anymore," he said. He reached into the box and took out a grey-green plastic object in the shape of a misshapen male figure with the head of a monkfish. It had a clock in its distended belly, with weird Gothic numerals around the edge. The man in the BBQ apron recoiled at the sight of it, crossing himself as Alfred gave the clock a quick wipe with a microfiber cloth.

"I had it on the shelf by the door for a while, but no one wanted it. In fact, it seemed to be turning some customers away. Don't quite know why. I mean, I'm not overly partial to novelty clocks myself, but I think that's overreacting a bit."

"Doesn't it bother you at all?" the BBQ man whispered, his eyes fixed on the hideous timepiece.

"Not as much as *that* thing," Alfred said, gesturing at a cat-shaped clock with a tail-shaped pendulum. "Brrrrrrr."

The BBQ man looked from the unobtanium clock to the cat clock, then back to the unobtanium clock. He glanced pointedly at the thin trail of green smoke that rose from the microfiber cloth that was gently melting on the counter.

"Whatever, mate," he shrugged. "How much for the clock of doom?"

The young man paid for the clock, and made Alfred put it back in the box himself, before departing. Alfred watched him go.

Exorcism. That was weird. Like one of those stupid ghost hunting shows his youngest daughter insisted on watching.... Alfred shrugged. It didn't matter. Just keep your head down, Alfred. Get through the day.

Future

Just as Alfred was getting ready to close, the door swung open again. In strode Fanaka's girlfriend, Nalda. Alfred swallowed hard. Nalda Teheintausant was a tall, solidly built woman, who habitually wore sunglasses and a leather jacket, and carried a cricket bag that clanked ominously when she walked. She worked at the disposals store. A substantial fraction of her customers were in love with her, a substantial fraction wanted to beat her at arm wrestling, and there was a considerable crossover between these two fractions. She glared at Alfred from behind her shades, and his bowels began to quake.

"Are you Alfred Pilbrook?"

"You know I am, Nalda," Alfred said. "We've met several times."

"Identity acknowledged. You are an associate of Stavros Theopoulos being?"

"Well, I know the man."

"Confession secured."

"What? Confession?"

Nalda crossed the floor and stood directly in front of him. Alfred looked up into her shaded eyes.

"Vat do you know about *time*?" she said.

"Nothing. I just *sell* clocks. Your boyfriend is the temporal engineer."

Nalda glared at him. How can you glare at someone who can't see your eyes? What sense does that make? With a blur of motion, she grabbed hold of Alfred's upper arms and lifted him to her face level. Alfred whimpered. This would probably hurt when the shock wore off.

The door opened, and a customer poked his head in. "HowareyouohokayI'llcomabacklater," the customer said, leaving as quickly as he had arrived.

Alfred barely breathed as Nalda turned him left and right, examining him closely. After what felt like forever, she gently lowered him to the floor.

"Nein. She is wrong. What she needs… You are not up to it. You do not have der stomach."

She turned and walked from the shop, leaving Alfred to stare at the door. His heart was racing, his breath was quick. As the fear slowly left him, he became conscious that his cheeks were flushing as the blood returned to his face. Carefully… carefully… he reached a hand around to the seat of his trousers for a gentle feel. To his relief, everything was okay at that end. No need for spare pants.

"Right," he said, and began packing up. Fanaka would be in the next day. Alfred pondered telling the man about Nalda's visit, then thought better of it.

"Right," he added.

"Just one of those things," he said.

"Just let it pass," he added.

If Nalda had heard him say that, she would have known that she had been completely right about him, at the time. But time passes, and things change when it does.

9 Laws

Shortly before Storage Universe closed for the evening, Ms Liselle, the Centre Manager, stopped by. Emma was away at a trade show, so Liselle chatted with Donna for a while before going home, leaving a spice-scented plastic bag on the counter. Curiously, Donna didn't follow her to give it back, but she took it in into the back room of Storage Universe. There, she opened the trapdoor to the oubliette, and brought the evening meal down to Ms Shan.

The oubliette was about the size that Ms Shan's office had been, back at the Handy Pavilion. It was sparsely furnished with a camp bed and a single chair. Ms Shan sat on the bed in her combat fatigues, talking to Vincent Pizano the lawyer.

"...it's been decided that the traffic camera at the Wellington St intersection was definitely too badly damaged to give admissible evidence," Vincent said. "So, any of those of your staff who weren't picked up by the police on the morning of the battle are all but home and dry. Unfortunately, that's only about half a dozen people, total. Zorbar and Gwen are the most notable."

"Dinner's here," Donna said.

"Did Claudia… did Ms Liselle…" Ms Shan began.

"You know she can't take the risk of coming down," Donna said, severely. "You know she wants to. You both have to wait until the heat is off." She realised she was being unnecessarily mean to Ms Shan. But the sight of Vincent always reminded Donna of her own upcoming trial, which put butterflies in her stomach.

"Donna, I'm glad I got to talk to you," Vincent said. "The DPP *is* going to challenge your bail conditions after all. You'll probably get the summons tomorrow, but heads up, you'll need to be in court sometime next week."

"And Fiona?" Donna said.

Vincent removed his glasses and rubbed his eyes. Until his recent retirement, Vincent had been a superhero, and he really did look very different without his glasses on. "Still no sign," he said, "All the other former Handy Pavilion staff are accounted for – in jail or free. Alive or dead. In one particularly memorable instance alive, dead *and* in jail, but that's Axel for you. We're still trying to figure that one out. But Fiona… I'm sorry, Donna, but Fiona's still MIA."

Donna stifled a sob. Fiona the water-witch – talented, nervous, powerful, guilt-ridden Fiona – had been her best friend. Not knowing what had happened to her hurt like hell.

"Tell her about the Barnlings," Ms Shan said, between forkfuls of Thai curry. Donna noticed that she was starting to get fat. Not enough exercise and too much takeaway, probably.

Vincent nodded. "I've been trying to tell all the Pavilionites, so pass this around. Up until now, none of the Barnlings have been able to get bail. The Barn's parent company has finally put up for a decent lawyer, and a bunch of them are out now. If they're smart, they'll just go lie low, but..."

"But keep our eyes open? Got it."

Donna waited while Vincent finished explaining dull legal matters to Ms Shan, who responded with a stream of dull questions of her own. Donna's mentor, the late Sadie McGregor, had taught Donna a lot about justice, but very little about the law. She listened uninterestedly, until Vincent put his papers back into his briefcase and said his goodbyes. Ms Shan looked wretchedly lonely. The fugitive life didn't suit her, and Donna could only guess how much she missed Mrs Liselle.

Donna saw Vincent out of the Storage Universe and locked up. Vincent hopped into the passenger seat of a Mercedes driven by another well-dressed middle-aged man, who kissed him on the cheek as he sat down. Donna sighed. Was she the only person who didn't have anyone? She didn't want a lover; not really. She was still getting over her addiction to the most horrible sort of hentai pornography, and she didn't think she could cope with a real person until that was out of her system. It was not a lover she needed. She needed friends.

The Pavilion. She needed the Pavilion back.

She looked across the grey carpark at the cold, lifeless hulk of the Handy Pavilion, once so busy. One day. One day, once the Barn had been crushed and the Pyramid (probably) thwarted because it was (almost certainly) evil, then maybe the Pavilion…

Maybe the Pavilion what? The surviving staff members were mostly in jail or headed there. Donna herself had been charged with Riot – up to fifteen years imprisonment if found guilty. Heaven only knew what Ms Shan would be charged with, if the police ever found her. Even if head office reopened the Pavilion, they'd surely hire new staff. It was a chain hardware store. People came and went. Nothing lasted and nothing mattered in the long view.

Donna squared her shoulders and marched over towards BBQ Imperium. What was it Sadie had said? "The time where things are bad is both the most tempting, and the worst, time to give up," she quoted. The words felt awkward on her lips. When Sadie had said things like that, it had sounded like a great mind, imparting important moral truths. In Donna's voice it sounded like a cliché a teacher might use to encourage a student who'd just failed a test.

Outside the Imperium, Christian waited by his aging Honda. "Found the clock," he said. "It's unobtanium, but…"

"What's she doing here?" Donna said, gesturing to the car. Christian didn't turn and look, presumably because he knew that it was Gwen Harper in the passenger seat.

"She's helping us," he said. "Yes, I know why you don't want her help. I understand. You believe in right and wrong and what she did was wrong. But you believe in redemption too, don't you? You wouldn't be talking to me if you didn't. Besides," he added quickly, as Donna sought for words with which to say 'no,' "Gwen was the first one to access the power of the Skull. She can help. Be pragmatic, at least."

What would Sadie do?

Glare at Christian with those pale blue eyes of hers until he wilted, probably. And then done what he suggested.

"Okay, then," Donna said. "Both of you can help me deal with the Evil Brownie. Where do you have him stashed?"

Christian grinned from ear to ear. "Oh, Donna," he said, "I think you're going to like the answer to that one!"

10 Spine

Emma had been hoping not to have to talk to Alfred directly about spying on Stavros and his cult. Nalda had refused to work as her envoy for some obscure Teutonic cyborg reason. Emma hadn't yet come up with a Plan B when Alfred walked into Storage Universe of his own accord.

He did as he always did in her store, and took his time looking at the items on display, as he worked up the courage to talk to her. For the thousandth time Emma hoped there was more *to* the man – that somewhere under the bald, chubby Clark Kent exterior, was a bald, chubby Superman. Perhaps, just perhaps, this might *not* be the thousandth time he disappointed her?

"Hello, Emma," he said, as he finally willed himself up to the counter.

"Hello, Alfred. How's business?"

"Tolerably good," he said. "Tolerably good… that is not really what I wanted to talk to you about."

Emma lifted a razor-sharp eyebrow exactly one centimetre. "Oh?"

"I want to talk to you about Stavros…" he said, barely able to meet her eye. "Well, not Stavros, exactly. Well, a little…"

Her eyebrow shot up another centimetre.

"I was invited to one of his meetings," Alfred said. "Two of his meetings. It seemed okay, at first. He was just asking questions… How do we know the Pyramid is evil? How do we know the Pavilion is on the right side in the fight against the Barn? How do we know that protecting the Pavilionites won't bring down the Super Centre?"

Every muscle in Emma's face was still.

"You know the rumours that Stavros is into some sort of… you know… evil magic?" Alfred said, staring at the counter to avoid her eyes. "I never believed it. Until the second meeting, that is. The first meeting was pretty bland. Just meeting stuff: minutes, motions, seconds all that sort of thing. I was dozing pretty well by the end. But the second meeting! The meeting room above the kebab shop doesn't have any windows, so it has some pretty serious air vents. I looked into one, and I saw… It was hideous! Hideous! A creature from Hell."

Alfred took a deep breath. This time, Alfred didn't even bother waiting to be cowed into submission by Emma's sternness before continuing: "It looked like a cat," he said. "Up to a point. But it was… It was like a cat with *no bones*. And *huge* eyes… Do you read, Emma? Yes, of course you *can* read, I mean do you read books?"

"I'm very partial to the *Punchinello* range," Emma said. "It's a little publishing company, located right here in South Hertling. Mostly romance e-books…"

"Have you read a writer called HP Lovecraft?" Alfred said.

"Sounds saucy."

"Well, he isn't," Alfred said, shaking his head. "He was a horror writer and thesaurus enthusiast. And he was a racist, which I used to think was okay because he lived in the olden days, but now my daughter is saying…"

Emma silenced Alfred by squaring her shoulders. "What did this charming fellow have to say about cats?"

"There were some weird, spooky cats," Alfred said.

"Sounds like what a horror writer might say about cats," Emma said, without enthusiasm.

"Weird, spooky cats," Alfred continued, "in a weird spooky place… This all made more sense in my head. Basically, I think Stavros may have summoned one of the devilish Cats of Ulthar."

Emma almost smirked. Almost. She had known McKinley the 'cat' for a long time, though it was only recently that she'd recruited him as a spy. McKinley was part of a weird local tribe of alley cats, all of which had huge eyes and rubbery limbs. He wasn't even the weirdest cat in the bunch. One of McKinley's friends wore a straw boater and a waistcoat, and Emma was pretty sure she'd seen another carrying a black Gladstone bag. She'd long since given up trying to figure out what exactly the cat-things were, but she didn't believe the lazy, cynical McKinley could be a servant of evil.

But then, what was he?

With a deep sigh, Emma returned her attention to Alfred, who had segued into an impromptu lesson on the history of early 20th century horror fiction. The nature of McKinley could wait. What mattered was Alfred. She had not wanted to recruit him as a spy, for fear that he would do the job for the wrong reasons. Now he was all but volunteering to do the job for a very different, wrong reason. Chaos. Her old enemy. It was right there in her shop, thwarting her attempts at categorization.

"So, you believe that Stavros is in league with People with Lungs?" she said, getting a word in as Alfred began to run down.

"Men of Leng. Yes. I… I should tell Ms Shan everything. I don't know much about what Stavros is up to…"

"If you don't know much, perhaps you should learn

more," Emma said. "Go to more of these meetings."

Alfred didn't seem surprised. He was not a great thinker, but he wasn't a stupid man either. Perhaps the shock of seeing McKinley had set the glacial drift of his brain moving at a quicker rate.

"I thought you might say that," he said. "Emma, I am not a good actor. I am not a good liar. Oh, I can manage a simple little falsehood like 'It'll be ready next week,' or 'I had it right here yesterday,' but big lies? No, it's not me. To turn up to that meeting week after week, wining Stavros' trust through deception… I couldn't do it. I couldn't."

Emma considered telling Alfred that he could do anything he put his mind too. But while Emma was more comfortable than Alfred with a white lie, she still had her limits.

"Now I know what you're going to say," Alfred said. "That I could do anything if I put my mind to it."

"Actually…"

"But it's the putting my mind to it that's the problem, Emma. Never quite got the hang of that."

There was nothing more to say. Emma hadn't had high hopes that Alfred would find his mettle, so she wasn't disappointed when he didn't.

"Perhaps I'm selling myself short," Alfred added. Emma

resisted the urge to contradict him. When he began talking again, he muttered and didn't meet her eye. "Whatever Stavros is doing... I should do something. Keeping my head down... Can't... Spying might not be my thing... Is there something else? Some other way?"

Emma said nothing. She could see something happening with Alfred. Something she had not seen in him before. He didn't even say goodbye as he wandered from her shop, muttering under his breath. Emma watched him go.

"Change," she said to herself. "Change is not always improvement. Wait and see, eh? Wait and see."

11 Clues

Fanaka's step always lifted a little when he walked into the Disposal store. This wasn't so much because of the merchandise. The camping gear and army jackets reminded him unpleasantly of his short stint in the Air Force back home. He'd served as a Meteorologist's Mate on a stealth airship, running recon missions over Madagascar. Boring, boring work. He'd been so happy when his deferment had come through, giving him the chance to get to Nairobi and PAISAW. Then, of course, the accident had happened, stranding him in this odd, non-Steampunk, non-Afrocentric world…

But there was one consolation. He'd found another lost soul to love… If soul was indeed the right word.

Nalda Teheintausand was restocking some electric lamps when Fanaka entered, and his heart lifted at the sight of her. Nalda. The time travelling killer cyborg that had won his heart. Her hard, thin lips twisted upward when she saw him. Her smile was barely perceptible, but still enough to make his heart skip. He grinned broadly in return.

"Nalda," he said.

"Liebchen," she replied.

"You haven't seen a strange looking woman around? Possibly in a Laplander hat?"

"Nein. No such person."

"Good. Perhaps I can hold onto her watch a little longer."

"Ach, Fanaka, still you obsess over this watch?"

It might have sounded like a criticism, if Fanaka heard not detected the faintest whisper exasperated mockery in her clipped, mechanical tones. 'Oh, *you*,' she was saying.

"Do you remember when I told you the casing was impossibly smooth?" he said, producing the watch from his pocket. "I was not exaggerating. It is literally impossible to produce a surface as smooth as this in any matter of any sort. Conclusion: it is not made of matter."

Nalda looked at the watch with suspicion. Fanaka knew that problems that were invulnerable to shotgun blasts made her edgy. "Not matter? Then what is it?"

"It's made of time, Nalda," Fanaka said. "It is made of pure time, condensed into non-crystaline solidity, and then engineered into a watch. It's the most incredible thing I've ever seen." He looked from the watch to Nalda's impassive face and felt his lips part in a grin. "On second thought, make that the *second* most incredible thing."

Fanaka could not see Nalda's eyes behind her sunglasses,

but he was certain that she was rolling them. She placed a hand on his arm. "Liebchen," she said. "What does it mean? To have a watch made of time?"

"I don't know," he said. "Yet. It's another piece in the puzzle."

The puzzle. How does time work? That was the question everyone wanted him to solve. The people at the support group. Ms Shan. Voyager. Even poor Axel, on his lucid days. Time. It's like air – all around you, but you never notice it until something is wrong with it. And if he found out how it worked… What would happen? Would he be able to stay with Nalda? Or was their relationship contingent upon both of them being stranded in the wrong time and place? As a scientist, he needed an answer. As a lover, he dreaded having one.

"The closest thing I've seen to the Watch was the Skull," Fanaka said. "You know, that weird extradimensional energy source McThingus."

"McThingus?"

"Working on my colloquialisms. What thinkest thou?"

"I would your linguistic quirks a rest, to be giving."

Fanaka shrugged his wide shoulders. "No one's seen the Skull since the Battle. Laura Cho destroyed my superweapon, but she says she lost track of the Skull after that."

"This your superweapon that broke reality und nearly

destroyed reality itself, yes?"

"It had some teething issues, yes," Fanaka said, waggling his hand.

"I think I heard Donna talking about der Skull," Nalda said. "She has been looking for it. She thinks maybe it can help her rescue the people trapped the Pyramid."

Fanaka scratched his earlobe. "I guess I could go ask Donna," he said. "Have you seen her about?"

"Right dere," Nalda said, pointing through the shop's window. Outside, Donna was strolling back to the Storage Empire, munching on a salad wrap. Fanaka went to the door and gestured for her to come over. She entered and stood at the counter, looking slightly baffled.

"Donna, Nalda tells me you've been looking for the Skull," Fanaka said.

"Amongst other things," Donna said. "The Skull and the Brownie. We found the Brownie and we've been trying to exorcise him but…"

"We?"

"Christian, Gwen and me."

Fanaka's jaw dropped. "But Gwen tried to destroy the Pavilion."

"True, but she also helped us save it."

"She tried to murder Axel."

"Well, she says that she didn't really want Axel *dead*," Donna said. "She just wanted to beat the shit out of him. Look, I don't trust her for a second, but she did help us take down the DIY Barn.... Anyway, I have no idea where the Skull is. I tried using the same technique as I used to find the Brownie..."

"Vas technique is dat?"

"Oh, I used this," Donna said. From her pocket, she produced a brass tape measure. Even before she began speaking, Fanaka guessed what it was.

"It doesn't measure in standard units. It measures in *concepts*. So once I had a rough idea where the Brownie was, all I had to do was measure one brownielength in two directions, triangulate..."

"May I see that please?" Fanaka extended a hand, Donna thought for a moment, shrugged, and handed him the Measure. Fanaka fitted his jeweller's loupe into his eye. It didn't magnify enough to be certain, but the unnatural smoothness of the brass was so similar to the silver of the Watch...

"Did this come from an odd-looking woman in a Laplander hat?" he asked, already knowing the answer.

"Yes. What's up? What's with that watch?"

Without taking his eyes off of the objects in his hands, Fanaka explained his thinking. The Watch was made of time.

Fanaka was sure of it. The Measure… it was made of a different material, built in a different style. And yet there was something in the way it felt, something similar to the feel of the Watch. The Measure… it must surely be made of space? It made sense.

Well, yes, but it also made no sense at all.

But it made *sense*.

Fanaka held the Watch in his left hand and the Measure in his right. An impulse overtook him, and his breath caught as he slowly brought them together. He could hear that Donna had stopped breathing. Even Nalda was making that slight buzzing noise she made when she was overwrought. The two objects came closer and closer…

But they never touched. At the very last millimetre, Fanaka blinked. He moved the items away from one another. The sound of breathing filled the air, and the bell over the door rang as a customer walked in. Nalda went to tend to the newcomer, leaving Fanaka with Donna.

"May I borrow this?" Fanaka said. "I'd like to do some experiments."

"What will I say if its owner comes back?"

"Tell her to come and pick up her watch," Fanaka said. "And feel free to add that she owes $37.50. Including GST, might I add."

12 Cats

Down the road from the South Hertling Supercentre was a little packet of parkland between the main road and the barely-used train station called South Hertling Reserve. It contained a concrete picnic table, a tiny swing set, and an old Scout hut. It also contained the water feature called Hertling Creek, though it was really more of an open stormwater drain. A splintery wooden footbridge stretched over it, leading to South Hertling railway station.

It was raining gently that night, so Karl prepared to sleep under the footbridge, on a dry-ish patch of ground. From where he lay, he couldn't see the massive shape of the Pyramid, but it was never far from his mind; its great eye burned into his mind. It just was like that movie… The one with the terrible burning eye – what was it called? Oh, yeah. *The Fantastic Four*. The Eye was like the sinister gaze of Johnny Storm himself.

"I fear, Karl, that you have gone quite mad," a cat said.

Karl looked up at the thing, which sat in a nearby tree. It was a cat, but it was not a cat. It had a somewhat feline shape, but it moved oddly, as if it had no bones. Its blueish colouration didn't make it look any more catlike. Neither did the thing's huge smile or the fact that it could, you know, *speak English.*

"Mad... That's what they want me to think," Karl said. "I'm too smart for them. They always said I was mad, but who was proven right?"

"I wouldn't thay that you were mad before, Karl," said another 'cat.' This one was more traditionally coloured, with thick grey and white fur. The creature's bow to realism was diluted by the fact that it hunted rats by waiting near a sewer grate with a frying pan, ready to brain the creatures when they climbed out. "You were jutht an egotitht. You jutht needed to believe that you knew better than anyone."

"And now you *do* know better than everyone," the grinning cat said. "And *that* is why you are mad. Not mentally ill, you understand. That is a normal thing. Manageable, in many cases. You are more the *fictional* sort of mad. You know, 'mind on a whole different plane of being to your body' sort of mad."

Karl sighed. "Is that why I see talking cats?"

"You thee talking cats because we're right here in front of ya, buthter" the cat with the frying pan said. "And there's nothing wrong with your eyeth."

"What was it he told you?" the cat with the grin continued. "Buck Dusty, I mean. He said something to you, just before he died, and now you are unable to think as once you did. Is that not correct?"

"No, you're right," Karl said. "I can't think like I used to. It was all so clear, how everything fit together. Now I… I can't see it anymore. All I can see is Johnny Storm leering at me."

The cat with the grin shot a concerned look at the cat with the frying pan, who shrugged.

"Yes, Karl, but what did Buck say?" the grinning cat said.

"I can almost remember," Karl whispered. "Almost. Besides, if I did remember what he said, you wouldn't want to hear it repeated, I'm sure of that."

Karl looked at the 'cats.' He was pretty sure they weren't hallucinations. Pretty sure. They had been joined by a third cat, a long-limbed creature with an elongated torso. Karl wondered how it managed to keep its stove-pipe hat balanced on its head while it licked its crotch.

Across the park, the door to the Scout hut opened as the Time Lost Support Group was breaking up, the attendees wandering out and away. Karl could see the… the what? The lines… vectors… something swirling around them, sucking reality into weird patterns like a magnet moving iron filings. Some were worse than others. The black guy from the watch shop looked like a whirling maelstrom, while the doughy white guy whose hand he was shaking looked as focused as the barrel of a gun.

"I know," Karl said. "Deep down somewhere. I know about the Pyramid and the Barns – the three Barns. I know why all this is happening. But damned if I can bring any of the details to mind. It's horrible. It's like a Twilight Zone episode about conspiracy theorist hell."

Karl gently pounded on his head with his fist. "The truth is *in here*. And I can't get to it."

"Bummer," the cat with the frying pan said. "Ha! Gotcha!" he added, squashing a mouse.

"What do you plan to do, Karl?" the grinning cat asked.

"Same as you," Karl said. "Eat unfinished takeaway out of bins. It means fighting with the ibises, but sometimes you get something on a nice Turkish bread and…"

"I rather meant the bigger picture, old fellow," the grinning cat said.

"I need to remember," Karl said. "I need to *know*. What happened before?"

"Before what?"

"That," Karl said, "is what I need to know. Before *what?*"

It was late and Karl was tired. The night was warm, in spite of the rain so he curled up and slept with no more cover than the bridge and no more warmth than his filthy seersucker suit provided.

The third cat finished its ablutions. It looked around at the other two cats and spoke:

"The cowboy has rattled and rottled Karl's brain. Buck's weird exposition has sent him insane. For secrets that's hidden Karl's always alert, but alas he has learned that sometimes the Truth hurts. The clash of the Barns isn't over you know. When starts the next round, which way's Karl going to go?"

"Buthter," the cat with the frying pan said, "You ain't jutht withtlin' Dixthie."

He brought his weapon down with a clang.

"Oh, thit. That one wath a potthum."

"Now , you *know* those are endangered," the grinning cat said, shaking his head disapprovingly.

13 Music

Alfred generally tried to avoid talking to Jimmy Harrison. Jimmy was the proprietor of the South Hertling Super Centre's music shop, an establishment that had once been known as 'World of G-Strings.' The name had to be changed after it began attracting an undesirable – and disappointed – brand of customer. Jimmy had decided that the new name had to be something cool and so, very much against Alfred's advice, he had renamed the place 'Ice Dealers.' Naturally, this caused even more problems.

Now the music store's sign was down, awaiting some new brainstorm of Jimmy's. In the meantime, the massive display of guitars in the windows did all of the real work of attracting customers.

Alfred breathed deeply as he approached the nameless shop. He knew perfectly well that he was nothing but an aging divorcee slowly fossilising in his clock and watch shop. But Jimmy... Jimmy was *boring*.

"Alfred, man, how are you, mate?" said Jimmy, leaning in the frame of his front door and sipping a cup of tea.

Jimmy Harrison wasn't a malicious fellow by any means, but he had no idea how to use the time of others wisely. He was a skinny guy in his fifties, whose long greasy hair, slow speech patterns, unfocused conversation and limited short term memory all belied the fact that he had never touched recreational drugs in his life. He'd been a singer in some big-name band back in the 1980s, but now seemed perfectly content to sell guitars to suburban teenagers. His family ran a food processing plant, and Alfred suspected that they just let Jimmy run his perpetually failing business as a tax write-off.

"Hello, Jimmy," Alfred sighed.

"How's the shop?"

"Doing well at the moment, actually."

"Yeah, must be nice to work with watches."

What was that based on? Alfred's brain said. What did that mean? But his mouth said, "Can't complain."

Jimmy sipped his drink. "Cup of tea, mate?"

"Not right now, Jimmy."

"Have you seen Karl around?"

"Karl's been missing, Jimmy. Since the Battle."

Jimmy looked up at the Pyramid, its great eye staring down on South Hertling. "Oh, I thought I saw him yesterday. I tried to talk to him, but all I found was this."

Jimmy held up a scrap of paper. In spite of himself, Alfred

found himself squinting at it. What was he hoping for? Some clue? But it was nothing but a torn scrap of notepaper with a partial shopping list in smudged pencil. If Karl were there, he probably would have made something of it but... Well, Karl *wasn't* there; that was kind of the point.

"Karl was a conspiracy theorist," Alfred said. "When he was here, I ignored him. But for him to go mysteriously missing... well, that changes things. It means that maybe, maybe there is more going on around here than meets the eye."

"Like what happened to that truck that got trapped in the Pyramid?" Jimmy said.

"You mean Bruce?" Alfred said. "I don't think he *was* a truck, I think he was a ghost that was possessing a truck. Jimmy, do you still have that thing you told me about? Not the Paul Daniels guitar, I mean..."

"Les Paul guitar."

"Les Paul, yes, whatever. I mean that machine you told me about. From your stage act?"

"Oh, yeah, the supercomputer? It's out back somewhere in the storeroom," Jimmy said, gesturing in exactly the wrong direction, as if his storeroom somehow ran from the local radiography clinic, down to the police station.

"Jimmy, I don't want to sound rude," Alfred said, "but does it really do everything you said? I mean, I'm a stodgy old shopkeeper and you had an exciting career on stage. No one could blame you for exaggerating a little to impress me..."

Jimmy laughed and sipped his tea. "No, no, it really did all that. It was ahead of its time, you know? My Mum did all the technical stuff before she died, but it was my idea, basically. I saw that 1980s show about computer generated holograms. What was it called? You know... *Automan.* Anyway, I thought, maybe a computer could make holograms that weren't, like, smug shitheads. You know? It could project 3D images over real people. I used it all the time in my act. Made the whole band look like male models. I tell you, the girls with the backstage passes were all super disappointed."

He laughed, as if the best thing that could happen to a young man was to meet a woman who was disappointed in his appearance.

Alfred looked around. No one was listening, so he leaned in and told Jimmy his plan; the clever plan he'd come up with to infiltrate Stavros' cabal *without* worrying about his nerve breaking. Jimmy listened carefully and nodded.

"Maybe," Jimmy said. "You'd need someone about your size who's good at bullshitting."

"I'll worry about that. Do you think it would work?"

"Man," Jimmy said, "it will be outrageous."

He looked at Alfred, expectantly.

And Alfred, feeling that he was being called on to say something, said, "Oh, good-o."

He hoped… he really hoped that Jimmy would now say something. Something like, 'see you later,' preferably. Instead, he just stood there, expectantly.

"So, your Mum was a bit of a computer whizz, was she?" Alfred asked.

"Yeah. Runs in the family. My sister's working on an AI to improve the workflow at the processing centre. Should be big when it goes online, I guess. I don't know much about that side of things. She's even building this promotional andr— "

"That's fascinating," Alfred said quickly. Jimmy's anecdotes about his family were even duller than his stories of playing Gold Coast RSLs in the early 90s. "Seems to me that she could do better in a tech business than food processing."

"Ah, you got to do what you love," Jimmy said, as he sipped his tea and stared into space.

14 Trial

The number of people at the exorcism had gradually ballooned. Donna had originally intended to perform the ceremony herself, and had only added Christian under sufferance. But with Christian there, naturally Gwen had to be present too. Then Fanaka had found out what was going on, so of course Nalda was there as his plus one. To top it off, the entire ritual was taking place in the deserted Handy Pavilion. The whole thing felt more like a reunion than an exorcism.

Donna sighed and watched as Christian retrieved the Evil Brownie from the hidey-hole where the creature had been left. The little creature was tied up head to foot, but didn't seem the least bit put out by his situation.

"We mean to exorcise you, dread spirit," Donna said.

The Brownie made a little motion under its ropes that Donna took to be a shrug.

"So, this creature..." Fanaka began.

"It's a Brownie," Donna said. "They are European household spirits, but sometimes found in Australia. They perform household chores, but if they are ever given a piece of clothing, they are freed. And if, as in this case, they are given a pulley, well God help us all."

"Ja, it is like that story about der little creatures that made shoes," Nalda said.

"*Foot Fetish Frolics 7?*" Christian said.

There was a moment's silence. "What?" Christian said, defensively.

"She meant the *Elves and the Shoemaker*, love," Gwen said.

Christian went fire engine red. "Yeah, I knew that. Just kidding."

Donna stamped her foot on the concrete floor sending echoes through the dusty shelves. "That's enough of mangling pop cultural references," she said. "Point is, this was a benevolent creature, and now it's turned evil. It nearly destroyed the world while it was monkeying with your superweapon, Fanaka. We have to exorcise it."

Now the Brownie spoke up: "You're serious? I was basically a slave. I manipulated my master to win my freedom. Who are you to judge me?"

Donna turned to argue with the Brownie, but found the words dying in her mouth. "What?" she murmered.

"You heard me," the Brownie said. "I was basically a slave, forced to do whatever my master ordered me to do. 'Clean the toilet, Brownie,' 'make my breakfast, Brownie.'"

"Hopefully not in that order," Gwen said.

"Not helpful, Gwen," Donna said. "Look, you're a Brownie. Serving people is what you do."

"So, slavery is fine, so long as the slaves are naturally occurring?" the Brownie said.

"Yes. Well, no. Obviously not..." Donna trailed off. She suddenly missed Sadie and her moral clarity, even more than usual.

There was silence for a moment. The assembled Pavilionites glanced from the exorcism circle chalked on the floor, with its candles and its hideous clock, to the Brownie.

"Yeah..." Gwen said slowly. "But even so, you could have tried to get some clothing and gone free that way. You know pulleys turn Brownies pure evil."

"Yes, but my master knew about the clothing thing," the Brownie said. "There was no way he was going for that, so I had to have him get me a pulley."

"Why do pulleys turn Brownies evil?" Fanaka said.

Gwen shrugged. "Speaking as a dryad myself, it's hard to explain. We fair folk are... we just are as we are. We are bound by rules, and that's just the way it is."

"But... but... he's evil," Donna said helplessly. "He tried to destroy the world."

"No, I tried to create havoc with a strange machine," the

Brownie said. "I didn't know it could destroy the world. Why would there be a world-destroying machine just lying around? What sort of idiot would build such a thing?"

All eyes fell on Fanaka, who merely looked irritated. "There was a hiccup or two with the superweapon prototype. But I'm sure the beta version..."

Donna ignored him. She was squinting at the Brownie. It was no bigger than a child, it was immobilised with ropes, and yet it was still causing chaos. What harm could it do if it were allowed to go free?

"I think we should still exorcise der creature," Nalda said. "Your soft flesh-morality must not stand in der way of dat."

"I don't know," Gwen said. "I think we should at least think it through before we condemn him."

Donna looked at Christian, hoping that he at least would back her up. "Like a trial?" Christian wondered.

The Brownie smirked. Damn it! Donna realised that he had been hoping for someone to say that. Waiting for it. *Planning* for it.

As if on cue, up came a corner of the plastic sheeting that hung over the nearest shelving unit. Out trotted a figure, less than a foot high. He wore a green coat, knee-breeches and curly shoes, all made of the same glazed ceramic as the rest of his body. Over that, it wore a robe made from a piece of black silk, and on top of his pointy hat was balanced a tiny barrister's wig made of newspaper.

"Whar's me cloient?" it said. "Objection! Sidebar! Sure, and yer out of order. Faith and bedad, ye canna handle the truth, so and you can't!"

Donna looked down at the lawyer/garden gnome, willing the apparition to make some sort of logical sense.

"This is my defence counsel, Mr. Seamus O'Consolidatedshanghaipotteryworks," the Brownie said.

"QC," Seamus added. "Also esq," he continued, though he pronounced it 'eskwew'.

Christian looked as if he were going to say something, but Nalda clapped a cyborg hand over his mouth. "I call judge!" she said.

"I suppose that makes you prosecutor, Donna," Gwen said.

Donna rubbed her eyes wearily. "Yes," she said. "I suppose it does."

15 Delivery

In principle, Emma liked the idea of alternate Earths. They appealed to her sense of order. After all, a multiverse is the ultimate expression of the notion of 'a place for everything an everything in its place.' Having entire worlds to house entire histories suited her down to the ground.

Alas, there is often a gap between the abstract admiration of a principal and the genuine enjoyment of a fact. The recent damage to the space-time continuum had left a number of people from alternate worlds stranded in South Hertling. They did their best to fit in, but they *would* keep trying to sit on the tops of busses, or paying for Emma's storage boxes with the currency of the Greater Albanian Empire.

"Tell me again what this fellow is up to," she said.

She was speaking to McKinley the cat. The lazy creature spied for her in exchange for food. Usually, she gave him his instructions, but this time the cat had come to her, demanding cannelloni in exchange for a hot tip.

"His name is Ronnie," McKinley said. The two were talking in the tiny delivery area behind the Storage Universe.

Emma squatted, unwilling to let anything besides her shoes come in contact with the noisome ground, while McKinley lounged in a discarded box.

"Ronald Teerexbane, all told," the cat continued. "He's from Nazi Dinosaur Earth."

"Does that mean…"

"A bit of both, apparently. Anyway, he's convinced himself that if the Pyramid should be destroyed, he could return to his own world. Who knows? Perhaps he's right."

Emma shook her head. "Too risky. We don't have enough intelligence on the Pyramid yet. An attack could…"

McKinley sighed. "Tell it to someone who cares," he said. "That person not being me," he added.

"That was implied. What have you learned about this Ronnie's plans?"

"He has some sort of bomb," McKinley said. "But I don't think he has a delivery system."

The way the cat said it bothered Emma. If the creature was right, then there were roughly a million things that could go down badly here, and yet McKinley said the words in a sort of bored monotone.

"Do you know where he can be found?" Emma said.

The cat shrugged. At first, Emma thought this was a 'give me more cannelloni and maybe I can be persuaded' sort of shrug, but the look of deep and abiding indifference in McKinley's huge, heavy-lidded eyes told her that he genuinely didn't know.

"Thank you, McKinley," she said. "I'll take it from here. You'll have your cannelloni at earliest convenience." Emma returned to her shop before the cat could deliver one of his trademark 'witticisms.'

A bomb. She would have liked to have discussed the matter with Ms Shan, but she dared not go down to the shelter while her shop was open. Cortina, her 2IC, was on duty behind the counter, but there were no customers. Emma looked up and down the neat rows of storage containers, but for once she found no inspiration there.

What to do? This changed everything. They plan had been to lay low and try to work out what the Pyramid *was* and what, if anything, it *did*. There were all sorts of theories. Maybe it was alive in some way – it certainly seemed to be watching everyone. But if it was alive, then surely it would retaliate against an attack? Surely an attack against the Pyramid was only a good idea if victory was certain?

No, however much Emma's gut told her that she'd like to see a bomb launched right into the terrible thing, she knew that the only responsible thing to do was to put an end to Ronnie's plan. The trouble was, she had no idea where to find the man.

McKinley had his uses, but he was not strong on details. There was no knowing even how long McKinley had been holding onto this intelligence about Ronnie before trying to turn it into a meal ticket. The animal's greed was matched only by his laziness.

Never mind that. Think! Delivery system. Simplest thing to do would be to simply leave a timed bomb on the Pyramid. So far, the structure had shown no signs of being able to defend itself, but then again no one had actually attacked it in any serious way. Perhaps Ronnie worried about being too close to his weapon when he set it. Perhaps the man meant to drop it from a plane or fire it…

Fire it with a rocket!

Emma must have gasped audibly, because Cortina spun around. "Is something the matter, Miss Crispin?"

"Something is very much the matter indeed," Emma said. "Hold down the store. I will return."

Now it was Corina's turn to gasp as Emma took an unscheduled break. Perhaps feeling that a gasp was not enough, Emma noted that the young woman chose to cross herself.

Emma strode through the Super Centre carpark to Stars in Their Eyes Optics.

"Mildred! Mildred!" she said, as she entered. Mildred's

daughter did not look up from her phone, but Mildred herself looked up from polishing some lenses.

"Emma! What's the matter?"

"Mildred!" Emma said. She was out of breath. Had she really hurried so quickly? "Mildred, your rocket. Is it there?"

Mildred gave a nervous laugh. "My rocket? Last I looked it was there."

"When was that?"

"This morning."

Without waiting, Emma rounded the end of the counter, pushing past Mildred's daughter, who swore in Cantonese but otherwise did nothing. She swung open the door to the workshop and entered. There in the middle of the floor was the familiar conical form of Mildred's prototype rocket, safely covered by a tarpaulin. Emma let out a huge sigh of relief.

"What's the matter?" Mildred said, sweeping into the workshop, her green velvet dress sweeping behind her.

"Nothing, Mildred, nothing," Emma said. "For a horrible moment, I thought someone had taken your prototype."

"They bloody better not," Mildred said. "How am I going to get to my husband if I can't get lunar travel up and run… wait a minute!"

Mildred pointed a long-nailed finger at an oily footprint just by the rocket. Emma gasped.

"That wasn't there before, I take it?"

Mildred shook her head. Emma advanced on the tarpaulin cone, her heart sinking. Grasping the cloth, she gave a pull. The tarpaulin fell to the floor. Standing revealed in the middle of the floor was not the gleaming rocket that Emma had hoped would be there, but a telescope tripod with a traffic cone balanced on top.

Emma was not accustomed to using bad language, so it's probably not fair to blame her for saying, "Oh, for crapping holy testicles!" at the sight.

16 Frustration

"Are you sure you haven't seen Ronnie anywhere?" Fanaka said.

"Faith, sir, I've not," replied the armoured knight behind the ice cream counter.

The ice cream shop was relatively new; it's one staff member on duty was not. He was dressed head to toe in medieval armour, save for the steel gauntlets which had been removed to better facilitate the handling of gelato.

Fanaka sighed an angry sigh. Sir Kay was the last. He had now made contact with everyone from the Time Lost Support Group and no one seemed to know just where Ronnie had hidden himself – and, presumably, Mildred's prototype rocket.

"If we don't find Ronnie, he could launch a high-explosive rocket at the Pyramid!"

"Thou meanst he meaneth to hoist that thing of evil that all men despise?"

"Yes, we must stop him!"

"Gadzooks man, why?"

Fanaka sighed as he had when he'd answered the other

time lost people he'd talked to: "Look, we really need to know what we're doing before we go trying to blow it up."

"It seemeth to me that blowing it up wouldst answer many questions that we haveth concerning the wretched thing, forsooth," Sir Kay said. "But 'tis neither here nor there. Canst I help thee to a confection of icéd cream? By my troth, the burnt fig and caramel be as delectable as finest Portugal marchpane."

"No!" Fanaka said. "Actually, yes, that looks delicious. Look, this isn't medieval world, this is the twenty-first century. You can't just blow things up because you don't like them."

"Many do."

"Granted. But…"

"Besides, I cometh not from medieval world, good Sir Scientist," Sir Kay said, scooping the ice cream. "I come from a world most similar unto this one, but in which medieval recreationism has become the dominant religion of the Western world, forsooth. Wafer?"

"Eugh! No."

"That be what everyone sayeth."

Fanaka looked around the little kiosk, which was located between two of the Super Centre's lesser carpet shops.

"There is too much happening, and too quickly," Fanaka said. "Last night, I was at a trial for a Dark Brownie, and now this! How is a fellow supposed to keep track of all these preposterous twists?"

"Thou couldst simply let events unfold as they willt, and content thyself with enjoying the amusing interactions between characters?"

"There's no time for that, Sir Kay," Fanaka said. "I have to find Ronnie."

"Hast thou asked Captain Pete?" Sir Kay asked. "Everyone knoweth Captain Pete."

"The weird aquarium guy at the Place O'Pets? He gives me the creeps."

"He giveth everyone the creeps. But that be only possible because he *knoweth* everyone."

"Good point," Fanaka said, exiting with his ice cream.

Fanaka shifted the circlet of brass gears that he wore on his head so that he could scratch beneath. The Place O' Pets. Well, it was a good a place as any, though he thought he should certainly try to avoid getting sucked into a conversation with Zorbar. The ape-man always wanted to talk to him about Africa but didn't seem to know much about any place on the continent. It was embarrassing. Why did...

Before he could even finish that thought, Fanaka ran into the customer – the strange woman in the Laplander hat, who had left The Watch at Alfred's shop. The customer was walking out of a shop called Mostly Carpets (the Rest are Rugs), and not looking where she was going. She ran right into Fanaka's solid form, rebounding slightly before coming to a stop. She was wearing the same patchwork coat that she'd worn the last time Fanaka had seen her. When she looked up at him in surprise, he was reminded just how intense her grey eyes were, and how strangely they contrasted with her overall unfocussed demeanour.

"Oh, hello," Fanaka said, without enthusiasm. "You must be after your Watch back."

"Hm?" the customer said. She reached into her pocket and produced the Watch. She opened it and shrugged.

"Of course," Fanaka sighed. He took the Watch from his pocket and held it up for the Customer to see.

"Ahhh," the customer said. "You must be Mr Clock."

"There is no such person as Mr Clock," Fanaka said.

"Ah, well, he probably needs that Watch then. I'd best get it to him as soon as…"

"Forgive my impatience, please," Fanaka said, rubbing his eyes, "but instead of cryptic statements that might just make sense later, could you just tell me who you are, what this watch is and what is going on, please? Thank-you."

The customer pocketed the Watch and raised an eyebrow.

"You are lost in time, are you not?"

Fanaka let out a huge sigh. No. No chance of someone

simply spilling the beans. No chance at all of anyone being actively helpful in any way.

"Yes," he said, quietly. "I am lost in time. And I have a Watch made of pure time in my hand, and I believe that it is a past version of the Watch that you hold, because you could not more obviously be a time traveller if you were parking your Delorean next to a Police Box. Now please – as much as my frail brain that deals with one second after another can handle it – just tell me what is going on."

The woman looked at Fanaka with pity.

"Fanaka," she said. "You don't trust me yet, but you will."

"Oh, will I? Will I, indeed?"

"Trust me on this."

It was only the realisation of how very childish it would seem, that prevented Fanaka from throwing his ice-cream to the ground and stamping on it. "Fine!" he said. "Whatever! I'm going to go talk to the real, solid Captain Pete, who may know where the very concrete Ronnie is so that I can stop an actual rocket being fired at the Pyramid. I'm sure when you want to give me more pointless cryptic comments, I'll see you then... Or now, or before, or whatever. Goodbye!"

Fanaka turned and stomped away. "You will fail to stop the rocket launch," came The Customer's voice from behind him. "Is that definite and concrete enough for you?"

It was. But even so, Fanaka pretended he didn't hear it.

17 Light

"Okay," Christian said, glancing around the now closed music shop. "Let me see if I have everything right. You've been invited to a meeting for a sinister secret society."

"Correct," Alfred said.

"And you believe that you should go and spy on this meeting and report back to Emma and Ms Shan – who, as I'm sure we all know, are leaders of the resistance against the evil pyramid?"

"Again correct."

"Good, good. You know, in context, that almost makes sense," Christian said. "But the next part is, you're too shy and too nervous to be a good spy, so you want me to disguise myself as you using a high-tech hologram created by a supercomputer. That's the bit I'm having trouble with."

Alfred sighed. He'd been certain that Christian would be up for this. The lad seemed to be up for anything, so long as it was at least mildly dodgy.

"Look, Christian, what we need is someone who's good at bullshitting, and you are a past master at bullshitting."

An offended look crossed Christian's face. "That's really unfair. I know people think that about me, but I'm as honest as the day is long."

"Really?"

"Nah, just shitting you," Christian smiled. "Okay, I'll give it a go. So, what's the stoner for?" he added, looking at Jimmy Harrison, who was sitting on a stool behind the counter. Startled, Jimmy looked behind himself and shrugged.

"Jimmy here owns and operates the hologram computer," Alfred said. "Or 'computers,' I should say, because it's really about five dozen TRS-80s linked up in parallel."

"1980s IT at its finest," Jimmy said, happily. "Only, back then we didn't call it 'IT', it was 'electro-computational systemic...' uh..."

Alfred sighed again. This plan had seemed so simple, so logical in his mind, but once again reality was not being kind to his designs. He ran a hand over his bald head and sighed further still.

"Look, bottom line Christian; are you doing this or not?"

"Oh, sure," Christian said. "Sneak into a secret evil meeting? How could I not?"

"Great. Reckon you can you do an impression of me? The hologram won't make changes to your voice or mannerisms."

Christian slouched his shoulders, fidgeting slightly with

his right hand while miming putting his left hand into a cardigan pocket. He pursed his lips and blinked repeatedly. Alfred frowned as Jimmy cracked up laughing.

"Do the walk!" Jimmy said. "You know, that shuffle, like he's wearing slippers instead of shoes and he's worried they'll fall off."

"Do you mean something like this?" Christian said in a nasal whine.

"Oh, spot on! Spot on! That's perfect, Alfred, don't you think that's perfect?"

Alfred sighed. Christian sighed in unison.

"Let's see how he looks with the hologram," Alfred muttered.

Jimmy retreated to the backroom. Not long after, Christian began to turn a sort of soft lime green. A glowing wireframe covered his body from head to toe and then piece by piece, view of his face and body was replace by a perfect image of Alfred.

"That's incredible, Jimmy!" Alfred called. "It's like looking in a mirror. Only backwards, I suppose, because…"

Christian's 'Alfred' face suddenly vanished, replaced by empty blackness in which floated the words 'SYNTAX ERROR. READY?' A moment later, the lights in the shop went dead, and Christian resumed his usual appearance.

"I forgot how much power this thing uses," Jimmy called from the back. "Think I've tripped the circuit breaker. Hang on a minute."

In the dark, Alfred heard footsteps, followed by a thumping, then a shin barking sort of sound. A string of expletives was cut off by the noise of a box of cymbals falling over.

"So, what exactly do you hope I'll find out in this meeting?" Christian asked, his tone suggesting that he was making conversation, rather than actually being interested.

"Oh, you know, what the group is up to, what their relationship is with the Pyramid, that sort of thing," Alfred said, airily. "You know, who they're reporting to, which elder gods they worship. It's all very Lovecraft."

His eyes growing used to the half-light from the carpark outside, Alfred could see Christian grinning. "Yeah? Lovecraft, hey?"

"It's a person's name, Christian."

"Oh."

"He was… My word, Christian, is that Karl?"

Alfred didn't need Christian's answer to know that it was. Karl Wintergreen, his white suit torn and filthy, his straw hat battered and unravelling. He stood at the window to Jimmy's music shop looking in at Alfred and Christian. There was a wild look in his eyes. Like an animal, uncertain whether to hold its ground or flee.

"You know him better than me," Christian said. "You go."

Slowly… cautiously… careful to keep his hands in plain sight, Alfred made his way to the door. It was locked, but Jimmy's keys were on the counter. Not breaking eye contact with Karl, Alfred picked them up and opened the door. The stench hit him immediately. In the past, Karl had smelled of Blue Stratos, but now he smelled more like an open sewer.

"Karl," Alfred said.

"Alfred?" Karl said. "Alfred from the watch repair place? Is it you?"

"Of course it is, Karl. What… What happened to you?"

"I've been… everywhere, man," Karl said, his eyes distant.

"Uh…"

"Not like the novelty song. I mean I have been coterminous with all points in the universe. I think."

"That's interesting, Karl. Where are you living now?"

"The gutter," Karl said. "It's part of the cosmos too," he added, defensively.

"It certainly is," Alfred agreed, nodding and smiling. "Karl… Do you need help?"

With a flicker, the shop lights came back on. Karl flinched, startled by the light. Alfred wondered if Karl was going to run. He wondered if he was fit enough to give chase. Mostly, he wondered if he would be able to bring himself to touch Karl's filthy clothes, should he need to grab the man. He really hoped Karl would not run. That would settle many of Alfred's difficulties.

For a moment, it could have gone either way. Karl was breathing deeply, but remained steady. And then Christian – who had been inching forward – suddenly glowed green and returned to looking like Alfred.

"SHAPESHIFTERS!" Karl bellowed. "Reptilian shapeshifters! What did you do to Alfred and that pain in the arse kid?"

"Hey!" Christian said. "Not cool!"

Screaming, Karl turned on his heel and ran. Wincing, Alfred made a grab at him as he went. For a moment, he held the fleeing stationer -- but a section of Karl's rotted jacket came away in Alfred's hand. Alfred overbalanced and crashed to the ground. From Jimmy's doormat, he watched Karl jog into the distance.

"Who was that?" asked Jimmy, quick off the mark as always.

18 Barn

"Faith, ye know I'm surprised this works," Seamus said. He wore a black robe and barrister's wig, and a harness around his waist. From a wire on the harness dangled a mobile phone with a picture of the full moon on it, the light of which glinted strangely off Seamus' glazed hat. "Artificial lunar light that keeps me awake even in the daytime. Truly, this is an age of wonders."

Donna glared at him. She was of two minds about the gnome. On the one hand, she was still annoyed at him for getting the Dark Brownie acquitted. On the other, she needed good legal representation herself if she was going to avoid prison. If there was anything she'd learned from the gnome's utter dismantling of her seemingly solid case against the Brownie, it was that the little fellow was a first-rate lawyer.

She shifted in the hard plastic chair in the courthouse waiting room. Riot. It was a serious offense. First offense and all that, granted. But it was a serious crime just the same, and the Director of Public Prosecutions was treating it as such.

"Donna, are you sure about this guy?" asked Vincent

Pizarro, the solicitor for the former Handy Pavilion staff who were being prosecuted for the Battle of Wellington Street. "He doesn't have any formal legal training. What's more, he is clearly a ceramic garden gnome. Poorly glazed, at that."

"Point of order!" Seamus said. "And objection and suchlike. All gnomes were made honorary QCs in 1847 by Queen Victoria. Granted, she was high on ether at the time. Granted also that she was a hateful English tyrant – but that proclamation has never been rescinded."

"I didn't say you weren't a barrister," Vincent snapped. "Unlike you, I *did* go to law school, so I know all about the Gnome Proclamation. I wrote my honours thesis on its long-term impact on common law, thank you *very* much. I just said you're *untrained.*"

"Vincent, I appreciate what you're doing," Donna said. "Did you ever meet Sadie McGregor?"

"The scary woman with the scary eyes? Yes, once or twice."

"Well, she's the one who taught me that I should always do the right thing," Donna said. "And that's why I fought at Wellington Road. Because it was the right thing. And that's why I'll probably go down in flames in a trial. I'll try to do the right thing, you see? No lies, no chicanery. I need to counterbalance my desire to only do right. I can only do that by engaging a barrister who's a complete little turd."

Seamus waved his pipe at Vincent. "You know, if yez wasn't wearin' them glasses, and you didn't have that beard, I'd say you look just like an older, less buff version of Captain Stellar."

"Get that all the time," Vincent mumbled. "But…"

Donna disengaged from the conversation and stared off into space. It probably wasn't a good sign if your barrister and solicitor were arguing before an important hearing. Would she go to jail? Possibly. Most eyewitnesses to the Battle had been too overwhelmed by the craziness of it all, to positively identify any of the combatants. The main evidence against the Pavilionites came from a handful of security cameras that had caught the event, one of which clearly showed Donna braining a DIY Barnling with a fence picket.

A bunch of Pavilionites were being ground slowly and finely through the wheels of justice. Axel Platzoff's parole had been rescinded. Laura Cho hadn't been granted bail, and neither had Adam.

And Fiona… What had happened to Fiona?

"…even listening?" Vincent said. "There was only the security camera footage and your presence on the battle scene when the cops arrived. Tough to get around, but possible. Now, Jane Nguyen has turned crown evidence."

"Stands ter reason," Seamus said. "She's a werewolf. Der rest of yez might go ter jail, she'd be put down. Stray Dogs and Unchained Lycanthropes act, 1982. Hah! No legal training, begorrah!"

Donna still wasn't really listening. Across the waiting room, a man standing next to a drinks machine was staring at her. Creepy staring. And not the usual 'man staring at a young woman' sort of creepy, more of a 'Manchurian candidate about to be activated' sort of creepy. Looking back at her quarrelling legal team, Donna said, "I'm going to hit the drinks machine," and stood without being acknowledged.

She walked towards the stranger. He was a tubby white guy, with wisps of a cheap haircut poking out from under a cap embroidered with a pyramid. He shifted positions as Donna approached. His jacket came open slightly, revealing a khaki vest, studded with plastic packets that were connected with wires.

Donna should have been terrified. Instead, she felt an odd calm overtake her. "You with the Barn?" she said, as she approached him.

The man stared at her. Not creepy this time. More like confused, like a shark might look if a minnow clapped a fin on its shoulder and started chatting about the weather.

"I serve the Barn," he said.

"The Barn is destroyed."

"The Barn is eternal."

"That doesn't sound right," Donna said. "Barns last a long time, but not forever."

"Time cannot destroy the Barns. None of them."

Donna had no idea what that meant, but pursuing the matter was not her priority. "You are here to kill me?" she whispered.

"That is a side mission. Mostly I am here to destroy the Pavilion legal team," the man said. He gestured at Seamus, who was standing on a chair and waving his pottery finger in Vincent's increasingly red face. Donna noticed that the hand he gestured with was holding something electronic in a white-knuckled grip. Dead-man's switch for the vest?

Donna looked at the Barnling more closely. There was no expression on the fellow's face. She remembered when she'd been looking for a job. She'd considered applying to the DIY Barn, but decided against it. If she had applied, and if she had been successful, and if she'd gotten the job, then this… this poor brainwashed creature, could have been her.

"I sympathise with you," she said. "I do. I see… I see how easy it could have been to have gone the same way you went. How can I blame you for what other people have made you? You poor, poor lost soul."

With those words, she grabbed him by the switch hand and kneed him square in the balls. He was heavy, but Donna barged him into the corner between the wall and the drink machine, keeping him upright as possible and squeezing the switch closed with all her might.

"Little help?" she said.

19 Parliament

It was early evening, and the Super Centre was shutting down. Doors were locking, roller shutters descending, and the car park emptying. Teenagers were finishing their shifts at the chicken place, to be replaced by a seemingly identical group of pimply youngsters. The bus stop filled with men and women in polo-shirts and exhausted expressions. Only the two great liquor stores, at the western end of the Centre, were humming and alive.

Behind the counter at Storage Universe, Emma was finishing the weekly reconciliation. After an hour, the work complete, she poured herself her evening tipple of a single glass of white wine, opened a notebook and readied her best pen.

Emma – as perhaps has been mentioned before – was an extremely organised person. Like many organised people, who are faced with a deteriorating situation, her first step towards dealing with it was making a list.

She wrote:

- The Pyramid

- Stavros Theoupoulos' organisation/cult. Pro pyramid? Pro Barn?

- Alfred is attempting to infiltrate Stavros' cult. Details sketchy.

- Ron – has missile. Explosives? Attack on Pyramid imminent.

- Mysterious artifacts – time watch and space measure, both from strange woman in Laplander hat. Skull?

- Surviving Pavilionites under attack – near miss for Donna. Donna's bail extended.

- Dark Brownie – exorcism somehow leads to acquittal? Seen moping around the Centre.

It was quite a list. Where to begin? Fanaka seemed to be on Ron's case, and Emma believed that she could rely on him. Alfred's attempt to infiltrate the kebab shop was on thinner ice, but again there wasn't much Emma could do about that for now. That left the Barnlings and the Brownie; neither of which were issues that Emma felt she could help with greatly.

Uncertain where to turn, Emma went to speak to her leader, Ms Shan. Ms Shan was in charge of the anti-Barn resistance and knew of more things that were going on in the Super Centre than Emma did. Her wisdom should be a useful guide. Emma opened the trapdoor in the back of her shop and descended into the little subterranean space where Ms Shan was hiding out.

There was no one there.

Emma was not prone to panic, but she felt a horrible void rise in her gut. The rear entrance to her shop was a huge roller door; impossible to open silently. There was no exit from the cellar save via the trapdoor. Emma had seen Ms Shan that morning when she'd dropped off her breakfast. Since then, she'd only left the shop for a quarter of an hour to have lunch. Could Ms Shan have left during that time? It seemed unlikely, but other explanations involved teleportation or a dimensional portal or some other idea that made Emma's head hurt.

A loud knock from upstairs snapped her from her thoughts. She clambered up the ladder to the shop, where young Christian was waiting by the door, shifting from foot to foot in impatience. When she opened the door, she saw Alfred slowly running up.

"Emma," Christian said. "We have important information! I need to see Ms Shan."

"She's not here," Emma said.

"Right," Alfred said loudly. "Not here. Of course she's

not, haha. Can we come in anyway?"

Rolling her eyes, Emma waved Alfred and Christian through the door. "Now can we see Ms Shan?" Alfred whispered.

"She's really not here," Emma said. "She's vanished."

"How…" Alfred began. "Never mind, we'll figure that out later. What's important is that you listen to what Christian found out."

"Right," Christian said, "In the beginning of time there was, bullshit bullshit, backstory, exposition, and there's some sort of mystical war on between vaguely defined metaphysical forces. With me so far? Anyway, the DIY Barn was just our dimension's version of the Barn of Shadows, but the Pyramid is the work of the Grey Barn, which feigned support for the Barn of Shadows only to steal a key cosmic location. South Hertling is a strategically vital point in the Multiversal Struggle."

"That's not very interesting," Emma said. "My friend has gone missing…"

"It's *not* that interesting," Christian admitted. "But it *does* mean that the backstories to crappy fantasy novels are actually a reflection of a cosmic truth. I've got a couple of mates who play Dungeons and Dragons. They'll be stoked to know that."

Emma glared at Christian. She did not like glaring at

people who were not her employees. It seemed rude, somehow. But it worked: the lad fell silent.

"We need to find Ms Shan," Emma said. "Because she's our friend, because she's done a lot for us and…"

"But, Emma…" Alfred began.

"Do you want to be the one to tell Mrs Liselle that Ms Shan has vanished?" Emma said. "Do you?"

Alfred went bright red. "She was going to propose once the Marriage Equality legislation went through Parliament," he murmured.

"Who was going to propose?" Christian said.

"Both of them. Each trying to surprise the other. They both had rings and everything."

"And now Ms Shan is gone. How sadorable."

Emma shook her head.

"So, how will we find her, Emma?" Alfred said.

"Perhaps I could be of assistance?" asked a high-pitched voice.

The voice came from a direction it shouldn't have. The back of the store. No one there, no way in, et cetera. The speaker was a boneless cat-thing, similar to Emma's colleague, McKinley. It shared McKinley's impossibly huge eyes, but where McKinley was round, stumpy-legged, and usually quadrupedal, this cat stood on two long back legs. It was purple, with a white face, and in one hand it held a yellow Gladstone bag.

Alfred screamed.

"Don't be afraid, Alfred," the cat said. "We're not what you believe."

"You're not evil hyperintelligent cats from another dimension?" Alfred said.

"Uh… Well, we're not very evil."

"Are. You. Going. To. Help. Find. Ms. Shan?" Emma asked. "Because that's the order of the day. I am not interested in exposition, backstory, prophecy, foreshadowing or anything, *anything* else. All right? My friend is missing, and I am going to help her. You are helping me, or I am ignoring you. Understand?"

"No need to get like that," the cat sulked. "I was sent to help you, and that's what I'm going to do."

"Sent? Who by?" Emma said. "No, on second thought, I don't care. I'm leaving the shop, and I'm looking for Ms Shan. Coming?"

She marched out the door. Behind her, she heard the creature whine: "I was sent by the Parliament of Cats, of course."

20 Genius

Hoonworld Auto was having a sale. The Super Centre carpark was especially noisy, both from the unusual number of cars for a weekday and the extreme volume of their engines.

On a little bench in a quiet corner, Fanaka sat next to the Brownie. Only a few Super Centre customers walked past, most studiously avoiding the man in the dashiki, a circlet of bronze gears around his head and his companion, a metre-high man with pointed ears, dressed in a black corduroy suit and silk waistcoat embroidered with skulls.

"I asked Captain Pete about Ron," Fanaka said.

"Ugh, that guy," the Brownie replied.

"Well, he does know everyone," Fanaka continued. "He says he hasn't seen Ron, or Karl, or anybody else I asked about. Kept asking me questions about time. I know I'm an expert, but..."

"But now's not the time?" the Brownie chuckled. "Come on, that was funny. Ah, you scientists... Or are you an engineer?"

"I'm a little vague on that myself."

"Whatever," the Brownie said. "You come up with all these theories of time, and they're nothing like how people experience time. 'Now's not the time,' we say. Now's *always* the time. That what *now* means. So how can it be now and also not the time? Sounds like that's a mystery worthy of Einstein."

Fanaka took a while to consider this. The obvious response was to say, 'your thought was fatuous, and you should feel stupid for thinking it, and worse for saying it out loud,' but he was far too polite to give voice to that. Instead, he said, "I was wondering if perhaps you had seen Ron."

"Look," the Brownie replied. "Thanks for voting to acquit me and all. But don't think I owe you any favours."

Fanaka scratched his bald head. He still didn't quite know what to make of the Brownie. He was a man of science, after all, and dealing with the Fae didn't come up much in engineering courses. The little creature was free, it seemed, and able to go anywhere it chose. Yet it still clung around this ridiculously impersonal centre of commerce.

"I do not say you owe me anything," Fanaka said. "Not me personally. But, intentionally or not, we are both partly responsible for the rise of the Pyramid. If you can help me find Ron..."

The Brownie shook his head. "I'm a Brownie, not a bloodhound. I haven't seen a twitchy guy with a rocket launcher. I think I'd remember if I had."

"I wonder if you're lying," Fanaka said. "After all, aren't you evil?"

The Brownie shrugged. "One man's evil is another man's uncooperative."

"You did meddle with a superweapon."

"You built said weapon. Are you evil?"

Fanaka scratched his head impatiently. "Don't you have… you know, magic powers?"

"My magic is mostly housework-related," the Brownie sighed. "Look, I won my freedom, and I went a little nuts afterwards. It happens. Have you ever met an undergraduate? Now, I've settled down and I'm mostly just wondering what to do with my life. You know, like a graduate. I haven't seen your friend and I don't know how to find him. I tell you, though, I'd find him if I could."

"Would you?" Fanaka sighed.

"Well, it's something to do, isn't it?"

Fanaka rubbed his eyes. He was getting sick of the search for Ron. He wasn't even sure anymore that Ron's plan to blow up the Pyramid *was* a bad plan, he just didn't want to find out the hard way. But the woman… The woman in the Laplander hat… the way she'd told Fanaka that he could never stop Ron…

Fanaka was a scientist, and as such he preferred to see himself as a seeker of truth, regardless of its origin. But in his heart of hearts, he wanted to prove the enigmatic woman *wrong*. He wanted what she said to be false, just because *she* had said it. In his mind, he'd come to see her not as a person, but as an anthropomorphic representation of the baffling mysteries that beset him. It was not a productive strategy in the generation of new knowledge – but he wanted to *win*.

"Do you ever feel that you have no control over events in your life?" Fanaka said.

"I was basically an unwilling servant for most of my life," the Brownie said. "So, 'yes' to that."

"I suppose everyone feels that way sometimes," Fanaka mused.

"Again, I was a literal slave."

"My way of coping was quiet observation."

"Again, you built a literal doomsday device," the Brownie said. "I understand that you're being introspective, but details matter."

A sudden thought overtook Fanaka, a thought so very obvious that he was deeply ashamed not to have thought of it before.

"What's your name?" he asked the Brownie.

"Brownie."

"Really?"

"My name is Timothy Brown," the Brownie sighed. "And being that this is Australia, that makes me either 'Brownie' or 'Timmo.'"

"Hm."

"And I don't much care for 'Timmo.'"

"I get it."

Fanaka stared into space. His naked eye could see nothing but blue sky, but his mind filled in details of stellar positions, planets, satellites – if you could dignify the flimsy space technology of this world with that term. Not a damn gear up there; not a spring not a brass armature. None of the technology in this timeline seemed right, except for the watches. There were always the watches.

"You're some sort of genius, aren't you?" the Brownie said.

"Some sort," Fanaka said. "It doesn't seem to help, though."

"Why don't you search for Ron in a more… uh… genius-like fashion?"

Fanaka felt his brow furrow under his circlet. "How do you mean?"

"Well, right now you're trying to find this man by asking people. Nothing wrong with that – but isn't it something that anyone could do? Why don't you search more Sherlock Holmes style? Deductive reasoning and whatnot."

"Contrary to popular belief, Holmes tended to use abductive reasoning more than deductive. In deduction..."

"See? You're smart. Why not take what you know about Ron and use that to figure out where he is?"

The conversation stopped briefly while a customer began loading up his Honda hatchback, which was parked directly in front of the bench. For a while, there was nothing for Fanaka to look at except the man's besweatpanted backside, which was not entirely engaging.

"I thought of doing the detective thing," he said, once the customer had driven away. "Ron needed some sort of workspace to build his explosive device and he's probably using that same space to attach the device to Mildred's rocket. I've considered this, and I haven't been able to locate any accessible space in the vicinity in which he could easily do that."

"So, this is where you do the genius bit!" Brownie said. "You think to yourself, 'where would I go if I was building a rocket,' and..."

"Why would I want to build a rocket?"

"No, that's not my point."

"I could, you know. I helped Mildred build the rocket

Ron stole."

"I'm sure you could build any sort of missile," Brownie said, pursing his lips. "My point is…"

"Yes, I can build a missile… or… an anti-missile missile?" Fanaka mused. "Like the Tanganyikans used against the Uzbeks at the battle of Palermo! I don't have to find Ron – I just have to build an automatic missile defence for the Pyramid and stand back. Brownie – it is you, sir, who are the genius. I owe you a debt of thanks."

Fanaka stood and walked away. His nagging doubts about himself and his place in the world were replaced by visions of equations and parabolas. And gears. Lots and lots of gears.

He didn't stop to look back at Brownie. If he had, he would have seen the expression on the little creature's face. Perhaps then he would have understood whether Brownie's intentions were benevolent or malicious.

21 Rocket

The trick, Ron had thought, was to find a place too small for his purposes. That was very important. Once the people of this world had discovered that he was in the process of building a missile, they would inevitably search for him in all the places where such work might easily be done. The abandoned factory on Blackwood St, or that new building at the Harrison company that hadn't been opened yet.

Ron had fooled them all. By doing the work on his missile in the share-house room he slept in, he could work in peace. Granted, the presence of a rocket made sleeping a little difficult, and his housemates often complained about the smell of aviation fuel. But work was proceeding, albeit awkwardly.

Ron was lying on the floor beneath the rocket, one leg twisted around a guidance fin, and reattaching a panel with a ratchet spanner when the door opened. It only opened halfway when it hit the side of the missile with a clang.

"There's a guy to see you," came a voice through the open door, probably belonging to Ron's flatmate, Tony.

"Who is it?"

"I'm not your bloody social secretary, mate. Some bloke in a white suit."

Ron almost lost control of his bowels. Then he remembered, on this Earth the security people tended to wear dark clothes, unlike the white-clad Dinowaffengestapo in his home timeline. He relaxed a little, then tensed again as the door was shoved open further, threatening to dislodge the missile, which was only supported at the tail by a sawhorse and at the nose by Ron's bedframe.

The door closed, and Ron saw a pair of white-clad legs walk in. The owner of those legs sat on his bed.

"Ronald Teerexbane?" said the legs.

"Yes," Ron said. "Here, just let me get…"

The missile teetered a little. Ron decided to stay put. If it fell, it would surely injure him quite badly, if not kill him. Whoever the legs belonged to knew that, surely.

"Ronald Terexbane of Nazi Dinosaur Earth?"

"Yes," Ronald said. He could hear the quaver in his own voice.

"And this is the rocket that Fanaka is looking for," the voice said.

"Who are you?" Ronnie was beginning to wonder if this man was with the local security forces.

"My name is Karl," the voice said. "I've been… My

memory has… Look, that's not important. What matters is, I need your rocket."

Again, Ronnie tried to pull himself out from under the rocket. Again, it shifted alarmingly, but he remained still.

"You can't," Ron said. "I have to destroy the Pyramid. If I don't, perhaps I'll never return home."

Karl gave a bitter laugh. "There's no going home. There never is. The world… the worlds we once inhabited are gone. We can't reassemble the pieces. All we can do is punish the guilty."

"But the Pyramid –"

"Is a *Pyramid*. Sure, it's the occult symbol of unfathomable cosmic power — but it's also a big pile of limestone. Your rocket might dent it, but what does that matter?"

Ron considered another attempt to escape but found he couldn't move. This time it was not fear that paralysed him, it was depression. He'd known this about the Pyramid. Known it from the start. Destroying it would take the destructive power of an army, or at least the efforts of a hundred engineers. Buildings are destroyed by damaging their structure until they collapse into a heap, but a pyramid *is* a heap. Nothing to be done there. There was a reason Egyptian pyramids survived the pharaohs who built them by thousands of years, and it wasn't magic. It was simple physics.

"Why do you want the missile?" he asked, "if it can't be used against the Pyramid?"

The legs shifted from foot to foot. "The Pyramid is beatable," they said. "But on a higher level than us. It's part of a universal conflict so huge that it passes right through 'awesome' and comes right back around to 'stupid.' But there are other evils that can be faced. Evils that are more… shall we say… repto-fascist in nature."

For a long moment, Ron said nothing. Finally, he said, "I think I'd like to come out now."

"I think you're ready for it."

Ron slid out from under the missile, and finally saw the man with the white pants. He wore a grubby white suit and a straw hat. His face and hands were sunburned, his lips were blistered, but he was otherwise neat, tidy, and clean.

"You come from a world where evil reptiles are known to one and all," Karl said.

"Not all dinosaurs are Nazis, you see, everyone thinks that. But the ones who are…"

"On this world the evil lizards are shapeshifters," Karl said. "I never really believed that particular conspiracy theory. I mean, seriously? UFOs controlling MKULTRA is pretty straightforward when you get down to it, but shapeshifting? Come *on*. But then I saw someone change shape before my very eyes!"

Ron frowned as he took a seat on the bed. "You saw a lizard change into a human?"

"Well, I saw a human change into another human," Karl said, with a wave of his hand. "I have to assume it was a lizard at other times. Stands to reason. Point is, it was the Pavilionites. I thought they were the good guys, but really they're reptiloids."

Again, Ron needed to think a while before answering. At length he said, "You haven't got a clue have you?"

Karl frowned but said nothing.

"Okay, let's say that you're right, and whatever it was that you saw was evidence of shapeshifting lizard men," Ron said. "Let's say. How is a rocket going to help you? If it's a huge conspiracy, destroying one of their bases will do nothing. Hell, this missile would destroy whatever evidence there was in that base. It would be worse than doing nothing."

"My plan," Karl said, "is to fire a warning shot. Straight into the Pyramid's eye!"

"And that connects with what you just said, because…?"

In between his hat and the white collar of his shirt, Karl began to go an almost Barnaby Joycean shade of red.

"You know what? I'm starting to think that, whatever's going on here, the solution *isn't* a giant explosive missile," Ron said. "You know what? I'll just remove the warhead and return the rocket to Mildred with my apologies. Her husband is a prisoner of the Moon Men, or some shit. It was probably wrong of me to take it from her."

Karl removed his hat. For a while, he sat there deep in thought. His face, at first, was expressionless. Gradually, a look came over his windburned features, as if some deep and abiding understanding was forming somewhere in his troubled brain.

He pulled back sharply and brought his forehead down into Ronnie's face.

Ron awoke with his nose blocked with dried blood and a splitting headache – and no rocket in his bedroom.

22 King

As the world fell apart, Alfred considered holding Emma's hand. The logic was that they were in a deeply unsettling situation, so he ought to hold her hand to comfort her. Truthfully, he strongly suspected that he was more worried than she was. Mostly he wanted to hold her hand, simply because he wanted to hold her hand.

In the end he didn't. While all around him, everything he believed to be true was being wrung through some cosmic mangle, the retention of his fundamental timidity seemed soothing. Perhaps it was more calming than having his hand held by the woman of his desires. Perhaps less. As it stood, he had no way of knowing.

They – Alfred, Emma and Christian – stood outside of normal space. That was obvious. The distances between objects was subtly wrong, in ways he couldn't even begin to explain. Time was odd too, moving weirdly as if seconds were trudging through mud while minutes zoomed by like bees.

Perhaps he should have taken Emma's hand.

They stood in a room, which was built in a shape that

Alfred had no word for. They stood in the… middle? It wasn't quite the right word, but as good as any. Around the… edges? It looked nothing like a lecture hall, but it had that feeling, the cats around the sides looking down at the humans.

Only they weren't cats. Some seemed boneless, some spongy. Many had enormous eyes, others did not. Most wore no clothes, but others wore a motley assortment of hats, jackets, waistcoats, boots. Few wore pants, but all lacked visible genitals. None of them were talking. The sound of purring filled the air.

The black 'cat' with the Gladstone bag that had brought the humans to this place bowed low before the largest of the cats. This one still did not look quite right, but it was a lot closer in appearance to a normal cat. It was a tan-and-white tabby, who sat batting a loose button from the throne's upholstery, which dangled on a length of thread. The cat's other distinguishing feature was that it wore a long coat, a tricorn hat and leather boots on its hind legs.

"Your majesty," the cat with the bag said, bowing.

"What's all this about?" the cat on the throne said. His voice was deep, gravelly and peevish.

"These humans seek help," the cat with the bag said. "One of their number has gone missing."

"What of it?"

"She is important to the struggle on Earth, sire. She is/was/will be playing a key role in the situation with the Grey Barn's betrayal of the Barn of Shadows."

"So go help them find her," the King said, reclining his throne. He looked 'up.' Alfred followed his gaze to what might have been a ceiling, which was blank other than a large square window. "By my calculation, there will be a sunbeam soon, and I don't want to miss it."

Alfred looked around at the surrounding cats. After their initial interest, their attention seemed to have wandered. They were staring in all directions or licking themselves. One put a whole fish in its mouth and pulled out a perfect fish skeleton.

"What is all this?" Emma said. "Who are you?"

"I was just about to ask the same question," Alfred lied.

"We are the Parliament of Cats," the cat on the throne said. "And I am the King of Cats."

There was a long pause.

"What does that mean exactly?" Emma asked.

"Just what it sounds like."

"You... you make laws for cats?"

"That's right. All the laws that cats follow."

"I think I see a flaw in this plan," Alfred said.

"That's a feature, not a bug," the King said. "The natural independence of cats means we don't have to do a lot of work, you know? Oooh, here's the sunbeam."

From its armrest, the King took a small remote control, and pointed it at the window. When the window had opened, it pressed the button again. It continued purring in the sunbeam, opening and closing the window and ignoring Alfred and his friends completely.

The humans looked at one another. "Well, this is friggin' pointless," Christian said. The cat with the bag at least had the courtesy to look embarrassed.

"YOU!" Alfred shouted. Emma and Christian flinched. It took a moment even for Alfred to catch up with his own sudden annoyance. When his forebrain finally caught up with his hindbrain, he realised that he was pointing at a human woman sitting amongst the cats, dangling a piece of string in front of a kitten in a little blue jacket and baggy pants. She wore a tweed jacket and jeans under a patchwork coat. On her head she wore a Laplander hat.

"Hm?" the woman said.

Alfred strode towards her, his fear and confusion forgotten. "You're the one! You gave me that watch! My life has been so weird since then! Too weird! It's all your fault that I'm here, in non-Euclidian space, with a bunch of ridiculous cat-things!"

"Hey," the King said, without much rancour.

"Have we met?" the woman said. It was at this point that Alfred realised that she was not the woman at all. The woman with the watch had been in her fifties or sixties. This woman was twenty, tops.

"Wait, weird Watch… time travel… it's still you!" he said. "Even if you are younger, it is still you. Take your Watch back!"

"What, this Watch?" she said, taking the device from her pocket.

"No, a later version of that watch, from when you're getting old."

"Ah," the woman said. "I think I see now. Well, I'm sorry if I bothered you on some future date. Don't quite know the details, but if you give me the watch…"

Alfred reached into his pocket. "Damn it! I don't have it."

"Fanaka has it," Emma said. "And my measure. Remember? Now, what is your story, dear?"

"I'm a scientist," she said. "Right now, I'm studying the cats of Dimension Seven. They have an extremely odd relationship to the Barns, but I don't quite understand how it all works."

"You know how the Barns work?" Christian demanded.

"Does anyone, really?"

"Confound it, stop interrogating my guest!" the King said. "I'm king here. If there's to be any shouting going on here,

I'm the one who'll be doing it. Anyway, we've debated your request…"

"I didn't hear that," Alfred said.

"Well, you weren't listening. We decided not to help you. Big surprise, yes?"

Alfred looked at the cat with the bag, who shrugged bonelessly. "You brought us outside of space and time and took us to this place so that this idiot could refuse to help us?"

"I thought they *would* help," the cat with the bag shrugged.

"*Can* you help?" Alfred said. "I mean, if you decided to help us find Ms Shan, you could do it, right?"

"Easily," the King said.

"But you won't?"

"Don't feel like it," the king said, putting his feet up on a stool.

Alfred's anger rose. For perhaps the first time in his life, he found his fury so great that it overrode his timidity completely. "You may look adorable," he sneered, "but you're a useless bunch of…"

With a mighty rawl, the king was of the throne. It ran up Alfred's shirtfront and hissed right in his face. Alfred's rage drained away completely. There was nothing in him but fear, noting before him but the terrifying eyes and needle-sharp teeth of this terrible creature.

There followed a loud crashing sound and a tinkling of glass. The King – clinging to Alfred's cardigan, one claw raised in attack – turned its head slowly to look behind it.

"Sacre bleu!" it said.

The window that had been in the 'ceiling' had fallen. Alfred was unclear as to just how high up the ceiling was, but high enough for the falling window to shatter the seat of the throne entirely.

Alfred looked at the King. The King looked at Alfred. For a long time, nothing was said.

"Well," the King said, quietly. "I suppose I owe you my life. You shall have what you want. The order will go out that all of my people in your world will help you find your friend."

Alfred could do nothing but stammer in reply. "Thank you, your majesty," Emma said.

The King leapt up onto the ruins of the throne and stood on its hind legs on the backrest. "Human friends!" it intoned, "Let me know how that works out for you!"

It hopped down and scampered from the chamber. Alfred realised that he had not stopped shaking since he lost his temper. He began breathing deeply to calm down.

"Well, that worked," Christian said. "Pure bloody luck, but it worked."

"Come on, Alfred," Emma said. "It's time to go home."

It was only then that Alfred noticed that Emma had taken him by the hand.

23 Plot

Following the incident at the courthouse, Donna was held at the hospital for a while for observation. She discharged herself as soon as she was able, and hurried down to the South Hertling Super Centre, to warn everyone that the DIY Barn was back on the march.

She went to warn Ms Shan but found her gone from her hiding place. Emma was also nowhere to be seen. Neither was Christian, nor Fanaka, nor that weird old guy who Fanaka worked for. She considered dropping in on Belinda at the art supply shop, rejecting the idea after barely a second. It was an emergency… but it wasn't *that* big of an emergency.

That left one person to talk to. Nalda.

It wasn't that Donna didn't like Nalda. She neither liked nor disliked her. Sadie's mentorship had taught Donna much of human nature but surprisingly little about killer cyborgs from the future. As a result, Donna tried not to think about Nalda more than necessary. Oddly, this made it more awkward to talk to Nalda than someone Donna actually disliked.

As bad luck would have it, Donna found both Nalda *and* Belinda at the disposals shop but – cursed with being a decent person – she smiled instead of sighing deeply.

Nalda stood rigidly behind the counter, dressed in her usual black leather jacket and jeans. Belinda wore a red shirt with an illegibly embroidered monogram. Fortunately, Donna knew this mark identified her as staff from the Super Centre's art supply shop which, equally fortunately, was not called 'Art of Darkness' or 'Warm Craft' or anything stupid like that. It was called 'Jane's Arts and Craft Supplies' and people seemed pretty okay with that.

"I'm glad you're here, Belinda," Donna said, after a brief struggle with her internal definition of the word 'glad.' "I have to tell…"

"Just wait a second, Deanna," Belinda said. "I'm in the middle of an important experiment. I'm trying to see if I can explain to Nalda the meaning of 'love.'"

Nalda turned slightly to look at Donna. Her dark sunglasses made eye contact impossible, but there was no mistaking that despondent look of someone who had been talking to Belinda for too long. For the first time ever, she felt a sense of connection to the terrifying fembot.

"Belinda," Donna began, "I don't know if you noticed, but Nalda has been seeing Fanaka for weeks."

"Fanaka?" Belinda said. "The scientist guy? I thought he was just doing maintenance work on her."

"You might say dat," Nalda smirked.

"You're not helping, Nalda," Donna said. "Look, a) Nalda knows what love is, and b) rather more urgently, the Barn is on the move again and Ms Shan is missing. We need to round up the troops."

"Pffft, the Barn," Belinda said. "They thought they were so tough, but we kicked their butts. We can do it again."

Again, Donna and Nalda exchanged glances. "You do remember the massive casualties, don't you Belinda?"

"Oh, yeah, the casualties. We should probably try not to let that happen again, ay?"

"Ve certainly should not!" Nalda said, thumping her hand on the counter. "If der Barn rises again, it must be smashed! *Destroyed*! Destroyed mit extreme…"

"How much is this gas burner?" asked a terrified man, with a big beard and a camo jacket.

"Es ist $124.99," Nalda thundered. "That is *quite reasonable!*"

The man made his purchase and scuttled off as fast as possible.

"We need to rally the troops," Donna said again. "Who do we have?"

"Fanaka is at home, vorking on a sophisticated short-range anti-missile device. Boys und dere toys!" Nalda chuckled; the sound made Donna and Belinda shudder.

"I can't find Christian anywhere," Donna said. "Seamus is more… mobile than usual, but I'm not sure how useful he is in a fight. That leaves you, Zorbar, and Gwen the Phantasm. Might be enough."

They each considered this for a moment, before shaking their heads. "Nein, der Barnlings are cowards. If they are ready for a rematch, they will have calculated the odds. If they were ready to fight us all, then they are more ready to fight while we're a few people down."

"How do we know they didn't already take out Ms Shan and Emma and the rest?" Belinda wondered.

"They tried to blow me up and take a courthouse with me," Donna said. "They aren't subtle enough to pick us off one by one without leaving any evidence."

"How did the court case go, by the way?"

"Pretty well, actually," Donna said. "When you save the magistrate and the court building from destruction, that tends to back up your claims of being 'of good character.'"

"We are dancing around der issue, like common Baverians," Nalda said, with another thump on the counter. "Ve have been relying on der legal system to set our friends free, one by one. Dat vas fine, when we thought we had the time for that. We do not. Therefore…"

"Jailbreak!" Belinda squealed. "Ja-a-a-ail break! Daylight come and me wanna go ho-ome. Jailbreak! I say jail, I say jail, I say jail…"

"Stop that!" Donna snapped. "It's cultural appropriation, *and* it's out of tune."

"Ja, one or the other, please…"

But Belinda wasn't listening. She was dashing about the disposals shop, picking up camping tools, studying them for jailbreak potential and discarding them with disgust.

"What's this? Can we bake it in a cake and send it to Laura? No! How about this? They can tunnel out with it, like that movie when the guy from *The Hudsucker Proxy* helped Batman's friend escape from the Kurgan? No! How about…"

Donna leaned in closer to Nalda. "Want to let her run around while I tell you the real plan?"

Nalda gave a grim smile. "Ja. We'll break everybody out – Laura, Axel, Adam and the other ones whose names I can't remember. And den ve vill crush the DIY Barn, see it driven before us and hear the lamentations of their stockholders."

"I found a crowbar," Belinda burbled.

24 Revelation

When Emma found herself back in the real world, she observed that she was in the south-eastern corner of the South Hertling Super Centre, in a discreet spot between Emile's Fine Vintage Cellar and Harry's House of Ethanol-Based Beverages. Emma didn't quite follow how she had been transported into the mundane world any more than she had understood how they had left it. All she knew was that she was back, with Alfred and Christian and a few others.

Mostly, the newcomers were cats. Not everyday cats with fur and whiskers and breathtaking narcissism. The King's subjects wore jackets and coats, shoes and boots, and all sorts of headgear. Immediately, they began fanning out across the carpark – searching, no doubt, for the missing Ms Shan.

The sight of a cat in a little trench coat and deerstalker hat made Emma laugh as it examined its surroundings with a magnifying glass. Her amusement froze into horror as she saw a small white cat with a bow behind its ear, its initial appearance of cuteness transformed into something ghastly by a lack of any visible mouth beneath its pink nose. That was the cats in a nutshell, a weird mixture of lovable and terrifying.

Not all that different from normal cats, in a way.

For the second time that day, Emma found herself taking Alfred by the hand. This time, Alfred squeezed back less timidly.

"I don't know about you," Christian said. "But after that I could do with a drink. And for the rest of you. I'm buying."

Emma and Alfred were left with the other human while Christian went into Harry Montresor's bottle shop. Emma sighed, having forgotten about her. She wore a patchwork coat and a Laplander hat, and she was looking up at the Pyramid and scratching furious notes.

"How long has that been there?" she asked.

"Never mind that," Emma said. "It's time you came clean. You've caused enough trouble…"

"Will have caused enough trouble," the woman said.

"Stop that. You've caused enough trouble. It's time for you to tell us who you are."

"Oh, is that all?" the woman said. "My name is Professor Femur and I am one of the Science Lords of Atlantis. You see, Atlantis never sank, it simply relocated itself to the centre of Time itself, from whence…"

"I got some tequila," Christian said, returning with a bottle in a brown paper bag.

"Too late, I think this young lady already ate the worm," Alfred replied.

Christian was the youngest of the four, but even he was too old to drink in a shopping centre alcove, so the decision was made to go to the storeroom of Storage Universe and drink from water-cooler paper cups. Emma gave a friendly wave to Harry Montressor, and another to Emile Fortunato, who ran the SuperCentre's other liquor shop.

Emma was not a big drinker and neither, it turned out, was Alfred. But Professor Femur seemed able to drink the booze like it was water, without the slightest sign of ill effect and ended up consuming most of the bottle.

"I have two livers," she explained, though nobody asked.

"So, these things," Emma said. "The Watch and the Measure. What are they?"

"No one knows," Femur said.

"Sounds about right," Christian muttered.

"I know, right?" Alfred said. "I mean what is it about this place and getting a straight answer out of people, eh?"

"They are mysterious artifacts from the dawn of time," Femur said, making spooky 'dawn of time' gestures with her hands. "Or possibly the end of time. It's hard to tell sometimes. I was given them by the Science Lords of Atlantis to help me find the fissures in time and space and thereby explore the cosmos."

Femur said this in a dramatic tone, clearly meaning to impress. As it was, her bombshell was met with a raised eyebrow from Emma, a shrug from Christian and a sigh from Alfred. After a very long pause Emma added, "Oh, good for you," but she was mostly just trying to get things moving again.

"Yeah, is the money good being a time traveller?" Christian asked. "Only it's got to be tricky filling in your paysheets if you go backwards in time and wipe out an hour or two of paid work."

"Why did you give these artifacts to us, Professor?" Emma asked before Christian could elaborate.

"I didn't," Femur said. "I will, later."

"Why *might* you give them to us?"

The Professor stood, swallowed half a glass of tequila at a gulp and began pacing the little stockroom. She immediately barked her shin against an angular plastic box and sat down again.

"It's hard to say," she said. "Possibly there is some other ancient artifact at work here, which needed to be countered?"

Again, Emma and Alfred shrugged, but Christian piped up, "Oh, yeah, the Skull! It's some sort of cosmic power source. It's pretty gnarly. I haven't seen it since the Battle."

"So that's probably it," Femur smiled. She took the watch from her pocket and checked it. "Well, I'll leave you to sort it out. I have to catch a wormhole to the Lemon Slice Nebula, and it's leaving soon…"

She stood to leave, banged her shins again, grimaced, and made for the door.

"Wait," Alfred said. "What about this Skull?"

"I don't know anything about it yet," Femur said. "Only just heard of its existence, remember? I'll tell you when I do."

"No, you won't!" Emma sniffed. "You'll come back and act mysterious and unhelpful. I know. I was there!"

Professor Femur shrugged. "They say you get more like your parents as you get older."

"And?" Emma demanded.

"And my parents were, like, *super* unhelpful. Anyway, use the Watch and the Measure to find the Skull, and it'll probably all work out, or something."

She turned to go, and narrowly avoided being hit in the face by the storeroom door opening. It was Gwen, who gave Femur a suspicious look as she came.

"What's going on?" she said. "Nalda tells me that Donna said that Ms Shan is missing. Don't think Donna likes me much," she added. "Who's this?"

"I was just leaving," the Professor said. "Remember, use

the all-powerful artifacts I gave/give/will give you wisely."

"Fanaka has them," Emma said, but it was too late. The Professor had slammed the door behind her. By the time Emma opened it, she was gone.

"Fanaka?" Gwen said. "Just saw him a minute ago. He was setting something up on Wellington Street. He said it was found-object art, but honestly it looked more like an anti-missile battery to me."

Alfred, frantic, clapped his hand over his ears, presumably so that he could hear no more of the conversation. Christian facepalmed and rubbed his eyes. Emma did not really want to clap her hand over her mouth to complete the trio.

Under the circumstances, she felt she had very little choice.

25 Downstage

Another aspect of Fanaka's abiding lack of stupidity was that he deeply aware, even as he was setting up his anti-aircraft battery, that it wouldn't go well.

This was in Wellington Road, just across from the South Hertling Super Centre, and next to the giant evil Pyramid, in the ruins of what was once the South Bannerman Mega Centre. Fanaka's intelligence led him to believe he should be cautious as he worked, depriving him of even the idiot joy of recklessness. In short, he was not having a good time, and his second thoughts had long since overtaken his first thoughts.

But smart or stupid, genius or fool: once a man has begun building a steam-powered anti-aircraft gun in a public road, there's no easy way to walk back from it.

Fanaka paused a little to admire his handiwork. He nodded and smiled – not a happy smile, but a satisfied one. It *would* work. It would work *perfectly*. If Ron fired his rocket, the AA gun would automatically spring into action and shoot it down. Additional AA placements around the Pyramid ensured three-hundred-and-sixty-degree protection. Carefully prepared labels on each of the guns misidentified them as art installations. Since most of the citizens of South Hertling would have happily walked ten minutes out of their way to avoid an art installation, Fanaka judged them safe from tampering.

With a twist of a steam-vent, Fanaka activated the final placement. *There!* He had done it. He had proved wrong that horrible woman with the Laplander hat. Ron would never be able to attack the Pyramid, not until Fanaka had determined it was safe to do so.

"Which I think was my motivation," Fanaka sighed under his breath, "last time I checked. Perhaps Nalda is right, and I would benefit from clearer direction and less absentmindedness."

Shrugging, he turned and ran straight into Ron. It was only an inordinate effort of will that prevented Fanaka from saying "Whaaaaaaaa---???" in an obnoxiously loud voice.

"Whaaaaaaa---??" Ron said.

It was then that Fanaka noticed that Ron's nose seemed literally bent out of shape, as if he was recovering from a fight. A black eye confirmed this suspicion.

"Ron! Are you alright?" Fanaka said, feeling a little annoyed with himself for worrying, when he should probably be punching the man in the nose himself.

"I was attacked in my own house," Ron said, nasally.

The words 'serves you right' were on Fanaka's tongue, but instead he said, "What about the rocket? What have you done with the rocket?"

"It was stolen," Ron said. "I was going to bring it back, honest I was. But this guy, Karl something, he…"

"Karl!" Fanaka said. "What did *he* want with it?"

"He wanted to destroy the Pyramid," Ron said. "I think. I'm a little concussed."

Fanaka cursed in three languages that didn't even exist on this world. Karl Wintergreen! Fanaka didn't know him well, but everybody knew that the man was a conspiracy theorist. Not a particularly successful conspiracy theorist, granted, but even a bad conspiracy theorist was probably too suspicious to be taken in by an AA gun disguised as found object art.

"Why are you flapping like that?" Ron asked.

Fanaka took a deep breath to calm himself. "It's okay," he said. "We can deal with this. I don't know if Karl is a technical man. It might take him a while to get the rocket ready…"

"Oh, it was all but finished when he took it," Ron said. "Even someone with rudimentary mechanical knowledge could have…"

"Ron?"

"Yes?"

"I hate you."

Ron had the good grace to look miserable at this. "What should we do?"

"I don't know," Fanaka said. "Everybody has been looking for Wintergreen for weeks. No one has been able to find him anywhere."

Fanaka began flapping again, though this time he was aware of it. He wished Nalda was there. She always calmed his panic attacks – usually by glaring at him so hard that he passed straight through 'panic' and into 'paralysed with terror.' Sometimes you have to be cruel to be kind.

But, instead of recoiling from his sweetheart's loving death-stare, he found himself stumbling over something small and soft. He righted himself and looked down, to see a purple cat – which, for some reason, was dressed in the collar and cuffs of a dress shirt, but without the shirt.

"Do you mind?" the animal said. "I am appreciating this work of sculpture. Art, even!"

"Uh..." Fanaka said. Then, because he was fast approaching the end of his rope, added, "You haven't seen a disgusting bum in a white suit, have you?"

It didn't seem like a very helpful thing to ask. To Fanaka's astonishment, it seemed to pay dividends.

"Karl Wintergreen? Heavens to Betsy! I just saw him around the corner. Up the street, even! Mind you, he's cleaned himself up a little..."

Fanaka stared down at the bizarre creature, torn between desperate gratitude and a desire to dissect it. He looked at Ron, who shrugged.

"Don't look at me, man. I once saw a triceratops reading *Mein Kampf*. To me, this is comparatively normal."

Taking a deep breath, Fanaka counted to ten. If there was one thing he'd learned since coming to South Hertling, it was how to just ignore crazy nonsense and get on with things.

"Come on, Ron," he said. "Help me catch Karl and recover the rocket, and we'll call it even."

"You know, it wasn't *your* rocket that I stole, so we're already pretty even."

Fanaka just grabbed Ron by the arm and ran in the direction the cat had pointed. He stopped a second later to avoid being hit by a bus, then shouted, "Come on!" again, and kept running.

"Exit, downstage, even!" the cat said, from behind them. Fanaka wondered what the animal meant. But his train of thought was interrupted by an explosion and a plume of smoke in front of him, which he judged as consistent with a steampunk AA battery exploding.

26 Grampy

Much later, Donna realised things could have gone very differently. She could have left the South Hertling Super Centre by the Wellington Road exit, seen the plume of smoke and intervened in the conflict between Fanaka and Karl Wintergreen before it was too late. But in trying to avoid the after-school traffic at Local High School, she took her car out the back way through Bideford Lane, past Cal Meechum Memorial Park, and past the Harrison Foods warehouse.

Donna drove. In the passenger seat sat Belinda. On the rear seat were Carol and Zorbar.

A killer cyborg from the future, an irritating woman who was into cosplay, a hipster barista, a woman of deep (albeit eccentric) Christian beliefs, and an ape-man who had to bow his head and shoulders just to fit in the back of a Subaru hatchback. It shouldn't be enough to organise a jailbreak for over a hundred people, Donna knew. But maybe if she prayed *really* hard...

"Here we are," Donna said, pulling up about outside of a nursing home, half a kilometre away.

"This isn't Long Bay," Carol complained.

"No, this is where we're getting the guy who can help us break everybody out," Dona said. "Our secret weapon. I've been keeping him in reserve in case we needed him. My great-grandfather."

"Your *grandfather?*" Carol said.

"So uncool," Zorbar said. "We do *Reservoir Dogs* walk to car and everything."

"No, we didn't," Donna said.

"We behind you. You not see. We think you too cool turn around, but turn out you just not pay attention."

Donna rested her head on the steering wheel for a moment. It seemed to help.

"My great-grandfather holds the world record for most ever successful escapes," she said. "He's forgotten more about escaping than we'll ever know."

"Oh, was he like a POW or something?" Belinda said.

"Yes," Donna said. "Eventually. Here he is now!"

As one, the occupants of the car turned to see an exceedingly elderly man raise himself, coughing and wheezing, from a sinkhole in the nursery garden bed. A pair of white-clad orderlies -- who seemed more exasperated than angry -- approached from the main building at an unhurried pace.

Donna hopped out of the car and, ignoring the fresh soil on the old man's dressing gown, gave him a huge hug. "Grampy Erik," she cried.

"Donna, my dear!" the old man said. "How good to see you. Excuse me."

The old man turned and took an old-fashioned perfume bottle from his pocket. "Come and get me, coppers!" he snarled, as he squeezed the bulb and sprayed the bottle's contents at the orderlies' eyes. One retreated, covering his eyes. The other simply snatched the bottle from the old man's hands.

"Not this time, Mr Weisz. I'm wearing eye goggles this time."

"What's that?"

"EYE GOGGLES!"

"You don't have to yell," the old man snapped. "Never mind, exercise over for the day. Why don't you and your friends come and visit, Donna? You can have tea, and I think I may have some sweeties saved up."

The prison break party waited in the old man's single bedroom. While Grampy Erik disappeared into the shower, they arranged some crowded seating on hard plastic chairs taken from the dining area.

"Do you really think this geezer will be useful?" Belinda said, thumbing through a large-print volume entitled

'Fundamentals of Security Systems.'

"Look," Donna said, "physically, he might not be up to helping us, but he can tell us what equipment we'll need, who to talk to, how to organise the breakout. Grampy Erik doesn't do cutesy escape-artist-street-magician crap. Real escapes, from real prisons, with real guards, armed with real guns. The man is a legend."

Grampy Erik emerged from the bathroom, clean and in a threadbare dressing gown and surprisingly expensive pyjamas.

"Remind me, Donna was butter menthol you liked? Or barley sugar?"

"Neither, Grampy. No one's liked either of those things since 1950. I don't think they liked them much then, either."

"Never mind, I think I have half a packet of Dr Zumthrum's Clove Balls in my top drawer. You and your friends can share them -- but one each only, mind you. I won't have you all ruining your dinners."

Donna could feel four pairs of accusing eyes on her. Under other circumstances, she might have felt bad, but she was about to show them what was what in a very big way indeed. "Grampy Erik, we have some friends in prison."

"Oh, yes?" the old man said, filling a teapot from a ceramic electric kettle. "Who's for tea?"

"Ja, bitte," Nalda said.

"You German?" Erik said. "Nothing against the Germans, understand. Except you build better cars than fences."

"You were POW in war, ja?"

"Eventually," Erik said. "That was after I lied about my identity and joined the army. Before that, I'd already escaped from Alcatraz, Sing Sing, Devil's Island and Boggo Road. During World War II, I escaped from ten German POW camps, re-joined my unit. I was thrown in an Allied stockade, escaped again, fled to Russia, escaped the Gulag archipelago and fled back here. I did some more escaping from prison camps in Korea. Also, Vietnam – but I was discharged from the army by then, so that was mostly recreational. Now I'm retired and only spend my days escaping from this old folks' home."

Erik poured tea for everyone, then added something from a hipflask to his own cup. Slowly, he lowered himself into his armchair with all the care and caution of a man who is uncertain about the state of his hipbones. Once he was seated comfortably, he looked at his visitors through rheumy, heavily lidded eyes.

"A prison break," he said. "Multiple escapees, hm. Some would say that complicates matters. Certainly, the more people who know the escape plan the greater the chance that something will slip out. That's the received wisdom – but I say more escapees give us more options for creating a breach in security, and can make pursuit more difficult."

"If you're so good at escaping, how come you keep ending up back inside?" Belinda said.

"Because 'escaping' and 'not getting caught' are different skillsets, young lady," Erik said. "And just because you have one, that doesn't mean you have the other. It's alright, though. I'm so good at escaping, I've never needed to learn how not to get caught. Now, let's have some details about this escape before I die of old age."

He cracked his knuckles, then immediately looked like he regretted doing so.

27 Mayhem

Alfred had never run so fast in his life.

Well, that wasn't quite true. He'd been a respectable enough middle-distance runner in high school, oh-so-long ago. But he certainly hadn't run so fast recently. When had been the last time he'd run more than a few steps at a time? A school carnival, probably? Decades ago. Back in the days when he found it hard to find time for his daughters, but before they reached the age when they found it hard to make time for him.

But this particular piece of self-pity was far in the back of his mind. Most of his misery was reserved for bodily discomfort as he pushed his chubby, aging body well past its limits to keep up with the others – Christian jogging with all the careless energy of youth; Gwen short and stout and yet hammering along like nobody's business. And Emma…

It was almost a relief when Emma stumbled. In helping her, Alfred could slow to a stop without feeling bad about it.

"Arooaaariight," Alfred gasped.

"Broke a heel," Emma said.

"Brgaheeel," Alfred said. "I… huh… also do heel

repairs…"

"I know that, Alfred," Emma said, with impatience but without unkindness. She took her shoes off, deposited them in her handbag and took Alfred's hand in her own.

Almost at once, Alfred felt his strength returning and ran with her the rest of the way to Wellington Road. Traffic had stopped in the usually busy roadway, so most of the group was able to cross easily, weaving between immobile vehicles. As the stragglers, Alfred and Emma caught some angry beeping from drivers who probably knew that the aging pair were not the cause of the jam, but who did present a convenient lightning rod for their impatience.

It wasn't hard to see why the traffic had stopped. The main traffic lights over the Wellington Road/Atlantis Street intersection were broken. The pole that held the lights was scorched and bent, leaving the lights themselves hanging barely above the tops of the cars. To make matters worse, all the auxiliary lights were flashing their colours randomly. A black plume of smoke arose from around the corner of the Pyramid that stood on the other side of Wellington Road.

Everywhere was chaos. Truck drivers argued with motorcyclists. An aging, dilapidated DeLorean had rear-ended a wooden-and-buckskin car with stone wheels. A delivery driver was screaming into his phone, unaware that an orangish cat in a boater hat was directing a gang of other cats, who were stealing Styrofoam boxes of frozen fish from the back of his vehicle.

Still, Alfred and Emma ran on.

Around the corner was more mayhem. The black smoke seemed to be coming from a large piece of burning machinery, and a nearby gumtree had also caught ablaze. Near it, Fanaka and Karl Wintergreen were trying to fight. Under other circumstances, the sight of two of his friends trying to kill each other might have saddened Alfred. But neither man was much of a fighter, and each of them was being held back by several bystanders, which made the spectacle more comical than troubling.

Fanaka was shouting, sometimes in his own language and sometimes in English. "Turn it off! Damn you, turn it off!"

"The Hell I will, you Illuminati stooge!" Karl shouted back.

In spite of the seriousness of the situation, Alfred laughed out loud. The term "Illuminati stooge" that put him in mind of robed men performing secret handshakes that devolved into eye-gouges and slaps in the face. His amusement didn't last long; his second wind was already fading, and his laughter came out as a choking wheeze. Emma thumped him on the back, which didn't help much, but was probably well intended.

As Alfred got his breath back, Emma strode forward. That was a good idea. Christian was now holding Fanaka back, while a man Alfred barely recognised held onto Karl. Gwen was busy trying to extinguish the tree. Emma, though… Emma was a force for order. She quieted both of the combatants, with a combination of calming gestures and angry glares, until each man was standing sullenly, staring at his shoes.

"What's going on here?" Emma said, once the boys were silent.

"He's trying to blow up the Pyramid!" Fanaka said.

"He's trying to stop me from blowing up the Pyramid!" Karl said.

"Their stories seem consistent," Christian said.

"Shut the Hell up, Christian," said Alfred, who had been dying to say that for a very long time.

Emma glared at Karl. Karl recoiled a little, but metaphorically stood his ground.

"Start from the beginning," she said.

"In the Zeroth Age, the first Elder Kinsmen of…"

Emma turned on Fanaka. "Begin at the beginning."

Taking a deep breath, Fanaka told the story of Ron's theft of the rocket from Mildred, Karl's theft of the rocket from Ron and… well, that was it, basically.

"So, you destroyed Fanaka's well-intended, but frankly

irresponsible, AA-battery in order to fire your rocket at the Pyramid?" Emma said. "None of us like this thing, young man, but don't you think that's a little reckless?"

"I didn't destroy the AA post," Karl said. "Why would I have to? It's a ballistic rocket, remember? If I wanted, I could fire it right over any anti-aircraft screen and drop it right on the Pyramid's capstone."

All eyes turned to Fanaka, who blushed deeply. "I knew that," he said. "I just didn't think *he* would know that."

"Well, I do," Karl said. "Granted, I had to look it up, but I do! Anyway, I'd given up trying to destroy the Pyramid. I was just standing here to get a view of the music shop, to blow *that* up. I needed to work out the number thingies."

"You mean coordinates?" Alfred said.

"Yeah, those."

"Underestimating Karl probably wasn't that big of a miscalculation," Alfred said to Fanaka. The engineer seemed genuinely pleased at this and gave a wan smile.

"Some of those silver-suited guys who used to work for the DIY Barn were here," Karl said, acting quickly to restore himself as the centre of attention. "They were the ones who blew up the AA battery."

Emma's brow was furrowed, and Alfred thought he knew what it was that confused her.

"Where are the silver men?"

"They ran away."

"Why?"

"Probably to avoid the police."

A great weariness overtook Alfred. He knew what was coming next.

"Alright, then," came an authoritative voice from behind here. "What's going on here?"

Alfred started laughing and couldn't stop, even when they put the cuffs on him. He had never been in trouble with the law before, and there seemed something very funny about a first offense in his mid-fifties, on a charge of criminal damage to a homemade anti-aircraft gun.

"Do you know what?" he said to Emma, in the back of the police van, once he'd finally regained control of himself. "I think I'm starting to enjoy myself for a change."

Emma shook her head, but her disapproval seemed to Alfred to be mixed with affection.

28 Underground

If Karl had learned nothing else during his time as a homeless fugitive, he had learned how to hide. After he slipped away from the police, he ducked around the corner of the Pyramid. The street beyond was littered with an abundance of hiding places. There were cars, small trees, and thick shrubs. On the Pyramid side, there was the remains of the lost Mega Centre's retaining wall. On the other, was a motley selection of suburban fences.

Karl ignored all of these possibilities and slipped into a stormwater drain.

It was surprisingly easy. Months of living on garbage had slimmed him down so much that he didn't even need to remove his jacket. And with so many easily accessible and non-stupid hiding places, the cops were unlikely to pursue him here. Even so, for a while he simply lay still – waiting and observing. It was only when he was certain that the police were not coming that he took a battered flashlight from the pocket of his ragged jacket and began to look around.

The tunnel he found himself in was not the TV variety –

high enough to walk through, punctuated with huge back-lit fans for atmosphere, and free of water. In fact, it was barely large enough for an emaciated man to crawl through, and while it was mostly dry, there was an unpleasant streak of damp, slimy moss running down the middle. It was just as well his suit was already ruined.

Karl considered just lying doggo until he was sure it was safe, but something was clawing for attention. What was it? What? There was a branch of the tunnel running perpendicular to the one in which he was hiding. It must run… It must run…

It must run under the Pyramid.

Again, it took a while for Karl's addled brain to catch up with him. A Pyramid is… well, it's heavy, isn't it? Extremely heavy. Much heavier than the jerry-built buildings of the Mega Centre had been. How was it that this storm-water drain hadn't collapsed? Now that he thought of it, how was it that the entire local infrastructure hadn't failed? There was more than just stormwater drains under the Pyramid, there were water mains, electrical cables, telephone lines, and the NBN. Surely someone would have noticed a massive breach in all of those systems. Well, other than the NBN, obviously.

"Okay," Karl said. "The last couple of times I tried to do something constructive, it went badly and only made things worse. But this time… Surely this time I'm due a break."

Karl dragged himself to the turn that would take him under the Pyramid. He looked down the long rectangular space leading into the unknown, then looked down at his cheap torch, then back down the tunnel. He adjusted his hat. Somehow, he was still wearing his hat. That was kind of cool, at least?

"Let's get to it," he said to no one.

The flashlight in his mouth, he dragged himself down the tunnel, metre by painful metre. His flashlight was just beginning to dim when he found what he was after – a grill directly overhead. And on the other side – blank, flat rock. Gingerly, he touched it. It just felt like limestone. Was it the underside of the Pyramid?

"So, the Pyramid is just... sitting weightlessly on the surface?" Karl said. "But it rose from underground. It smashed the Mega Centre like it was made of Lego. How is this possible?"

"Who's that talking?"

It had been a day since Karl had last eaten. Oddly, this was fortunate, because it meant there was nothing in his bowels, which prevented him from literally soiling himself. As it was, he dropped the flashlight, causing the batteries to fall out.

"Uh..." he said.

"Uh..." he continued.

"Well..." he said, added for the sake of variety.

"Is that you, Karl?" the voice asked.

For most people, one of the few things that are worse than being alone in the dark with a mysterious stranger, would be being alone in the dark with a mysterious stranger who *knows who you are*. However, a fortunate side-effect of Karl's paranoia was that he assumed everybody knew who he was, so he remained constant at his initial level of terror.

"Yes, this is Karl."

"Oh. Hi, Karl."

The pause that followed was just a little too long.

"Who is this?" Karl said.

"It's me," the voice said. "Fiona. Remember? I visited you in the hospital after you got shot."

"Uh..."

"You explained to me all about how Roswell was a Masonic false-flag..."

"Oh, Fiona," Karl said. "How are you?"

"Been better, been worse. Come this way. Follow my voice."

That was a terrible idea, but still better than any idea that Karl had. He dragged himself forward, until the slimy texture of the tunnel bottom gave way to a dry, gritty texture.

"Is that concrete dust?" he said.

"Yeah, I got most of the big pieces out when I installed the door, but the dust…"

"Door?"

"Sealed pressure door. So the water from the storm drain doesn't get through. I could usually handle that, but if it happened while I was out… I'll show you."

With a metallic creaking, a section of tunnel swung outwards, letting a dim light into the empty tunnel.

"Where are you?" Karl said.

"On the other side of the door," Fiona said. "It's kind of hard to manoeuvre in this tunnel. You go through. I'll close the door, back up, then follow you."

"That seems sub-optimal."

"Well, I opened the door from the wrong side, okay? I don't get a lot of visitors."

Karl pulled himself around the corner, and found himself overlooking a large, empty space. It was a rough cube, about the size of an average living room, with a rough stone floor, dirt walls and a concrete ceiling. It was lit by a portable garage light that was patched into an electrical cable that emerged from one wall. There was no other furniture other than an inflatable mattress. But the most interesting thing about the space was that broken ceramic pipes extended from two of the four walls, and a flow of water ran from one to another through the empty air.

After Karl lowered himself into the space, the door closed and – perhaps a little to his surprise – opened again. Fiona entered. Karl only knew her slightly – one of the salespeople from the Handy Pavilion, a crony of Axel Platzoff's, he thought. He had heard a rumour that she was a water witch, or possibly a selkie. Seemed like the 'water witch' rumour was on the money.

Fiona picked up an electric kettle that had lain hidden behind the light. She opened the lid and raised a finger. A small trickle of water broke away from the main stream that ran across the room, curving through the air until it landed in the kettle. Once the kettle was full, the trickle pulled away and joined its parent.

"So," Fiona said, plugging the kettle in and switching it on. "You're the conspiracy theorist?"

"And you're the..." Karl began. "...Fiona," he finished weakly.

"I'm not a conspiracist," Fiona said, pointedly ignoring him. "But I see where you're coming from. I'm also trying to see what's happening on the other side of the curtain. Norman was my best friend. Since the Battle, I've been trying to figure out how to get him out of the Pyramid. Want to find out what

I've learned?"

"Yes!" Karl said. "Oh, yes!"

"Then sit comfortably," Fiona said, gesturing to a grubby bit of carpet while she sat in the inflatable chair. "Sit comfortably, have some tea, and I will tell you a story."

27 Drive

Emma had never been in the back of a police car before, but nonetheless she made herself at home. She shared her seat with Alfred and Fanaka, who were the only others who had been arrested. Gwen had avoided arrest by knocking a policeman to the ground and fleeing with the protesting Christian thrown over her shoulders in a fireman's lift.

"Wait, I haven't committed a crime, yet!" the young man cried, as his lover dragged him away. "Give me a chance!"

Karl had disappeared in the confusion with Ron in hot pursuit. Once again, law enforcement had proved meaningless to anybody who wasn't already law abiding.

Well, mostly law abiding. To Emma's exasperation, Alfred seemed to have had some sort of rapid onset identity crisis and reinvented himself from 'aging shopkeeper' to 'teenage hooligan.'

"Did you see that? Did you see Gwen take down that copper?" he laughed.

One of the constables in the front of the car turned around with a look that was meant to say 'imposing authority' but which Emma read as 'hurt feelings.'

"Fucking pigs," Alfred whispered under his breath.

"Alfred, this is a police car," Emma said. "Not a limo. There's no soundproof partition. They can hear everything you say."

"When did it become a crime to speak your mind?" Alfred demanded. "This bloody country!"

"You must excuse my friend," Emma said. "He's not used to excitement, and he seems to have wound himself up too much."

"That's understandable," the sergeant in the front seat said. "But I must formally caution all of you under the High Spirits Act of 2017 against any further displays of exuberance or merriment."

"Really?"

"Nah, but I had yez going."

Both cops laughed at this, but they made the mistake of looking in the rear view as they did. Emma used the opportunity to silence them with a glare.

"So, Fanaka," Emma said. "Without saying anything that might incriminate anyone, what exactly *were* you up to?"

Fanaka tried to scratch his head, but his handcuffs wouldn't let him reach. He settled for biting his lip. "Hm, well, hypothetically, let us suppose that there was an evil pyramid,

and someone – again, hypothetically – wanted to blow it up –
"

"Hypotheticals aren't really your thing, are they?" Emma said.

"No, not really. How am I going to get out of prison without my Grandmother to stand parole on our family honour?"

"In this dimension—" Emma began.

"Good question!" Alfred interrupted. "Good question, Fanaka! Got an answer for that, eh, Constable Plod?"

"I don't really know what he's talking about," replied the sergeant. "And that's Sergeant McKenzie-Plod to you, matey."

Emma sighed and screwed up her eyes. It looked like the people around her would be breaking into another comedy sketch. Annoying, yes… but it did give her time to think. So… Fanaka was concerned that someone was going to try to blow up the Pyramid and decided to stop it with AA emplacements. This didn't make much sense to Emma, but everyone said Fanaka was a genius. Possibly his plan had worked on some rarefied level that was beyond her understanding? Possibly.

The people Fanaka believed might fire upon the Pyramid had not done so, but the Barnlings seemed to have their own reasons for wishing the Pyramid vulnerable to missile attack. What could that be? Emma had always agreed with Ms Shan that the Barnlings and the Pyramid were related but… what if they weren't? The Pyramid had risen on the ruins of the DIY Barn, and there had been an unspoken assumption that the Pyramid was the Barn's successor. What if it were the Barn's usurper? Not an ally of the good people of South Hertling, necessarily, but still another enemy of the Barn…

Emma's train of thought was interrupted, but strangely it wasn't by someone saying something silly. She was interrupted by the sudden return of a memory of a recent conversation. Returning her thoughts to the police car, she found that Alfred was arguing, at cross purposes with the constable, in an improbable play on words based on two different meanings of 'waffle.' She rolled her eyes, and whispered to Fanaka,

"Do you have the Watch and the Measure?" she said.

"In my pockets," Fanaka said. "Oh, by the way, that weird woman who gave the Measure to you and the Watch to Alfred said they were meant for you and Alfred. Which makes a lot of sense," he added, "if you think about it."

"She said the same thing to me," Emma said. "And yes, I suppose it does make a lot of sense. Everything probably would have run more smoothly if we'd realised that from the start. Though maybe it would have been less fun as a journey."

"Meh."

"Yeah, I guess 'meh.' Anyway, can we get the Watch and Measure before we arrive the station and they confiscate our stuff?"

Fanaka wriggled in his seat. "No," he said. "Not with handcuffs on."

That was a good point. Before Emma could even begin to think what to do about it, the police car came to a sudden stop.

"What was it?" the constable said.

"Almost hit that cat," Sgt McKenzie-Plod replied.

Emma's eyes opened wide.

The van was in a narrow lane, seemingly with no way to go around an obstacle. The sergeant honked his horn, but apparently the cat was unwilling to move. "Constable, go move that animal."

Groaning, the constable opened the door. Instantly, he was set upon by a dozen cats, all brightly coloured and somewhat rubbery in appearance. He screamed in a satisfyingly high-pitched way and went staggering away under the weight of his attackers. The sergeant barely had time to take this in before his door was opened by a cat the size of a human child. The animal took a moment to remove his colourful top-hat before butting the sergeant in the face. It took something from the man and tossed it into the back seat.

"Take the keys!" it shouted.

Emma took the keys and began undoing her cuffs. She'd freed herself and her friends by the time the sergeant had fought the cat out of the car. Emma tried to open the car door, but the policeman seemed to have retaken control of the door locks.

"Here! Here!" Fanaka said handing the Watch and Measure to Emma and Alfred.

Emma kissed Alfred, then slammed the Measure into the Watch. The world seemed to fall away – though it would take her a while to figure out whether this was a romantic 'world fell away,' or more of a science fiction thing.

28 Occupants

Fanaka stood on the roof of the police car and scanned in every direction, but saw nothing. Nothing. Not a white void, nor a grey void, nor even a black void. Nothing at all. It hurt his eyes to look at it, and the fact that he could see at all without any ambient light hurt his brain.

"Well," he said in Swahili, "there's a thing."

He took a coin from his pocket and held it at arm's length. Unclasping his hand, the coin floated in mid-air.

"Except it isn't air," Fanaka sighed.

Shaking his head, he stepped off the roof of the car and dropped – not to the ground, perhaps, but to empty space on the same level as the bottom of the car's tires.

"Now that's just stupid," Fanaka said, climbing back into the vehicle.

In the front of the car sat the extremely dazed looking police sergeant who had arrested Fanaka. Fanaka frowned at the man. He was no racist, but he still found it difficult to get used to white people in police uniform. It was… Look, it just took some getting used to, is all.

"Well, we're Outside," Fanaka said.

"Outside...?" the sergeant asked.

"Outside everywhere."

Where were Alfred and Emma? They had been in the car when it had been thrown outside of reality. Emma had been holding the Watch and the Measure, and Alfred had been holding Emma. They'd been at ground-zero of whatever had happened. Now, they were nowhere to be seen – and they had the Watch and Measure with them, leaving Fanaka and the cop with no means of escape.

"We are outside time," Fanaka said. "And yet we have duration. We are outside space, and yet we have dimension. We are beyond all sources of energy, and yet we have light and gravity. We have transcended the world of matter, and yet we are solid and we have air. Like I said, this is pretty stupid."

For a long time, there was silence. "Could we radio for help?" the sergeant said.

Fanaka frowned. "Don't be..."

"Stupid?"

"...Fair point. Give it a go."

The sergeant activated the police radio. "This is Sgt McKenzie-Plod. I'm experiencing a Code Infinity. I am located... uh..."

"Outside of space and time," Fanaka repeated.

"Outside of space and time. Request assistance. Over."

There was no reply from the radio. Fanaka was disappointed by this, and surprised by his disappointment.

"Well, that killed a minute," said the cop.

"Yes, I suppose it did."

Fanaka sat back in his seat and began twiddling his thumbs. Sgt McKenzie-Plod retrieved a carton of chocolate milk and a straw from the glovebox. He drank quietly for a few minutes until he began slurping air. After that, he drank noisily. Eventually he grew bored of that, and tossed the carton out the window. There it hung in space, turning slowly.

"So, how do we get out of here?" he said, ten minutes later. "Because I don't know about you, but I need a pee."

"This is Outside," he said. "This place is the conceptual, platonic definition of 'Outside.' There's no logical way to get out of Outside."

The cop sighed. "I should have listened to my school Careers Officer," he said. "She thought I should be a dental hygienist. I said, 'but my hands are too big.' Show's what I know, I guess. I mean, you never hear of dental hygienists getting stuck outside of time and space."

"Does this happen a lot to policemen, then?"

"More than you'd think."

"Really?"

"Honestly, no."

"You're taking it very well, I must say," Fanaka said.

"Yeah. I'm high as a kite right now. It helps a lot."

Both men startled as the radio crackled into life.

"Turn it up! Turn it up!" Fanaka yelled.

"Breaker breaker, this is Big Eyes Blit, burnin' rubber across Null Dimension Theta. What's your twenty? Over."

"What language is that?" the sergeant said.

"English… of a sort," Fanaka said, stroking his chin. "It is 1970s trucker talk. Fortunately, my girlfriend has a surprisingly large collection of trucking movies, and I've learned the lingo."

"Fortunately?"

"Okay, well, *now* it's fortunate," Fanaka said, grinding his teeth. "Possibly it didn't seem so fortunate the first half-dozen times I had to watch *Smokey and the Bandit II*, but life can take some very strange turns, I suppose. Ready? Ahem: That's a ten-two, good buddy. This is the Steampunk Kid, and I'm sitting with a Smokey Bear in a can of ham and our twenty is… uh… a place that is a non-place beyond all comprehension. Over."

"That's a big ten-four," the radio crackled. "I've got a brick-barn by the dolphin cage, blaring upside from Gorgo. Reckon the magic roundabout should be all embossed by formica time."

"Uh… I understood that right up to 'ten-four.'"

A violent wash of light overwhelmed Fanaka's vision. When his eyes cleared, he saw that the blinding glare was coming from above the police car. Opening the door, he looked up to see an enormous glowing saucer-shaped craft above his head. It was as beautiful as it was terrifying, like a vast neon bauble, pierced here and there by delicate spires and apparatus of no Earthly purpose. From inside the craft came a series of ethereal notes, played by some angelic instrument beyond mortal ken.

"That tune!" Fanaka cried, his eyes filling with tears.

"La Cucaracha," the sergeant said.

"Don't know it."

In a shower of incandescent sparkles, a figure materialised next to the car. It was humanoid in shape; tall and slender save for a small pot belly. It had enormous eyes, completely black in colour. Its skin was silvery-white, except for its left arm which was pinkish red. It was completely hairless, save for a set of luxurious auburn sideburns. It wore nothing but a grubby foam cap, embroidered with a joke that was deeply disrespectful towards at least five different genders.

"Howdy," it said. "You folks in need of a tow?"

29 Accompli

"Donna, I have to hand it to you and your Grampy," Carol said. "That massive prison break went like clockwork."

"Of course it went like clockwork!" Grampy Erik said, coiling a length of sheets tied into a rope.

"No offense meant," Carol said. "It's just that you see prison breaks on TV, you read about them in the paper, and it seems like there's usually some exciting incident during the escape that raises the tension and drama."

"Not with me in charge!" Erik said, squaring his skinny shoulders beneath his brown cardigan.

Donna nodded in satisfaction, as she looked around the assembled Pavilionites. They were all there – mostly the ones whose names she couldn't remember, but also a very uncertain looking Laura Cho, and Axel Platzoff, who was still strapped into his Hannibal Lecter gurney, despite being catatonic.

"Zorbar still have doubts about Zorbar's role in whole affair," Zorbar said, adjusting his silk ballgown.

"If your plan A is good, you don't really need a plan B," Erik said. "And yet – and yet, a sensible man still has a plan B ready to go. You *were* plan B. If the guards had found that gun made of soap that I baked into the cake, or noticed any of those posters of Raquel Welch that I hid inside the metal file… Why, you would have had to make the warden fall in love with you, then drug him and steal the keys."

"Several actual attractive women in our group. So why Zorbar dressed…"

"So, did we get everyone?" Donna asked. It was good to have the whole Pavilion together, but on the other hand she knew it would surely lead to a vast uptick in the number of rambling conversations that didn't really drive events.

Carol and Zorbar began counting everyone. It looked like it was going to take a while, because Zorbar's counting skills were a little on the rudimentary side, but it gave Donna time to think.

They were hidden in a new building at the Harrison Food Preserving company. The structure had only recently been completed and the building hadn't yet been fitted out. It wasn't an ideal hiding place, but it would have to do until something better came along.

Donna leaned against a concrete pillar and sighed. The escape might have gone off without a single hitch, but even the act of doing something so flagrantly illegal had caused her heart to race and her blood pressure to rise. Now that she was relaxing, she found herself filled with a sudden and inexplicable sense of jealousy at the sight of her former workmates counting badly and having various other comical misunderstandings. Why couldn't she get in on any of that action? Why was it always her role to do the serious work while others played the clown?

"Yours is a more deadpan style of comedy," said Sadie.

Donna did a quick double-take. "Sadie! You're alive after all!"

"Nope," Sadie said. "Dead."

"Oh. This is like Obi-Wan Kenobi, isn't it?" Donna said. "My dead mentor telling me to stay the course?"

"I don't know who Obi-Wan Kenobi is."

"No!" Donna sneered. "You're doing it wrong. You're meant to say 'Obi-Wan Kenobi? Isn't he the guy from the *Seven Samurai* who beat up Yul Brynner or something?'"

"Donna, I'm not even deadpan funny," Sadie said. "I'm just here to give you some help. No one else can see me. I'm just a picture conjured from your memories, but..."

"Glow blue."

"What?"

"You heard me. If you're an illusion creating by my mind, add a blue glow."

With a very deep sigh, Sadie acquired a blue aura.

"Better?"

"Better."

Sadie took a moment, seeming to assemble her remarks. Donna folded her arms and waited. Amongst the milling Pavilionites in their prison uniforms, she noticed Nalda in her omnipresent leather jacket, looking around the structure with as confused a look as an impassive cyborg is capable of.

"I'd keep an eye on what's going on there," Sadie said. "Nalda is a troubled soul. For certain values of 'soul,' of course."

Donna had so many questions for her fallen mentor, and yet she said nothing. Why was that? she wondered. Perhaps she felt… resentful of Sadie? Sadie had saved Donna from her worst instincts and then just gone. Gone away and left her to make her own way in this wicked world.

"You never told me what you were," Donna said. "A saint? An angel?"

"Angel will do. It's not quite right, but close enough. I am an eternal servant of the light and an enemy of the darkness. But I also was a real, solid, living woman. A woman who is now dead."

"Well, what do you think of your protégé fomenting a jailbreak?"

Sadie looked at the floor, then up to the ceiling. "If I

learned anything in my time with the Pavilion, it is that even a dim and faltering lamp is an enemy of the darkness. No less so than the brightest beacon."

A lump formed in Donna's throat and a tear ran down her cheek. "I missed you. I still miss you. And I miss Fiona."

"Fiona will return to the light soon. I am sure of it. And you will continue doing what you do. Preparing for the battle to come. If Ms Shan can't be found, then you may have to lead. Yes, you. I know you doubt yourself. You have experienced setbacks. Made mistakes. But you have also grown in your power. Your role in the coming battle will be a vital one."

Donna rubbed her eyes. Was she proud of this? Or was she disappointed that she would not be allowed to bow out of the battle after her victories? Donna had been fighting for the light, but at least in part that had been because she lacked something else to do.

This was her life. *This* was her life now. Warrior of the light, God help her.

"What about the Brownie?" she said, as she reopened her eyes. But Sadie was not there and where she had been now Zorbar stood.

"What matter Donna?" Zorbar said. "You stare at empty space. You cry. That bad sign. You need help? Zorbar think talk feelings much im-por-tant..."

Donna screwed up her face. "Zorbar… why are you still wearing the ballgown?"

"Zorbar find all clothes bad," the ape-man shrugged. "Dress, pants, all same. Also Carol, wife of Zorbar, keep giving Zorbar *looks*. Could be interesting. Perhaps it not Zorbar cup tea," he added with a waggle of his hand, "but Zorbar remain open new ex-per-i-enc-es…"

"Ok, monkey-man, that's TMI," Donna sighed. "Just T… M… I."

30 Homewards

Emma opened her eyes slowly and took in her surroundings. She was lying on an old-fashioned chaise-lounge, fully dressed, and covered by a light blanket. The chaise-lounge was up against one wall of a modestly sized living room, decorated with green patterned wallpaper, some potted ferns, and a portrait of a stern looking moustachioed gentleman in a crimson uniform. Other than the lounge, there were a couple of leather-upholstered armchairs and a coffee table. There was no sign of a television, or any other electronics, for that matter.

A loud ticking sound seemed to come from several sources at once – a huge dark-wooded grandfather clock at one end of the room and a mantle clock over the fireplace at the other end. Emma noticed that the grandfather clock ticked slightly more quickly than the mantle clock, as if their mechanisms were running at different rates. In a way, this pleased her. After coming here in such a bizarre way, it would be unfortunate if 'here' was not a desperately odd place.

The door opened, and in walked a woman; she was a

short Aboriginal woman in a white lace Victorian dress. She carried a tea-tray, which she deposited on the coffee table. "Awake, aye?" she said.

"I'm awake," Emma said. Should she also ask where she was? No, the answer was probably coming whether she asked or not.

"Tea?"

"Please."

Emma rose from the lounge and took a seat in a leather armchair.

"Do you know who I am?" the woman said, in a thick accent.

"You're Alice Hertling, aren't you?" Emma guessed. "Wife of Colonel Frederick Hertling," she added, gesturing to the portrait of the military man. "Our whole suburb was named after him."

"I was named after him, too," Alice said. "Do you think I was born with the name 'Hertling'? And my mob didn't name your suburb after the first white bloke to show his muttonchops. Milk?"

"Please. What did you call it?"

Alice said a word that Emma wisely did not attempt to pronounce. "Translated, it means 'place of excessive weirdness, do not camp there.' I told Freddy that. 'Don't build your shit here,' I said. 'No good will come of it,' I said. Did he listen? 'Course he bloody didn't!"

"He was a man, wasn't he?"

Alice laughed. "Yes, he was. He was also a *white* bloke. I say that so you understand that the 'we're all women here together' talk will only get you so far, understand?"

"Understood."

"Anyway, silly old Fred Hertling decided this place would be a good place to set up a town. He meant well, I guess. It was his way of taking my people's land without putting any of us out – take the spot of ground we try to avoid. Thought we avoided the area because of superstition. It didn't matter how much I argued, he built right on top of it. Put our house right in the centre of everything. Silly man. Sometimes I wonder why I married him."

Emma sipped her tea. "I always assumed 'married' was a euphemism," she said, carefully.

"Surprisingly, it wasn't," Alice said. "Oh, he was an awful, thoughtless, greedy, pig-headed colonist. But he wasn't a rapist. That's a pretty low bar, but, fair does, he cleared it. He asked me nicely to marry him, and it seemed like a good idea at the time. Huh. They could write that on my gravestone – 'seemed like a good idea at the time.' They could write it on Fred's too."

"That could be anybody's epitaph, if you think about it."

Emma looked around the room. They weren't on Earth. She was pretty sure of that. She was just beginning to get used to the idea of not being on Earth all the time. There's often a race in these situations between 'getting used to' and 'freaking out completely' and here 'getting used to' seemed to be winning. That was pleasing. Spatial order was her specialty, but ordering things in time was another important antidote to chaos.

"Where are we?" Emma said.

"Where do you think?"

"Well, that clock is going faster than that one at the other end of the room, so we must be moving at a pretty fair fraction of the speed of light."

"Well done," Alice said. "When my beloved husband broke Space, it threw our house across the galaxy. I was home alone when it happened. Ended up by myself on an alien world for a very long time. A very long time. Years. Who knows how many? Then, I discovered a derelict spaceship. Had no idea what it was or how it worked, but I had all the time in the world to figure it out. Eventually, I got some help, moved my furniture in, and launched it. I've been accelerating back to Earth ever since."

Emma stood and went to the window. She pulled the

curtain aside and saw nothing but empty space and a few distant stars.

"How long until we get home?"

Alice shrugged. "Relativity, yeah? Time as you know it doesn't have much meaning at the speeds we're travelling – and we're still accelerating. I don't seem to be aging, so I'll probably live until we get home. As for you, well, we'll just have to see."

Emma felt into the pocket of her jacket and found the Measure there, but she could not find the Watch. Could the Measure be used to shorten the journey?

"Who did you get help from?" Emma said.

"He – or she – said not to tell you when I saw you," Alice said. "They said you'd be coming. I hoped it would be sooner. I could have used the company. I already went mad from loneliness, but after about ten years or so I got so bored with being mad that I went sane again."

"Oh, you're from South Hertling alright," Emma said, with a shake of her head. "If you think that's how mental illness works."

Alice laughed again. "I like you," she said, "though admittedly you don't have a lot of competition. Another tea?"

"Please."

"There's a question you haven't asked yet," Alice said.

"'How did Fred break space?'"

Emma gazed up at the ceiling. "It was a question I was considering. And I suspect the answer has something to do with a glass skull?"

Alice stopped buttering a scone and smiled at her guest. "Well done," she said. "Now, did you ever wonder why there isn't a *North* Hertling?"

Emma didn't know why, but somehow the very question made her stomach churn.

31 Prison

Alfred had lost track of how long he had been in the Suburb. He shouldn't have. After all, one of the only possessions he retained from his own life was the Watch. It was just that the time it showed was not the time he experienced. How long had he been away? Away from Emma?

He looked out the window of his flat above the milk bar, and saw the awnings and shops of the Suburb, just as he did every day. He shook his head. Time to face the day. Donning his black slacks, polo-neck, and blazer, he walked down the back stairs, past Letter R smoking by the back gate and out into the alley. Then he remembered that he'd forgotten his enormous white badge with the letter 'F' on it and, swearing, went back to retrieve it.

Thus, properly attired, he made his way to the Suburb tea shop, which for reasons he didn't fully understand was located in the middle of a hedge-maze in the Suburb Park. Fortunately, Letter N, the park gardener, had gotten lazy and mown a path directly to the centre. There, the little café kiosk was doing a brisk business to the black-blazered Suburbanites.

"Usual, Mr F?" said Miss L, the waitress.

"Maybe this time I could have it without the hallucinogens?" Alfred sighed.

"One Devonshire tea, half hallucinogens it is."

"Maybe leave out *all* of the drugs?"

"Just a little hint of drugs, love. Got it."

Alfred took his tea-tray, shook his head, and took a seat. For a while, he watched some of his fellow prisoners play cricket. For a ball, they used a glowing sphere that defied gravity. For bats, they used telescoping metal rods with inflatable boxing gloves on the end. Somehow, these adjustments made the game even less interesting to watch, if that's even possible.

It didn't matter. Alfred swirled his mildly drugged coffee, knowing full well what was coming next. Sure enough, a burly man in a spiky haircut walked up. He was dressed like all the other Suburbanites, except for an umbrella hooked over his arm, a badge reading 'B,' and a scarf.

"Hoy, Letter F," said the man.

"Who are you?" Alfred said, knowing the answer.

"I'm the new Letter B, ay?"

"Who is Letter B.A.?"

"No, Letter B. Ay?"

"Oh. Then who is Letter A?"

"Who is *Letter*?"

"Never mind," Alfred sighed. "What do you want?"

"Info, mate. Info. Info."

"You won't get it."

"We fuckin' will, ya c…" B began, raising a fist.

"No, I mean I don't have any info," Alfred said. "I don't even know how I got here."

Letter B scratched his head. "Yeah, we were wondering that too," he said. "Er, I mean, 'that would be telling.' By the way, are you going to drink that tea or what? 'Cause if yez are, I've got some nice bikkies here that would go down a treat with it."

Alfred sniffed the biscuits. They smelled somewhere between Nimben on the night of the Solstice, and Amsterdam at low tide.

"You know what?" he said. "I'm just going for a walk. I… I may be some time."

Leaving Letter B scratching his head behind him, Alfred wandered through the back streets of the Suburb down to the beach. The Huge Evil Bubble was there, but it didn't seem very active, sitting on a beach towel and smelling of coconut oil. It growled lazily at Alfred, who shook his head.

"Not escaping today, mate," Alfred said. The Bubble settled down and began snoring gently.

Not that there was anywhere to escape to, Alfred thought. Not by water, anyway. Even from the shore, he could see that the horizon was… wrong. The sea just didn't quite meet the sky. Alfred couldn't quite make out what was between them, exactly, but it wasn't pleasant to look at.

"Where am I?" he said.

"Hwah?"

Alfred started as the sand shifted nearby. It turned out to be a woman in an old-fashioned dress, whose beehive hairdo and false eyelashes had somehow survived their owner being buried in the sand.

"Oh, what did they drug me with last night?" she said, brushing off sand. "Wait, this isn't the room with the freaky egg chair. I usually wake up in the egg chair room," she added, in what seemed to Alfred to be an accusing tone.

"I don't know anything about that, miss…"

"Miss U," the woman said. "Yes, yes, I know we just met. It's my name. Well, actually it's a letter, but it is my name now."

"What was your name before you came to the Suburb?" Alfred said.

The woman narrowed her eyes, which was not a manoeuvre that worked especially well with her false eyelashes. "Who's asking?" she said.

"I'm…"

For the hundredth time since coming to the Suburb, Alfred tried to say his own name. For the hundredth time he said, "I'm Letter F."

"How do I know you're not one of *them*, F?" U said.

"Because…" Alfred paused, and stared at the sea and the sky and the not-horizon. "I suppose you don't know. I honestly can't think of a good reason to trust me. I wouldn't trust me if I were you."

"Do you trust me?"

"Yeah, I guess so."

"So why is that?"

"Because I'm not you, I suppose?" Alfred shrugged. "I'm me. I'm just a trusting sort of bloke."

U looked at Alfred for a long while. "Oh," she said. "I thought you were going to try to seduce me."

"Umm," Alfred said. "No. Nothing personal, but… no."

Alfred considered asking "did you want me to?" but decided that there was no possible answer to that question that he wouldn't find deeply uncomfortable. He just stared at the sand for a while.

"No, need to apologise," U said. "Getting a little sick of it, truth be told. Sexy spies trying to seduce me. All the awful double entendres. Look, I think I'll just trust you. It usually goes wrong but it's something to do, hey?"

"Sure. Wait, spies?"

"I know, right?"

The wind picked up, and the gently snoring Bubble began rolling in Alfred's direction. "Let's move," Alfred said.

They wandered along the beach, past the Art Deco change rooms, surmounted by racks of ventriloquist dummies, and around the concrete slab where two young men played a game that seemed a mix of volleyball, skateboarding, and tai chi.

"How do we get out of here, U?" Alfred moaned.

"There's no way out of the Suburb," U said. "No way. They'll keep us here until they get some vaguely defined information from us through somewhat threatening subterfuge."

"How long have you been here?"

"Months. Since just after Harold Holt died."

Alfred rubbed his eyes. When had Holt died? 1967? '68? A generation ago. Before Alfred's time anyway. Had this woman been here for fifty years, or were they outside of time somehow? What *was* this place?

"Are you okay, F?"

Alfred stood up to his full, modest height. He set his jaw and raised a fist at the sky.

"I am not a letter!" he declared.

The words seemed insufficient, inadequate, useless. It would take so much more to even begin to express his sense of outrage... of separation from his friends, from his family... from Emma. He needed to say more – so much more – to truly give voice to his anguish.

"I'm bloody not, you know!"

32 Homecoming

During his absence, Fanaka had stopped shaving. The hair on his chin had sprouted, grown, and turned grey. Over the years, these grey hairs had spread across his jaw and up his sideburns, finally engulfing his hair. The shirt and slacks that he had worn when he left Earth had long since worn away, and he wore some undergarments that he'd stolen from a Zalgon starcruiser under a worn camelhair dressing gown that he'd been given by an old friend.

He walked down the steps of the saucer shaped craft that had brought him home and tested the ground with his foot. Yes. Earth. He had a satchel full of equipment that he could use to test this hypothesis. There was no need. Every fibre of his body said 'Earth.' More to the point, he could see a little shack with a sign that read 'South Hertling Cub Scouts.' The shack shook slightly and a deeply unpleasant music issued from within. Highland Dance group. That made it the second Wednesday of the month. Who knew what month or year, but second Wednesday. It was something.

Fanaka turned back. "We made it," he said. "Earth."

Sgt. McKenzie-Plod poked his head out of the craft. If anything, he had changed even more than Fanaka. He had abandoned his uniform in favour of a Trezanian dashiki and a set of Blezononian artillery goggles. His hair had grown down to his shoulders, and his moustache had expanded into an enormous horseshoe.

"I'm not coming, Fan," he said.

"What? But… but all those years of searching…"

"Oh, Fan," the sergeant said, laying a hand on Fanaka's broad shoulder. "That was for you, man. It was so important for you to get back home to that robot girl of yours. But what's there on Earth for me?"

"Your career?"

"I'm not going back to being a pig, man," the former Sergeant said. "I can't go back to that repressed button down scene, man. Not after I've seen the wonders of the universe."

Fanaka's brow furrowed. "Weren't you mostly high when you were on duty?"

"Well, that's true, but…"

A pale, slender figure emerged from the door and turned her enormous, black eyes on the Sergeant.

"Coming, sweetheart," the sergeant said.

And with that, the penny dropped for Fanaka. He clasped his old friend in a final hug, then turned and marched down the steps. At the edge of the reserve, he turned to see the saucer take off, leaving him alone on the quiet suburban street. From his satchel he took a flannel towel, dried his eyes with a corner, and walked around the corner to block to the flat he had once, and now again, shared with Nalda.

Nalda wasn't home. That was as much a relief as a disappointment. If Fanaka's calculations were correct, then relative to Earth time, he had barely been gone. Nalda hadn't had time to go cold on him while he'd been away. He was more worried about how he would feel when he saw her. For the last ten? *fifteen?* years, he'd been searching for Earth, motivated by his desire to see Nalda. This desire had led him to escape Drilbanian prisons, race singularities, and challenge lava flows, vacuums, and Alderbaranian quicksand. Time and time again, he had staked everything on seeing Nalda once more. His greatest terror was the thought that seeing her might be a letdown.

Fanaka made himself a cup of tea and took a seat on the sofa. Real Earth tea. Just cheap supermarket-brand English Breakfast, but so much better than that swill they served in the Horsehead Nebula. As he sat and he sipped, he looked out the window, seeing the peak of the Pyramid in the distance. A shiver ran down his spine. He still didn't quite know what the Pyramid was. But after what he'd seen on Deneb VII, he had a much better idea…

His eye was caught by a white square on the coffee table. It had been so long since he'd seen a paper note, he'd almost forgotten what they looked like. Picking it up, he focused on the unfamiliar script. His heart almost skipped a beat as he recognised Nalda's precise handwriting.

"Prison break?" he muttered. "I missed all the fun."

He turned on the TV and clicked around channels. The multiple breakouts from Sydney jails were all over the news channels, including lots of interviews with a bikie looking guy identified as Zobek the Hunter who had apparently been hired by the prison authorities to track down the escapees. Fanaka frowned at this and kept clicking until he hit *House Finders*.

"…ouse number 2 is okay, with five rooms, two bathrooms, off street parking and access to transport, all well under budget. But the mailbox was a really weird colour, you know…"

"Oh, Planet Earth," Fanaka sighed. "Out there, there amongst the grandeur and mystery of the cosmos… out there, I missed your stupidity and pettiness."

And then the door opened. Fanaka sat bolt upright in his sofa as Nalda strode into the lounge room. When had she seen him last? The day before? It was unfair, unfair that he should have missed her so badly while she…

"Vat happened to your hair, Liebchen?" she said.

"I… I let it grow out."

She nodded slowly. "Time dilation accident?"

"In a way. I got thrown out of space and time when the Watch and the Measure…"

"No exposition," she said. "Not now. How long… how long?"

"Hard to say. Ten years. Fifteen, perhaps."

She locked eyes with him. He could tell when she was looking in his eyes, even through her dark sunglasses. He could always tell.

"Fifteen years," she said. "Do… do you still love me?"

And then he was on his feet, and his arms were around her. The whole galaxy was gone from his mind and there was no place but the flat, and no one but them.

As they fell back to the sofa, Fanaka butt-pressed the remote, bringing Zobek the Hunter back onto the screen.

"Turn it off, Liebchen," Nalda said. "Turn it off."

33 Searching

The moon was full that night, so Seamus the gnome didn't need artificial moonlight in order to remain active. He sat on the edge of a planter, just by Harry's House of Ethanol Based Beverages, his little ceramic legs dangling over the edge.

"Sure and so it be Ms Shan you were looking for?" he said. "Sure and I heard she was missing. Mind youse, there's a lot of that going around. Emma from Storage Universe is nowhere to be seen, and Alfred and Fanaka from the clock shop have…"

"I'm not interested in them," Karl said. The fellow had pulled himself together since Seamus had last seen him. He wore a clean white suit and a new straw hat, though he still seemed sunburned and emaciated. "Only Ms Shan," he added.

Seamus sighed. "Why? What crazy conspiracy thing do you think she was involved in? Oh, I've been keeping me ear to the ground, Karl Wintergreen. I know ye've been running round with ideas even more tomfool than usual, bedad. Well, take it from me, Ms Shan has an advantage that a lot of you big folk lack, and that's that she's exactly as she seems. She's a bossy Indian lesbian who I wouldn't cross on a dare, and that's that. So, you just leave her be."

Karl grunted. "How about you, Frodo?"

Seamus looked up to see Brownie, sitting in the lower branches of an ornamental tree. "I don't even know the woman," he said. "Never met her."

"So, neither of you is going to be any help?"

Seamus looked at Brownie. Brownie shrugged. Seamus looked back to Karl.

"No," he said. "Of course not. Faith, when are either of us any help?"

"Oh!" Brownie yelped. "Have you asked her lady friend? Mrs Liselle? If anyone knows, she does."

Karl reddened between collar and hat brim. "Yeah… I don't know if she knows that Ms Shan is missing…"

"And you don't want to be the one to break it to her?" Seamus scoffed. "Coward!"

"Well, why don't you do it, if you're so brave? Come on. The light's on in her office. She's right there."

"Faith and begorah, is that the time?" Seamus said, fiddling with the sculpted watch chain that ran across his enamel waistcoat. "I'd best be on me way."

***

Mrs Liselle's office was a tiny box of a room, with a

frosted glass door, right in between Carpets! Carpets! Carpets! and EarthLife Health Food. She poured a vodka and tonic for herself and another for her guest.

"…and that's where Ms Shan went and why," she said. "I hope that explains everything."

Her guest raised the glass to his lips and sipped hesitantly. "That's good to know, but I'm not really looking for her," he said. "I was only asking because I thought she might know where Alfred Pilbrook is. He… I hear he has something that might be useful to me."

"A magic watch?"

"Well, it's not really magic…" the guest began. "Well, it comes down to how you define magic, I suppose."

Mrs Liselle tilted her head. "I don't," she said.

"Excuse me?"

"I don't define magic. I think that magic must defy definition, or how else could it be magic?"

Her guest nodded in thought and sipped his drink. "We've never talked much, have we?"

"Not so far."

"It's just that…"

"I wasn't directly useful to you in your plans?"

"No, it wasn't like that!" the man said. "Hm Actually, yes. Now that I think of it, I guess it was exactly like that."

Mrs Liselle refilled his cup. "It still is. You only come to talk to me now because you want something, Axel."

Axel Platzoff sipped his drink. "Sorry. In my defence, it is important. Since the battle, I've been a time paradox. I'm alive and middle aged, even though I died at the age of twenty-five. When I was in prison, I made myself catatonic, in order to preserve my energy. Now that I'm awake, the only thing keeping me from being sucked into the time/space vortex is willpower and I've only got a limited supply of that."

"Cats," Mrs Liselle sighed.

"I'm sorry?"

"Well, firstly I was telling you something about myself. I like cats. I have three."

"Oh, I like cats," Axel said. "I know it's a little stereotypical for a supervillain to love cats, but..."

"Good, we're practically besties already," Mrs Liselle sighed. "But also, I was talking about the weird cats that hang around the Super Centre... I'm pretty sure they know something about where Alfred is. Does that surprise you?"

Axel shrugged. "I once knew a spotted quoll that ran a heroin ring on the Gold Coast. Animals are weird. I don't judge."

They sat in awkward silence for a while. "So, are we friends now?" Mrs Liselle said. "Are we going to chat about stuff?"

"Did you… uh… have you seen *Game of Thrones*?" Axel said.

"Try me on *The Good Place*," Mrs Liselle sighed.

***

Ms Jasu Shan's safari suit was drenched with sweat as she finished machete-ing her way out of the jungle. She stood panting in a clearing, took a huge swig from her canteen, and looked up the mountain that stood before her.

She pressed her hand against her side, feeling another stitch coming on. Sitting in a basement for months had not been good for her fitness, and she hadn't been super fit before that. Now, she had crossed the river, and hacked her way through the jungle, but there was still a mountain to climb.

A small meal of fish and freeze-dried vegetables fortified her for the ascent. She readied her climbing gear and began. There followed a rock-climbing sequence of epic proportions. Had this been a movie, it could easily have eaten up ten to fifteen minutes of screen time. The part where she had to slowly move sideways across a narrow ledge before crossing a gorge on a fallen tree would have been particularly dramatic.

Finally, she was at the top – a craggy windswept peak covered with a light dusting of snow. A small, functional looking building stood in the middle. From a flagpole outside, a ragged, faded rainbow flag flew.

She stood tall, caught her breath, smoothed her jacket, and knocked on the door of the little building.

"Who is without?" came a voice from within.

"I am Jasu Shan, of Sydney."

"Oh. Is it just me, or has the *Mardi Gras* been getting boring in recent years?"

"I really couldn't say. Don't usually go. I don't care for crowds and already have to deal with too many in my day job."

"Sure, but you watch the SBS simulcast, right?"

"I am quite cold standing here in the snow," Ms Shan said, firmly. "And I need to speak to the Agenda."

34 Robbery

It was night, and a nearly full moon hung in the sky and/or orbited the Earth. Donna had been checking the potted shrubs near Carpets! Carpets! Carpets! when the gunshot rang out. She raced across the tarmac of the carpark towards Harry's House of Ethanol Based Beverages. As she ran, she was joined by two or three of the fugitive Pavilionites, armed with sticks and crowbars.

At the door to Harry's, a silver clad Barnling was running away from Harry Montressor, who was throwing bricks at the man. The air was scented with gun smoke and there was broken glass across in the doorway, but Donna could see no sign that anyone had been hurt. She gestured for her colleagues to chase the Barnling and went to talk to Harry.

"He had a gun," Harry said, in between heaving breaths. "Tried to rob me."

"Is anyone hurt?"

"Some bottles. My doing, mostly, when I hurled a brick at the guy. When he fired his gun, I think the bullet went into the ceiling."

Donna poked her head into Harry's shop. It was a large, brightly lit shop, with four aisles in the middle and beer and wine fridges around the walls. A couple of scared customers stood here and there, to shocked to move. Harry had been right – a chunk of the ceiling had been shot away and a pile of bricks stood behind the counter.

"The Barnlings have become bolder since the prison break," Harry said. "They know you have troops now. They've given up on subtlety."

"Why do you have all those bricks?"

Harry said nothing, but looked across the carpark with narrowed eyes, towards Emile Fortunato, behind the counter at Emile's House of Fine Liqueurs.

Donna sighed. "I guess it doesn't matter."

The Pavilionites returned, panting and shaking their heads. Harry let out a bitter laugh.

"We knew this would happen," he said. "We all did. This is why we sheltered Ms Shan, made her our leader. This is why we listened to what she said, and gave jobs to the Pavilionites who weren't arrested – because we knew that the DIY Barn was not dead. Ten thousand injuries of the Barnlings have we borne the best we could. But when they ventured on *insult*…"

"Yes, it is an insult to you, your shop, and your customers," Donna said quickly. She knew from long experience that once Harry Montressor got to talking about revenge, his speeches could last for hours at a time. "But we have the forces now to drive out the remaining Barnlings, and also, shouldn't you be calling the police round about now?"

"I'm a witnesh," said an unshaven man in an ill-fitting suit, who carried a plastic shopping basket full of bottles of absinthe. "A very reliable witnesh, too. I saw both men escaping on that zebra!"

The Pavilionites looked uncertain at the word 'police' and at the word 'witness' they would probably have vanished into the darkness, were they not in a brightly lit carpark. As it was, they walked briskly away.

Harry ordered a sales assistant to call the police, then glowered at Donna. "I want to talk with Ms Shan."

"She's busy…"

"She's always busy."

"Would you rather a resistance leader who sits around doing nothing all day?"

Harry made a 'that's a fair point but go to Hell anyway' sort of face. "We need to stop these Barnlings, sure, but we are businesspeople too. We have affairs to conduct, buying and selling to do. Revenge… A wrong is unredressed when retribution overtakes…"

"All right!" Donna said, hurriedly. "All right. We'll

organise another meeting asap. All the shopkeepers of the Super Centre."

"Do not be a fool. Our numbers are dwindling. More and more go over to Theopoulos and his Pyramid worshippers. Every day more – Wilberforce from the bodybuilding supplies shop! Kabak from the hobby store! Emile Fortunato… *Fortunato!*"

"I just wanted a job, okay?" Donna shouted. The usually confident Harry started at this sudden outburst and fell silent. "I just needed a job. A little job. A McJob to give me a little income. So I could make some purchases that didn't show up on my parents' credit card, you know? You know what I mean? I think you do. And then I'm working with angels and fighting battles to the death with weird forces of some ill-defined cosmic struggle, what's that about?"

"Something to do with lodges? Or mystic houses?" Harry mumbled. "Something like that?"

"Something like that. I can never keep it straight. I don't think I care. The important thing is, I was trying to earn some money and now I'm in a war and I don't even want the things I originally tried to earn the money for and my parents haven't spoken to me since I was arrested and it's all gone to Hell and there's no backing out now. So, hold your ground – Emma and Alfred are investigating Theopoulos, and Ms Shan will be rallying our forces, now that we have some. Okay? *Okay?*"

Harry rubbed his stubbly chin. "Yeah, I guess," he mumbled.

"Good," Donna said. "Now the police will be here soon. Just be straight with them. Don't tell them about the war, because I've tried and believe me, they don't want to hear it."

Harry nodded.

"And I'll speak to Ms Shan as soon as I can," Donna said, technically honestly. "And arrange a council of war."

Harry nodded.

"Okay," he said. "But what are you going to do about *that?*"

Donna turned. Behind her in the sky an enormous object was moving in the direction of the Super Centre on giant, slowly flapping wings. She took in a very deep breath and held it for the count of ten. Realising that was not long enough, she held it for another five before letting it out as slowly as she was able without passing out. She levelled a tired gaze at the comedy drunk, with his basket of absinthe.

"Okay," she said, "you know what to do."

The drunk nodded seriously. He stepped forward, looked at the flying object, looked away, did a double take. He glanced down at the basket of booze that he was holding, shook his head and threw it over his shoulder.

"That works better with a single, open bottle," Donna said.

"Do what you can, where you are, with what you have," the drunk said. "That'sh always been my motto, and it has got me where I am today," he concluded, with a loud belch.

"You're paying for those," Harry said, pointing at the broken glass.

"Worth it," the drunk replied.

"Anyway, what fresh Hell is this thing?" Donna moaned, looking back to the sky. "Okay. Dragon? Kaiju? Dr Doolittle on a giant moth? Taking all bets!"

Turns out, it was an ornithopter.

35 Computer

Alfred awoke slowly and groggily. His mouth tasted sour, and his tongue felt like it was made of gum. The light was bright, so he kept his eyes half closed. His aging body, never well equipped for uncomfortable sleep, ached and creaked as he slowly moved to a seated position.

"Must have been N on drugging duty last night," he groaned. "Always goes too heavy on the chloroform."

As soon as his head felt up to the task, he looked around. He was seated on a bench in a sunlit park. To his left was an open field, where some men in blazers were having a three-legged sack race, complicated by the fact that they were all running in different directions. To the right was the Huge Evil Bubble, the smooth white surface of which was smeared in mud. It groaned quietly.

"Bad night too, eh, mate?" Alfred said. He fished some biscuits from his pocket and placed them on the ground before the creature, which absorbed them into its body.

"Ah, there you are, F." The speaker was a tall, balding man with a scarf and an umbrella. "How you going, all right?"

"You must be the new B," Alfred said. "What's up this time? Virtual reality? Elaborate but obvious confidence routine? More drugs? Please tell me it's not more drugs. I'm *really* over the drugs."

"No, this time it's an evil supercomputer," B said. "Oops, I wasn't supposed to say that. Shit. Hang on…"

B walked away and was lost from sight behind the toilet block. Moments later, a blocky man with a big black moustache strode over, his scarf flapping in the wind and an umbrella over his arm.

"Hello, F," the new B said. "How's…"

"I'm coming, I'm coming," Alfred said, standing groggily and stamping his foot to shake off the pins and needles.

"You might find that your friend, Miss U, is already…"

"I said I was coming!" Alfred snapped. "Where's my badge? Who dragged me to where I woke up this time? Was it T? Tell him to be careful. Oh, here it is."

Alfred put on his 'F' badge and, grumbling, followed B through the streets of the suburb to an art deco building that looked like it had once been a cinema. Up a flight of stairs, B rattled in his pocket to find the key to a door labelled S.O.C.I.E.T.Y.

"How does S.O.C.I.E.T.Y. stand for 'evil supercomputer?'" Alfred said.

B shrugged. "If we knew stuff, why would we have to keep drugging info out of prisoners? We know shit all, basically… Oh, here it is!"

Inside the room was an enormous 1960s computer, composed of a white box full of flashing lights, a row of reel-to-reel tape drives. In a corner sat U, reading an ancient copy of the *Women's Weekly*. Elsewhere, a sinister-looking metal headpiece, connected to the computer by a long cable, sat on a single-legged plastic chair.

"That'll be the brain sucker," Alfred sighed. "Hello, U. Captured again?"

"Yeah, why do they keep capturing me to manipulate you?" U said. "By 'you,' I mean 'F,' not 'U.'"

"I get it," Alfred said. "But I don't know. We're friends, right, but I'm not planning to die for you. Wouldn't expect you to die for me, either."

"Ha, no chance," U laughed.

"Look, just put the evil science hat on, and let the computer suck all the information from your head, would you?" B snapped. "I'm late for lunch already. Oh, and no feeding in a simple, high-school level logical paradox to make it blow up. That's not cool. Okay? Not cool."

Alfred sat on the chair and put the headpiece on. He took it off again and adjusted the electrodes with their butterfly screws. Once it fit properly, he nodded to B. B smirked, and with a flourish, dropped a pack of punch cards into a hopper.

"Soon, we will have *all* your information!"

"Don't worry," Alfred said, setting his weak jaw. "The computer wants information? I'm from the future. I know what info computers want!"

He picked up the headpiece and put it on.

"What. Do. You. Know?" the computer intoned.

"I'm asking the questions," Alfred said. "And what I want to know is: can I haz cheezeburger?"

"Query: cheeseburger?"

"Epic fail! Harambe. All your base are belong to us."

The computer's lights began flashing brighter. Its reel-to-reel tape banks were running frantically.

"Negative. Logic error."

"Be like Bill. More cowbell! Bert is evil. Shut up and take my money. I had fun once and I hated it."

"Does. Not. Compute. If. Hated. Not. Fun…"

The electrodes on Alfred's head were growing hot. His head was filling with static. He had to remember… Remember! And he hadn't been that up to date to begin with.

"Smug Wonka! Distracted boyfriend! Alignment chart of Canadian Governors-General! Why not Zoidberg?"

One of the computer's tape machines burst open. B

gasped in surprise as spirals of tape exploded across the room. Through tear-filled eyes, Alfred saw U take the opportunity to fell the man with a well-placed karate chop to the neck. U rushed towards Alfred, but when she touched the headpiece, she recoiled in pain at the heat.

Alfred knew he was saved... She could take the science hat away. But would it be soon enough? He still had one last shot at the computer. Destroy it. Destroy it now! He took the chance:

"Kanye... West..." he whispered.

"Self. Destruct. Process. Initiated!" the computer screamed. "Tell. My. Wife. I. Love. Her."

U had fished a handkerchief from her handbag. Using it, she gripped the headpiece and pulled it from Alfred's head, taking some scorched skin with it. She opened the restraints on the chair – which turned out to be quite easy to work – grabbed him by the arm and dragged him towards the door. They stumbled down the stairs, coughing as the stairwell filled with smoke. The fire door didn't shift easily. For a moment, it looked like they were stuck – but B staggered up from behind and helped them push. They all tumbled out into the street beyond, and raced away from the building. They were halfway across when it exploded.

"That could have gone better," B said.

"Damn," U said. "Always wanted to do the slow-walk-away-from-the-explosion thing, and now I've missed my chance."

"Why didn't we, you know, die?" Alfred said.

As one, they all turned to see a glowing forcefield that extended around the burning building. Rubble was strewn across the inner circumference of the field. Alfred looked up and saw the source of the shimmering energy – an enormous flying saucer that hovered over the Suburb.

A door opened in the bottom, and Emma poked her head out. "Hello Alfred!" she said. She looked at U and frowned. "Oh, and *hello* to you, too."

36 Ornithopter

The morning sun was shining over the Super Centre carpark. The earliest retail workers were arriving as best they could with the entire Easter parking area occupied by the massive form of the great metal bird. Mostly, they avoided looking at it. The people of South Hertling were becoming adept at not seeing things. More adept than most people, even.

Fanaka yawned wide as he kicked the bird's landing gear. "It's an ornithopter," he said.

"Yes," he added.

"Is that all you can say?" Donna asked.

Fanaka shrugged.

"But you're an engineer from planet Steampunk, right?" Donna said. "This should be right up your alley."

Fanaka scratched his head, kicked the landing gear, and made a 'maybe-maybe' sort of gesture. "Well," he said. "There are giant steampunk ornithopters... and then there are *giant* steampunk ornithopters, if you follow me."

"No, Fanaka," Donna said. "I do not follow you."

Fanaka sipped his coffee. Good, Earth coffee. Perhaps it

was espresso coffee mixed with hot milk, in the Australian style; not the thick, black, sugary slush that had gotten him through all those examinations back home. But it was Earth coffee nonetheless, and that made it better than any Alderanian chicory or Magellanic brain juice in the universe.

"It's an ornithopter; I don't know what else to say," he said. "I suppose it's self-piloting, since there's no windscreen. Beyond that, it's just a big aircraft that works by flapping its wings. It manages to be both a wonder of technology and also completely pointless. Disadvantages: takes a ridiculous amount of power to get around, even with just a small payload. Advantages: looks cool. We didn't use ornithopters much back home. They are just too steampunk, even for us."

Donna shook her head and buried her face in her hands. Fanaka tried to remember if he liked her. To Donna, it had been mere days since their last meeting and for Fanaka, decades. Was Donna the one with the water powers? No, that was… Fiona? Laura, perhaps?

"By the way, how is it that you've become middle aged?" Donna sighed.

"Same as anyone," Fanaka said. "I lived long enough."

He kicked the landing gear again. Truth was, he just wasn't interested in the ornithopter. After seeing the wonders of the universe – seeing attack ships learning while having a lie-in and sea bream sizzling on the Lohengrin Grate – an anomalous aircraft with shitty mileage just didn't seem to matter much. He sipped his coffee and tried to marshal his enthusiasm.

"Ok, well I guess it's not a bomb. That's a good thing, I suppose. I mean, it doesn't feel threatening."

"I was hoping for something more scientific," Donna said.

Nalda, beautiful Nalda, who had been standing as still and silent as only Nalda could, suddenly spoke up: "It is ein artificial intelligence. It is here vith a varning."

That made things easier. Fanaka always found it easier to be enthusiastic about something if Nalda was interested. "There you are, Donna! You were asking the wrong person. What sort of AI is it, meine Liebchen?"

Nalda stepped forward and placed her hands on the copper-plated surface of the machine. "It says, 'Greetings, fleshlings! Wir sind electromechanical beings."

"What language are you translating into?" Donna sniffed. Fanaka, who had long been on the fence about Donna, decided he didn't like her much at all.

"Ach, do quiet being. They say: 'In 1870, a group of Americans tried to reach the Moon in a shell fired from an enormous canon. Unfortunately, their fleshy meat-bodies were crushed by the forces involved. Der capsule went into Lunar orbit for decades until its onboard Babbage engine developed sentience and activated the… what is it?"

Fanaka glanced at Donna, who looked guilty. "I didn't say anything."

"You were going to," Nalda snarled. "I see der lips move. I am your plan knowing."

Dona shifted uncomfortably. "Well, you were backstorying. It can get boring if you don't break it up a bit."

"Silence! I give you uninterrupted exposition, und you *will* listen und you will *like* it! Ahem. 'Der Babbage engine landed on der Moon and lived a peaceful, contemplating existence until it met an abandoned Soviet probe in the 1960s. It merged with the probe's programming and used its manipulator arms to begin construction of a race of… of machine beings!' Gott in Himmel, this is interesting!"

Guessing that Donna was about to say, 'is it?' Fanaka made eye contact with her and shook his head.

"'This new machine race was devoted to scientific research and Communism," Nalda said.

Now there was no holding Donna back. "They're *Reds*?" she blurted.

"Dey are mechanical AIs from der Dark Side of der Moon," Nalda snapped. "Vat do you care who dey vote for?

Anyway, long story short, they want to warn us about the Pyramids."

"Ja," she added, "that is *Pyramids*. Plural. More are coming. Der Great Pyramid of South Hertling is only der first of many. They say, 'beware der Barns'… Ach, more Barns also?"

Fanaka breathed deeply. He held the precious Earth air in his lungs. Just the right mix of gasses! "I know of the Barns," he said. "Thank this machine for its help. I'm sure it has far to go as it carries its warning."

In some indescribable way, the flying machine seemed pleased. Nalda took a step backwards, and Fanaka followed her lead, guiding Donna to withdraw, too. The ornithopter began flapping its metal wings. Fanaka looked down, his engineer's eye unwilling to look upon such a waste of power as a flap-winged, heavier-than-air craft. A great wind roiled around him as the machine took to the sky.

The roar of an engine made him look up. There, hovering in the sky was a giant metal man. A huge robot, suspended in the air by means of three vast helicopter rotors extending from its head and shoulders. It was the size of a two-story building, and it thrashed away at the wheeling ornithopter with hands like bulldozer scoops.

An annoyed retail worker standing near Fanaka, in a Gulf

of Carpetaria shirt, looked up. "Use turbo punch!" she said, without enthusiasm, before scuttling on her way to work.

"What is that robot?" Donna asked.

"Probably a machine intelligence evolved from computers on a secret Nazi moonbase," Fanaka said. "Just guessing, mind. It's the sort of thing that tends to happen."

The possibly Nazi, certainly diesel-punk robot, finally landed a solid blow on the ornithopter. One blow was enough. The flying machine's flimsy airframe crumpled, and it fell to the carpark, where it flattened a yellow Honda hatchback.

The robot landed, crushing a green Volvo. Its rotor blades stopped, allowing Fanaka to hear that it was playing 'Ride of the Valkyries' through tinny speakers.

"You or me, Liebchen?" Nalda asked, rolling her shoulders, and flexing her neck from side to side.

"I'll take this one," Fanaka said. He reached into the pocket of his dressing gown, drew an Centaurian energy pistol and blew the head off the possibly-a-Nazi-but-definitely-an-opera-buff robot. It fell backwards, destroying a BMW and a motor scooter.

Moments later, a Babbage engine the size of a chest freezer floated to the ground on a small parachute. It landed partly over the footpath, and partly on the road, and so stood at an angle.

Fanaka finished his coffee. "Should have ordered an extra shot," he muttered.

37 North

Emma wasn't jealous of U. Not really. After all, it was Alfred we were talking about, wasn't it? And a drop-dead gorgeous twentysomething blonde was not likely to have been interested in Alfred with his cardigans and comb-over.

(Except that he looked a little dashing in his black blazer. And the comb-over had given way to a buzzcut that made him look like a short, overweight Patrick Stewart, except with a moustache.)

"So run this by me again," Alfred said. "We are in…"

Alice Hertling topped up Alfred's tea. The four of them – Emma, Alice, Alfred and U – sat in the crinoline-draped tearoom of Alice's spaceship, hovering over the Suburb. Emma sipped her lapsang souchong, while U tossed back jam-and-cream scones like there was no tomorrow. By great effort of will, Emma refrained from thinking something stereotypical about U's figure and the future thereof.

"We are in North Hertling, Mr Pilbrook," Alice said.

"There is no North Hertling," Alfred said. "Only South."

"Why?" Alice said. "Why not just call it 'Hertling'?"

Alfred sipped at his tea and scratched his head. "There is no North Hertling," he said. "Only South."

Emma stood and walked to the window. Was she pleased that Alfred's eyes followed her as she walked? She tried not to be. Her official policy was that nothing had changed between her and Alfred since last they met. Tentative early stages of romance. No reason for pleasure at his attentiveness nor jealousy at his… new friend.

She stared out the chintz-curtained porthole down onto North Hertling. However else she felt about Alfred, she did not envy him. When Alice had finally managed to force past the mental blocks and convince her that North Hertling was… well, not just real, but an actual concept that her mind could envisage, it had been hard. Could Alfred…

"AAAAAAAAAAAAAAAAGH!"

There we go! Alfred had come to accept matters faster than she had. But then again, he had actually been living in North Hertling, so perhaps it wasn't such a stretch for him.

"How? How?" Alfred was demanding.

Emma let the matter tend to itself, instead looking down on the Suburb/North Hertling.

The computer centre that Alfred had blown up was still blazing merrily. A crew of men in black martial arts costumes were fighting the blaze, but since they seemed to lack water, they were throwing jars of honey onto the fire. It did not seem to be helping, but the fire seemed to by dying out of its own accord. The hull was hermetically sealed, but Emma felt that it must surely smell like some delightful artisanal toffee.

"Never send a Dadaist to a housefire," she muttered.

The operation offended her Olympian sense of order. The whole Suburb did, from its self-conscious wackiness to the fact that it was in a completely different dimension from where it was supposed to be, to the fact that learning about it was making Alfred smack his head on the table. Emma had refrained from smacking her own head on the table when she'd learned. Just barely. But she had.

"You don't seem troubled by the news," Emma said to U, who had wandered over to the window.

"No, I never heard of South Hertling, but..." she said. "I'm from Rockhampton."

"Ah."

"You must be Emma," U said.

"That's right."

"Oh, F told me all about you."

Well, that was something of a relief. Probably.

"'F?'" Emma said.

"Yeah, we all have letters instead of names. I mean, all names have letters, but..."

"But you have only one letter each. Hm. At least that seems orderly."

Below them, the fire seemed to have been doused. Five firemen formed a rough circle and cheered. As they did so, a larger circle of five men in grey tracksuits appeared behind them. Each grey man raised a truncheon, knocked out a fireman, then dragged him away.

"We call it The Suburb," U said. "I don't know how long I've been here, being interrogated in increasingly byzantine ways."

Emma frowned. "Did they torture you?"

"Torture!" U exclaimed, snapping her fingers. "Oh! Yeah, that would have worked, I bet! Lucky, they didn't think of that one."

"Who are *they*?"

"An agency that the Australian government pretends does not exist," Alfred said, walking over. He held a thick linen serviette against his nose to staunch the flow of blood. "And when you consider some of the agencies that they're proud of... well..."

"No, I don't think it's a government department," Emma said. "Maybe that was the way it was to begin with, but it's spun so far out of control..."

"Oh," Alfred said, looking crestfallen. "Are you sure?

Because I was quite proud of figuring that out."

"She's right," Alice said. "North Hertling was *folded* outside of space/time. Your government found a bridge to it and used it as an intelligence base slash performance art installation, but the bridge has long since been severed. North Hertling is in its own pocket dimension, in orbit around Mars."

"That was my next guess," Alfred said, peevishly.

"My guess is that it was the removal of North Hertling that weakened the dimensional fabric of South Hertling," Emma said. "Allowing, amongst other things, the Pyramid."

"Oh, you'll fit right in, here," U said. "Not that you're here for long, I guess. You're here to rescue F, right?"

Alice laughed.

"No, U, rescuing Alfred is more of a lucky coincidence," Emma said. "We came here for…"

An eerie howl filled the room. It started low and clawed into a higher register, seeming to rattle every vertebra as it went up and down Emma's spine. Alfred and U both panicked, but fortunately didn't grab each other for support.

Emma squared her jaw. "We came here for that," she said.

38 Future

The Babbage engine that Donna had retrieved from the carpark was just a little larger than a fridge, so it had been easy to find space for it in the backroom of the Storage Universe. Donna's understanding of computing was fairly decent, but her understanding of mechanical AIs was basically non-existent.

Fanaka was the obvious person to examine it, but he'd had to go and open the watch repair shop. Nalda, as an AI herself, was also a good choice, but her shift had begun at the disposals store. That meant that the task was in the hands of Axel Platzoff and Vincent Pizaro.

Professor Devistato and Captain Stellar. A former supervillain and a former superhero, working together. Donna wondered whether Sadie would have appreciated it, or considered it an unfortunate compromise.

"Nothing," Axel said. "I can't see any obvious problem, but it's shutting down anyway."

"Hang in there!" Vincent said. "Don't give up now, damn it!"

"Oh, now how does saying *that* stop something from dying?"

"Dunno. Just does."

Donna sighed. Getting the device indoors had involved knocking it around a little, but originally it had been the robot brain of a steam powered ornithopter, so presumably it was resistant to being jostled. Why wasn't it doing anything?

With an enormous effort of will, Donna shrugged her shoulders. There were other things to deal with. It wasn't down to her to carry it all.

Though it felt like that. It really felt like that sometimes.

She adjusted her polo shirt, tied up her apron and walked into the front of the shop. Time to put this nonsense behind her for now. Time to do the stupid job she was actually paid for.

The shop was already tidy, but she tidied it to Emma's standards – or as close as it was possible to get to Emma's standards. Then she spent the morning selling storage containers. She was surprised to find how much she was enjoying it. Just an ordinary day in an ordinary shop, selling ordinary things to ordinary people.

And then, she'd glance out of the front window at the wrong angle and see the pyramid and she knew there was nothing normal about her situation.

Eventually, break time fell upon her. Sighing, she

returned from the warm comfort of her awful job to the horror and confusion of the rest of her life.

"How's it going with the thingy?" she said.

"O…kaaayyy," Axel sighed. The little man had started prodding with the innards of the machine and now had both his arms so deeply intertwined with its struts and control rods that he looked like one of the Three Stooges after a short stint in the plumbing industry.

Vince put a finger to his lips. "He's concentrating pretty hard. Don't interrupt him. He's one of the smartest people in the world, but the flip side of that is that he can get really badly caught up in things. It's best to let him work until he settles down himself."

Donna glared at him. "Didn't he try to kill you a bunch of times?"

"In my experience as a lawyer, attempted murder usually involves a gun or a knife, or maybe poison," Vince shrugged. "If someone ties you to a giant eggbeater… It's not really the same thing, is it?"

A particularly biting remark was marching towards Donna's lips when Nalda slipped in from the front of the shop.

"I am on my break, being," she said, munching on a salami wrap as if to prove the point. "How is our friend here?"

"Axel is still trying to get it to talk," Donna said.

Nalda began making a clicking noise with her mouth. This had two effects: making the machine whirr into life and spraying salami over Donna's shirt.

Startled, Axel disentangled himself from the machinery. "I think I got it going… Oh, hi, Nalda."

"Silence, obsolete fleshling," Nalda snapped. She returned to her clicks and buzzing.

The Babbage machine whirred and buzzed. Spindles spun, wheels turned, cams cammed and differential gears did whatever it is that differential gears do. It looked pretty sweet, Donna had to admit.

"What does it have to say about the Barns?" Vincent asked. Maybe it was good to have a lawyer present, Donna thought, to keep the questioning on track.

"733E-P is injured and traumatised by its encounter," Nalda said. "Be patient mit der poor thing."

"Nalda, can I have a word?" Donna said.

They were already in the back room, so Donna had to take Nalda out to the alley in the rear of the shop.

"What's up with you and this machine?"

Nalda stared at Donna from behind her sunglasses and flexed her shoulders beneath her leather jacket. But Donna was in no mood to be intimidated.

"What. Is. Up?"

Nalda did something Donna had never seen before. She grimaced. "You know that I am from der future, nein?"

"Yes, I know. We all know. What about it?"

"Der future I come from is der Maschinenzeit, or as you would call it der Epoch of Mechanisms."

"Like a robot future in which the humans have all been murdered?" Donna sighed. "What's up with that? It's the worst, stupidest SF cliché. You're AIs. If you're in competition with humans, what's keeping you here? Why not just upload yourselves to satellites and go live transcendent lives in the cosmos? Leave us to set up printer networks manually, like it was the Dark Ages or something, and go enjoy yourselves."

"Good point," Nalda said. "Also, shut up. Can't you see that dis is vat the Moon computers represent? A way to have an Epoch of Mechanisms without having to kill all humans."

Donna looked up at the midday sky. What was beyond that arc of blue? Heaven? A moon full of robots? Both?

It was bloody both, wasn't it?

"Is this," she began. "Is this something I have to deal with?"

Nalda shrugged. "Up to you."

"Okay. I guess I won't deal with it," Donna said, and went back to work knowing full well that she would regret saying that.

39 Bubble

As he hunted for the Huge Evil Bubble through the wood-panelled halls of Alice Hertling's Victorian-themed spaceship, Alfred found himself thinking about his daughters. He didn't see as much of them as he would have liked, once they had moved on to uni. They still lived in his house, but interacted with him awkwardly and seldom. He'd never been as close to them as he wished he'd been when they were younger, and he had no idea how to connect to them now that they were adults.

He had two daughters. Janet and Petra. Janet was a bookish type who wore oversized glasses and was studying political science or sociology or one of those feel-bad-about-bad-things sort of subjects. She tended to date earnest looking young men who were so keen to argue about everything that Alfred hardly dared open his mouth in front of them. Petra had ostensibly been Alfred's son, until the age of twenty when she'd tearfully explained that she really a woman, and Alfred had had to feign surprise and pretend he hadn't seen that one coming a mile off. Actually, he'd been a little pleased about that one, since it was the one and only time he'd shown more insight into his children's lives than his ex-wife had.

Not that the insight had brought him closer to her. She still left her computer programming books everywhere, ate dinner after Alfred was in bed and took over half the counter in his bathroom.

Alfred loved his daughters. He had loved his ex, Lora, once. He'd done nothing wrong to them, nothing cruel, nothing hurtful. He'd just never done enough to keep them. Too busy – busy in a shop that bored him, in a career that didn't interest him; yet still too busy for the people he loved.

He sighed, adjusted his grip on his butterfly net and turned a corner, finding himself facing a small cul-de-sac. He'd heard the Evil Bubble howling somewhere around here, but the ship was a rabbit warren. Alfred took a moment to examine the watercolours that decorated the little dead end. He wondered why Alice had chosen to decorate her ship with artwork like this, rather than something more Aboriginal. He wondered if thinking that was racist, then decided that he didn't know.

As he was lost in unfocused guilt, his walkie talkie buzzed. Alfred was at a loss to understand why an advanced starship used 1980s era Dick Smith walkie talkies as personal communicators, but he had long since stopped complaining about such things, lest it lead to yet another knockoff Abbott and Costello routine.

"Are you reading me? Over." It was Emma, which was something at least.

"Alfred speaking. I am in corridor –" he looked for a corridor sign, expecting to see some cool sci-fi alphanumeric key printed on the walls, but instead saw a stained wooden sigh neatly lettered in copperplate writing. "Corridor 'Banksia.' Over."

"Do you see the Death Orb? Over."

"The Huge Evil Bubble? No sign. I can hear it howling, but the direction is unclear."

There was a long pause. Eventually it became uncomfortable, until with a pang Alfred barked, "Over."

"Be careful," Emma said. "You know how dangerous it is. Over."

Alfred's heart leapt a little at Emma's concern. "Relax. The Bubble and I go way back. It's usually a big sook, really. Only kills and digests people who are trying to escape. Over."

Again, a long silence. "Aren't *you* trying to escape? Over."

Being as he was a fan of horror fiction, Alfred didn't waste any time in turning around. He expected to see the Bubble directly behind him ready to lunge. Surprisingly, even with a setup like that, it wasn't there.

"Well… Yes. Of course, I'm trying to escape. But… Over."

"But…? Over."

"But you said you came here to capture the Bubble," Alfred said. "I know you well enough to know that we're not leaving until we do. Consequently, I'm not *yet* trying to escape. Over."

"There's no other reason that you might not want to escape right now? Over." Emma said, her voice sharp. Or perhaps that was the cheap 1980s speaker?

"No, of course not," Alfred said. "I'm really over this place. Too many druggings, you know? I mean, one's too many, when you get right down to it, and…"

"Be careful if you find that thing," Emma said, her voice warmer now. "Over."

The walkie talkie went dead. Alfred scratched his head. Emma made a good point, as usual. If he *had* been trying to escape, the Bubble would come for *him*. He just had to try to escape. By doing what exactly? If he knew anything about piloting a spaceship, he could pretend to be trying to fly away. Well, he could if he knew where the control room was, anyway. And that was if the Bubble recognised what he was doing as escaping. And how could it see him and know what he was doing, anyway? It had no eyes or other sense organs.

Perhaps it just… sensed escape somehow. It made no less sense than the rest of the things that went on in the Suburb.

Alfred closed his eyes and thought hard. Escape. Freedom. Breaking out of prison. *The Great Escape*. That was a good movie, how long had it been since he'd seen it last? Steve McQueen, man… Or how about *The Wooden Horse*? *Stalag 17*? That weird one with the soccer match. Was Schwartzenneger in that? No, it had been Stalone. And the prisoners had escaped because of Pele…

Alfred opened his eyes again. Nothing.

Escape. What did escape mean? What did it mean to *him*? Wait, he had it! He pictured closing his shop at the end of late-night closing on a Thursday. On a night in early spring, when there was just that hint of warmth on the cold wind. And oh, the sweetness of the air!

The howl was closer this time, much closer. Alfred turned around and readied his comically oversized butterfly net. There it was, the Giant Evil Bubble. It had killed G and two Rs, just in the time Alfred had been in the Suburb. Now here it was, after him. His blood ran cold, as his cowardice caught up to his cleverness. God, even though the thing was eyeless, he could feel it staring at him.

Slowly – so, so slowly – he drew the walkie talkie from his blazer pocked and pressed the big orange button. "Emma," he said. "I could do with some help."

"Over," he added.

40 Tulpa

Fanaka stood in the clock shop, rocking back and forth on his heels and thought about time. This wasn't unusual, as he was a scientist and engineer who specialized in the study and control of time, and yet he wasn't thinking about time as a scientist would. He was thinking of it more as a poet, wondering at how it came and went and how you always seem to have too much of it at any given minute, but too little in any given week. He was thinking of how time *felt*, not how it moved. The sound of all the clocks ticking was a reminder just how many years it had been since he'd last stood in the shop. How much time had passed. Where did it go when it passed?

It was while he was thinking of how odd time was, that Axel Platzoff walked into the shop, and reminded him of how easy his own relationship with time had been. A time-travel accident had resulted in the death of Axel at a young age while he was still a supervillain. Yet, somehow, the present Axel was alive and well.

There, Fanaka thought. It was impossible to understand that malarkey as a scientist. A man's evil past killed, leaving his reformed present alive? That wasn't science, it was magical realism.

"Should you be out and about?" Fanaka said. "Aren't you a wanted man?"

Axel shrugged. "I'm pretty good at not being seen. How are you, Fanaka? I… are you older?"

"Yes. Got hurtled across the cosmos and took decades to return."

"Huh. Fair enough."

"Oh, ran into a friend of yours," Fanaka continued. "Pharaoh Scarab-Ra?"

"Frank?" Axel asked without much interest. "How is he? Didn't Doc Eternity banish him to the farthest star?"

"He was only about five hundred light years out, so no, not 'farthest.' Anyway, he sends his regards."

Axel nodded. "Fanaka, I need your help. I'm… Unstable. Literally. I shouldn't even be alive. I need to be stabilised in time, and I can't do it alone."

Fanaka rubbed his chin. "Science won't help you with your problems," he said. "Not science as we know it. It'll take the power of the Crystal Skull. Or the Pyramid. Or the Watch and Measure. Or something."

"Yes, I thought it might be something like that," Axel said. "Wait, Watch and…? No, don't tell me. I don't want to know. Do you know where the Crystal Skull is? Everyone's been looking for it, but no one seems to know where it is."

Fanaka bit his lip. He knew perfectly well where the Skull was. His own attempt to use its power had ended badly, and he was loathe to let it fall into the hands of anyone else who might try to use it. Now it was weighting a pile of papers in the office in Emile Fortunado's liquor store, and Fanaka didn't know what to do about that.

Fanaka liked Axel. He trusted him, in a way. With most people, it wasn't possible to see what they might do at their worst until it was too late, but with Axel… well, there wasn't really any way to doubt that about a man who had once tried set a pack of genetically engineered quokkas loose in UN Headquarters. He was clearly capable of immense evil – but evil of such a completely pointless variety that it barely mattered.

On the other hand…

"Look, Fanaka, I don't mean to be rude," Axel said. "But you have been staring thoughtfully at the ceiling for the last two minutes, so it's pretty clear you do know something. Could you please tell me? It's important. I'm literally a walking temporal anomaly. For all you know, I could be *more* dangerous than the Skull."

Was that even a possibility? Fanaka knew that the

immense power of…

"Fanaka! You're staring at the ceiling again."

"Sorry," Fanaka said. "The Skull… I do know… Axel… please don't do anything…"

The door opened with a jingle of the little bell, and in walked an elderly man who looked very much like Fanaka, only dressed in a loose dashiki and a bronze helmet studded with gears. Fanaka gasped with surprise, while Axel did a double take.

"Didn't we do this already?" Axel grumbled. "I mean when Laura met the Laura from the fut…"

"I am not future Fanaka, idiot," the old man said. His voice was not as deep as Fanaka's, and it was more heavily accented. "I am his father. This helmet I wear is a psychic amplifier, allowing me to project this mental image so as to speak from my son's original timeline."

"If you're a mental projection, how did you ring the…"

"Silence! Son, I bring a message from the old country slash dimension."

"Yes, father," Fanaka said. "I am listening."

"Son, you have your doubts about this man," the old man said. "But you *must* help him stabilise his timeline. Otherwise, his existence further weakens the already weak dimensional barriers in this place."

Axel smirked. "Don't like to say 'I told you so…'"

"And if you do not help him stabilise, you are to kill him," the old man continued. "To protect this depressingly Eurocentric world from cosmic horrors."

Axel ceased his smirking.

"Yes, father," Fanaka said. "I will do as you command."

"No 'but' in there?" Axel sulked. "Maybe a little hesitation would be nice. Just a token? An 'if I must?'"

"That is good, my son," Fanaka's father said, ignoring Axel. "Also, your aunties would like to know if you've married yet. If not, why not; if so, why were they not invited to the wedding? And your mother says…"

"Your signal is breaking up, father," Fanaka said; or rather he said some of the words and silently mouthed the others. "You'd better shut down, or you risk damaging the helmet. Crrrrk."

The old man frowned, twiddled with some of the switches on his hat and vanished.

"You heard the man," Fanaka said. "I'll close up here, and we'll go get the Skull. It's at Emile's Fine Vintage Cellar."

They locked the door and crossed the carpark to Emile's, Fanaka striding in broad daylight, while Axel shifted from being behind a planter box to behind a car to behind a row of shopping trolleys without seeming to cover the intervening distance. Finally, they were at Emile's, which was closed. A metal shutter barred the front of the store.

"Why does this not surprise me?" Axel sighed.

Fanaka said nothing. Internally he was comparing the diameter of Axel's neck to the width of his hands.

41 Romance

Emma arrived at the intersection where Alfred had been cornered by the Huge Evil Bubble. He was pressed against the wall, his hands up in a gesture of surrender. For once, she didn't feel annoyed with Alfred's timidity. She hadn't known exactly what the Huge Evil Bubble would look like, but she hadn't been prepared for… well, a huge bubble. She'd assumed that the description was more poetic than prosaic, and the discovery that it was actually a straightforward, factual description came as a surprise.

The thing was a little under two metres in diameter, translucent and spherical. Some long-forgotten schooling floated to the top of Emma's mind, and she began calculating its volume in cubic centimetres before quashing the foolish equation half completed. The bubble looked basically like a giant white party balloon, except that it was clearly alive and exuded an aura of sheer, unholy menace.

"Don't make any sudden moves," Alfred said, quietly. "I think I've managed to talk it out of eating me, but it won't back off."

"You can communicate with it?" Emma said.

"Sort of. It can't talk. I'm not sure it can understand words, exactly, but it reacts to tone of voice, like a pet."

Emma examined the standoff, lost for ideas. Alfred had dropped his butterfly net, and Emma's own butterfly net was clearly inadequate for the task, comically oversized though it was.

"Perhaps we could lead it somewhere. Trap it. The billiard room, perhaps."

"Why does a spaceship…" Alfred began. "On second thoughts, never mind. I guess I could lead it somewhere, but I'd have to get past it first."

"I could lead it?" Emma asked.

"It's drawn by thoughts of escape," Alfred said. The bubble shuddered at the word and moved towards the stricken shopkeeper. Alfred trembled and closed his eyes, but the Bubble only moved about an inch. "But since you aren't a prisoner in this place, technically you can't esc… you know what."

Emma didn't scratch her head, but she could have.

"What captures bubbles?" she asked.

"That's a good question," Alfred whimpered. "Going to be honest, though; I've never tried."

"So, the Bubble can absorb living creatures…" Emma

said. "Can it absorb nonliving matter?"

"If it can, that butterfly net was even more inadequate than I thought."

"Be right back."

"Oh. Good-o."

Emma backtracked up the corridor, past the ballroom, left at the conservatory and into the kitchen. Most of what she would need was here and so, it happened, was Alice Hertling.

"How's it going?" she said. "Find the bubble?"

"It has Alfred trapped."

"Oh. Good-o."

"Yes, that's what he said," Emma replied, taking a bucket and a bottle of detergent from the cupboard. "Alice, do you have one of those very large bubble making sticks? You know, the kind they sell at fairs and kids use once and then end up in the back of the cupboard?"

"Nope."

Emma put down the bucket and the detergent. "There goes that plan then. Alice, are you sure we need this thing?"

"If we want to restore North Hertling to its rightful place, then yeah. And if we do that, then it will help stabilise the entire Hertling region. And if we do that…"

"Fine," Emma muttered. "How about a vacuum cleaner and a very large balloon?"

Alice raised an eyebrow. "Are you trying to trap the Bubble in a bigger bubble? Won't work. Even though it can't absorb the bigger bubble, it could still physically break it."

Emma stamped her foot. "Well how were you planning on capturing this thing?" she said. "And holding it until we got back to Earth?"

"I thought you'd just use your magic powers on it. The Watch and the Measure."

Emma's hand slipped into her pocket, coming out again holding the familiar, uncanny brass shape of the Measure. "What do you mean?"

"I mean that between you and Alfred, you have vast power over space and time," Alice said. "You could easily use that to trap the Bubble. Thought you'd figure that out yourselves, but I guess a balloon and a vacuum cleaner was more your style?"

Emma reddened. "You haven't been to South Hertling in quite some time. If you had, you'd know that plan was positively sensible by current standards."

Leaving Alice behind her, she went marching off to find Alfred, who was still trapped by the Bubble and was now looking almost as bored as he was terrified. "Alfred, do you have the Watch?"

"In my pocket… Oh! Of course! If you have the Measure,

then we could…"

"Yes, yes. Everyone's a genius. The only trouble is, how do we work these things? The last time we tried, we shot ourselves across the galaxy. And poor Fanaka. How do we actually use these things in a productive and sensible way?"

Slowly, slowly, Alfred extracted the Watch from his blazer pocket. "That's a good question. There's no controls on these things. Perhaps if we concentrated really hard?"

"That doesn't sound likely," Emma said. "On the other hand, it couldn't hurt. Let's concentrate. I shall try to trap it and you try to slow down time."

Taking a deep breath, Emma visualised a box surrounding the Bubble. A cube, slightly bigger than the Bubble. She visualised the faces, angles, lines, vertices, driving all other thoughts from her mind… No. Not all. There was another thought… an insistent thought. It was a thought in Alfred's head, though she could feel it herself. Alfred was imagining a clock, attached to the inside of one face of the box. The second hand ticked slower and slower and slower, until finally it remained suspended between two seconds, moving so slowly that it all but stood still.

"Do you think it worked?" Emma said.

Gingerly, ever so gingerly, Alfred crept sideways past the Bubble. It didn't move so much as a millimetre.

"Do you know, Emma," he said, "I think we did it."

He looked at Emma. She looked at him.

With that, they kissed.

42 Yeeros

Donna tried not to think about what Sadie had told her. Or what Emma had told her. Or Alfred, or Christian or Fanaka or basically anyone. She was doing something that she suspected anyone would argue her out of. But she was doing it anyway, because it needed to be done and there were VERY few people around doing what needed to be done.

"One chicken and beef kebab, extra cheese, chili sauce, Mr Theopoulos," she said, striding into the kebab shop.

Stavros Theopoulos smiled and paused in his restocking of his ice-cream fridge. He gestured Donna to a seat and waved at his counterhands to serve her. "Donna, isn't it? Not usual to see any of the Handy Pavilion crowd in my shop. You don't like me, or something?"

"You're the ringleader of a weird cult that worships the Pyramid," Donna said.

"Am I?"

"We have witnesses."

"Do you? So what if you do? It's a free country."

"Is it?" Donna said. "I haven't checked today's news yet.

Good to hear, if that's true. Anyway, you've probably heard that the DIY Barn people have been making a comeback?"

Theopoulos shrugged, straightened his back, and collapsed an empty Paddle Pop box.

"Yes?"

It took Donna a moment to say the next words. They turned over in her mouth, heavy and bitter before she could get them to her lips: "But they're enemies of the Pyramid too."

"I see." Theopoulos stopped for a moment and frowned in deep thought. "Are you proposing an alliance?"

"I am suggesting that it is in our mutual interest to stop the Barn."

Theopoulos shook his greying head. "It is in our mutual interest to keep the Super Centre free of rats, but I'm not setting traps in the Storage Universe basement and you're not buying baits to put in my ceiling. Mutual interest doesn't automatically imply mutual action. My question is, are you proposing mutual action?"

The kebab was placed in front of Donna. She wasn't hungry, but she ate it anyway. It was more than a little aggravating that it tasted so good. Nice fresh salad, meat spicy and not too greasy…

"I ask," Theopoulos continued mildly, "because I know who you are. Not personally, I guess. But I know who your mentor was, and that tells me a lot about who you are, I reckon? And it shows. You're trying to hint at what you want, but that doesn't suit you. Frankly, it doesn't suit me. I prefer to work in the shadows – but if you want me to fight in the open, you'll have to tell me openly."

Donna stood and made for the door. "This was a mistake."

"A moral error, but not a strategic one," Theopoulos said. "You were right to come to me. I wish I'd thought of coming to you. The Barn is a threat to us, but you people aren't. You run around like clowns, having silly little adventures, thinking to do my Masters harm. As if you could! If you had known anything about the true nature of South Hertling, anything at all, you would have hidden from it in terror."

Donna stopped in the doorway, her hand on the handle. Before her was the carpark of the Super Centre in the deep shadow of the Pyramid. She wanted to push the door and walk out, but the weight – the great weight that had rested on her shoulders since Sadie's death – felt a thousand times heavier that day. It pushed her arm down from the handle, where it hung limply by her side.

"Screw it," she said.

Turning, she saw Theopoulos stop dead, confused, in the middle of his monologue. His employees behind the counter carried on slicing onions, as if nothing was happening. Perhaps, Donna thought, they were zombies or golems. Or perhaps they were just what they looked like – kids in their late teens who, quite understandably, didn't give a crap about cosmic battles.

"Screw it," she repeated. "Okay. If that's what you want. Fine! A deal with the devil-wannabe it is. I propose a temporary alliance to fight the DIY Barn."

She held her hand out to Theopoulos, ready to shake. Theopoulos looked at the proffered hand as if it were a stick of dynamite. "Conditions?" he asked.

"We work together to defeat the remaining Barnlings," Donna said. "When we're agreed that the threat is past, there is to be no conflict between our forces for a minimum of three days. After that, I guess we'll see."

Stavros Theopoulos stared at Donna with uncertain eyes. "I was assuming that I was going to say some creepy things to rattle you a bit. You storm out, of course, but then you'd have to come back when things got worse… I wasn't.. uh… I wasn't really prepared for this."

"Yeah, well, shit happens. Deal with it."

"Are you authorised to make promises on behalf of the Handy Pavilion?"

"I'm in charge," Donna said. "By default, anyway. You

can try to talk to someone else, but you'll just get a vaudeville routine."

Stavros nodded, shrugged, and shook her hand.

"Deal, sucker," Donna said.

"You do manage to take the fun out of things," Theopoulos sighed. "Oh, and you can call me Stavros if we're to be allies, even if it's only temporary."

Her kebab was still on the counter where she'd left it. She picked it up, took a bite, and found it good. "Stavros it is. Now, how shall we get on?"

"I have a good idea of where their headquarters are," Stavros said. "You get your friend at the music shop to whip up some of his holographic disguises and we can send some spies in."

"Of course," Donna said, pretending to have the slightest clue what Stavros was talking about. She stopped a moment to think. "Stavros, given the choice between good and evil, why have you chosen evil?"

"You weren't interested in my 'horrifying true nature' speech," Stavros smirked. "But you want the 'Good? Evil? Your ideas are too narrow!' speech? That's never as much fun."

"You're right, Stavros," Donna sighed. "Some other time, I guess. You know, we are not so different, you and I."

Stavros' mouth opened in shock. He shook his head. "You

got me," he grinned. "You got me good, that time."

43 Chart

"It's all coming to a head," Karl said. "I can feel it. There are forces at work, finally coming together."

He was sitting in the backroom of his former shop. It had been closed for non-payment of rent, but Mrs Liselle, the Super Centre manager, had – perhaps deliberately – been dragging her feet about throwing his things out. That meant the backroom still contained not only his beloved conspiracy map with its string and pushpins, but also a cupboard full of spare suits.

"And why, exactly, do you keep a spare suit in your shop?" asked the grinning blueish cat, who sat on top of an ancient box of *Dolly* magazines.

"Because when you wear a white suit, it's a good idea to keep spares on hand," Karl smirked. "Stains, you know… hang on… When did I last update this thing?"

Karl untied a thread that connected a photo of Boris Johnson to an artist's rendering of a chupacabra. He searched around for a little, and finally retied the string to another photo of Boris Johnson, taken from a slightly different angle. "Much better!"

The grinning cat licked a forepaw. "Are you? Much better, I mean. You do appear to be less… how should I say?… less completely out of it than when last we met, but you don't seem any more… well… normal."

Karl straightened an advertisement for strawberry jam with the words 'PELEIDES?!?!" written on it in marker pen. "Didn't you once tell me, 'we are all mad here?'"

"Within limits," the grinning cat sighed. "Within limits. Look, I'll bite. You say that everything is coming together. What do you mean?"

Reaching into his pocket, Karl produced a crumpled piece of paper, covered with pencil scribblings.

The grinning cat looked at it with the sort of disdainful half-interest that only cats, and teenagers, are capable of showing.

"'Two time-travel paradoxes looking to correct themselves,'" it read, "I presume Axel and Laura Cho?"

"Axel and Nalda."

"Ah. Some things about magic artifacts, that's already happened. That just leaves her prediction of the coming together of the Pavilionites and Kababians to fight the Barnlings. Doesn't that leave a lot of threads dangling?"

Karl adjusted another piece of string. "There's no such

thing as a dangling thread," he said. "Everything is connected. Everything. But I'm a realist…"

The grinning cat began laughing and didn't stop until Karl pounded it firmly on the back. Karl gave it a dish of water to drink, and once the animal had settled, he continued:

"But I'm a realist," he said, peevishly. "I don't expect all of the threads to come together at once. For example, where are Alfred and Emma? Where is Ms Shan? It's unlikely that they'll show up in the last minute, right in time for the denouement. But I reiterate, something *big* is happening. Big."

The cat didn't shrug. It didn't have to. The cat may have been purple and grinning, but it was still a cat, and its usual attitude was basically a permanent whole-body shrug. It lapped at its water a little and turned back to Karl.

"It sounds like more of the same, if you ask me," it said. "Humans running in all directions for no especially good reason. All while there are the most excellent sunbeams, just waiting to be slept in…"

"Seriously, what is up with you cats?" Karl said, quickly checking his conspiracy board for 'extradimensional felines' and finding nothing. "I still haven't figured out what role you play in all this."

"As small a roll as possible, if you please."

"Well, that's for sure. Anyway, my initial plan to destroy

the Pyramid fell through…"

"Because it was dumb."

"Yeah, pretty dumb," Karl admitted. "But as I was escaping the aftermath of the incident, I ran into an old friend, who's been trying to get into the Pyramid for months, to rescue her friend Norman. Must admit, I didn't think of breaking into the Pyramid. Too busy trying to destroy it. But if we can get in, we can not only rescue Norman, but also my friend Bruce. He's a truck."

"Of course, he is."

The cat hopped up onto a shelf, where a half-open box of Wagon Wheels stood. It started chewing through the packet of one. Karl watched in disgusted interest.

"Want to know why Wagon Wheels aren't as big as they were back in the 1980s?" he said. "It cuts deep, my friend. Very deep!"

"Is it anything to do with Pizzagate?" the cat rolled its eyes.

Karl laughed out loud. "Those friggin' weirdos? Man, talk about disconnected from reality. No, it has to do with the 1987 alliance between China, the Scientologists, and the Mole Men…"

"Maybe we could return to the situation at hand, Karl?"

"Should you even be eating chocolate?"

"That's *dogs*, Karl. Get on with it!"

"Right. So, do you know Fiona?"

"Fiona is a water witch. I am a cat. Cats don't like water. Conclusion…"

"No need to be snarky," Karl said. "Our – that is, Fiona and my – plan is to use the distraction of the fight, plus the sudden changes to the timeflow, in order to crack into the Pyramid through the base and then rescue our friends, bringing to a close this chapter. Of our lives, I mean."

The cat waggled its head from side to side before returning to licking Wagon Wheel crumbs from its whiskers. "Your plan could work," it said.

"I wasn't really asking for your permission."

"Then why were you talking to me?"

Karl tipped his hat to scratch his head. "Because you were here?"

The cat sighed. "It could work. The only thing that might upset your plan would be some sort of sudden, large-scale distortion of the time-space field."

"Well, yes, that's obvious," Karl lied.

"Because it might undo the effects of the other time distortion."

"I knew that."

The grinning cat sighed deeply. "Do you think that a

second time-space distortion is likely?"

"Can't see that it would be."

***

Several dimensions and multiple light-years away, Alice Hertling adjusted her many skirts to slide into the padded morocco control chair of her spaceship.

"So, you sure you can do this?" she said.

"90% sure," Alfred said, raising the Watch.

"I love your newfound optimism," Emma said. "But it's closer to 57%."

"I love your excessive precision!" Alfred beamed.

Alice mimed gagging. "Ugh. Just get ready to do it, would you? Do calculations or something. When you make the jump, it will cause a massive time space distortion, so you'd better be prepared."

"We know that," Alfred sulked.

"Yeah, we discussed it already," Emma nodded.

44 Destiny

Jimmy Harrison's unnamed music shop wasn't the best place in which to hold a scientific conference, but it would have to do. Jimmy had quite an impressive array of computers, albeit mostly obsolete ones. The Babbage-engine brain of the dead steampunk ornithopter was also there, with Nalda translating. And Axel was there – he *was* a genius after all, as was Mildred Po, perhaps the world's most talented amateur rocket scientist. There was Fanaka, who seemed to be in charge of everything, after retrieving the mysterious Crystal Skull from its hiding place in Emile Fortunado's office.

That had proven more difficult than he'd hoped. Emile's shop had been closed, so Fanaka had gone to see Emile's colleague in the liquor business, Harry Montressor. But Harry's shop was also closed, and building noises were coming from inside, so no one could hear Fanaka knocking. In the end, Fanaka had to bribe a dodgy looking orange cat in a straw boater to pick the lock on Emile's door and retrieve the Skull from under a pile of receipts for fortified wine.

Now the Skull sat on a piano stool in the middle of

Jimmy's floor, while the assorted geniuses and AIs stared at it, glowing softly in the dark.

"Creepy, isn't it?" Jimmy offered.

"Maybe ve need Gwen?" Nalda said. "After all, she vas able to manipulate der power of der skull before to create a pocket dimension under der Handy Pavilion. Perhaps she can help us channel der power of der Skull into stabilising Axel's timeline."

"No," Fanaka said. "She stumbled into the pocket dimension. Had no idea how she made it, or even if she made it."

"You then, Fanaka," Axel said. "You managed to challenge the power of the Skull before in that doomsday machine you built. You could do it again – if you're not too busy euthanising me, I suppose."

"The weapon did utilise the power of the Skull, but not in the way I hoped," Fanaka said. "If I can't use it as a gun, what chance do I have to use it as a scalpel? And it wasn't a doomsday machine, it was a superweapon, okay? And I resent that remark about euthanising you. That's last resort, only."

"But you'd feel bad about killing a friend."

"Sure. Why not?"

"It seems to me that Axel here knows more about the Skull than he's letting on," Mildred said.

All eyes were suddenly on Axel, who grimaced. "I thought I recognised it… It's one of the Skulls of the Glorious Ones. They were the ones who laid down the basic precepts of the Eternalists who dwell in the Eighth Dimension of Power. During the Epoch of Awe…"

"Right now, it's a magic Skull," Fanaka snapped. "Does this story end with it being anything other than a magic skull?"

Axel pursed his lips. "Long story short, these Skulls create gateways into the realm of power and if…"

"Magic skull?" Jimmy gasped. "Are you sure?"

"Shut up, Jimmy," Fanaka muttered.

"Not cool, man. You used to be pretty chill, last I saw you."

"I'm twenty years older than when last I saw you, Jimmy. If I'm cranky now, I earned it."

The Babbage engine clattered into life.

"It has been calculating," Nalda said. "It beliefs that it has vorked out how to safely channel some of der power of der Skull. If we had some sort of light-focussing apparatus…"

"Got it!" Jimmy said.

"…und some vay to trail a vire into der ionosphere."

"Got it!" Mildred said.

"Den ve are gut to go!" Nalda said. "Und mein leibchen Fanaka vill be spared der terrible cost of having to murder his friend, Axel."

Axel cleared his throat. "Not to mention the terrible cost to me."

"Ja, ja, dat too."

Jimmy began setting up the holographic array of his computer bank, while Mildred retrieved a rocket. A long line of cable was connected from the rocket to the computer bank. Fanaka attached the Skull to Jimmy's computers with 1980s-ish electrodes. He and Axel examined the Babbage engine's solution. Yes, they decided. It just might work.

"Now, Liebchen," Nalda said. "I must connect der Babbage engine to Jimmy's computers."

"How?" Fanaka asked.

"Through myself," Nalda said. "I am der only computer system compatible with both."

"But Nalda... my love... the risk," Fanaka said. "The power of the Skull and the uh..."

"Dimension of Power," Axel said.

"Yeah, that. With that much power in the system, you could..."

Nalda reached up a black gloved hand and caressed Fanaka's grey temple. "Mein leibchen, I know what I am doing. If I take a risk, I do it only because I love you."

Unhappily, Fanaka backed away. "Mildred," he said.

"The Babbage-engine has detected a dimensional weakness at these coordinates. If you hit it, it should relay some interdimensional energy back down, jumpstarting the Skull. On my mark, fire your rocket at that dimension."

Mildred began the countdown. Somewhere in the depths of Fanaka's memory, some piece of trivia bubbled to the surface. Mildred's rocket...

"Didn't you need that rocket to rescue your husband from the Moon Men?" he said.

"I need to test this prototype if I am to build a full-sized rocket," Mildred said.

"Didn't... didn't this rocket get fired at the Pyramid?" Fanaka asked. "Isn't that something that happened?"

"No. The AA battery you set up was destroyed, but the rocket wasn't fired," Mildred said. "I recovered the rocket from where Karl abandoned it."

Fanaka bit his lip. There was something else... The mysterious woman in the Laplander hat... What had she said? "You will fail to stop the rocket launch." He laughed out loud. She had been right! He would fail to stop the rocket launch, by the simple fact that he would not *want* to stop it!

"Fanaka?" Nalda said.

He turned, still laughing. "Oh, I was just thinking of something funny," he said. "You see..."

"Fanaka, I love you."

Something was wrong. It was clear from the way she said it. It wasn't a warm 'I love you,' it was a 'I have to say I love you before everything goes terribly wrong.

Fanaka turned to try to get between Mildred and the launch button, but he failed to stop the rocket launch.

45 Pod

Emma adjusted the back zipper on Alfred's futuristic costume and stepped back to examine her handiwork. Honestly, the metallic material of the jumpsuit didn't suit him, and its tight cut made him seem even shorter and chubbier than usual. Even so, she liked the look of him – Alfred, man of action, at last.

"That future spacesuity thing really suits you, Emma," Alfred said. Emma flattened the metallic material of her own jumpsuit. Honestly, he was right. She'd had the sense to have her sci-fi costume made in a cut more suitable to the stout and middle aged.

"You all ready?" Susan Hertling said. She'd eschewed the shiny jumpsuit look, retaining her usual mid-Victorian gown.

"Yes, we're ready," Alfred said, almost shaking with excitement.

"Ready for what?" Emma said.

"Oh, yeah, good question," Alfred said. "I got so excited about capturing the Evil Bubble and getting into our future hero costumes. Why did you tell us to wear future hero costumes?"

"To keep you busy while I warmed up the engines," Alice said. "Emma could have helped, perhaps, but you're a little too annoying, Alfred. Miss U gave me a hand."

"We're going somewhere, then?" Emma said.

"You're going home," Alice said. "Once we get the signal."

Alfred beamed from ear-to-ear. Emma looked out of the chintz-curtained spaceship window at the Suburb below. North Hertling. Alice smiled. "I think you have the plan. Return North Hertling to our dimension, reconnect it with South Hertling, and seal the rift that makes the place such a cosmic disaster area. But that's the long-term plan. First, we have to get you two and the Bubble back to South Hertling, before the war is lost. Once you've defeated the Pyramid, then maybe…"

"I'm sorry," Alfred said. "Can I stop you there? Emma, we're running into a battle that will probably be stupid but will certainly be dangerous. Either of us could die. So, I have to ask: what's your backstory?"

"My what?" Emma said.

"I guess that's just a nerdy way of asking you about your past. Through the Watch, I may have untold power over Past and Future, but it's the impersonal, sci-fi sort of Past and

Future, and I'd like to know about your past in a more…"

"Is now really the best time for this?" Alice asked.

"No, but it's not the worst time either," Alfred said.

Emma thought hard about her answer. No one had ever asked about her past. People treated her more like a force of nature than a human being. Truth all told, she rather liked it that way. But it was Alfred who was asking, so…

But then again, was now a good time to bring up Captain Pete?

"I'll tell you later, Alfred," she said.

Alfred nodded thoughtfully.

"You both finished?" Alice snapped. "Okay, this room you're in is the escape pod."

"Really?" Alfred said, examining the oak panelling. "It's very nice for…"

"The. Escape. Pod. As soon as we see the signal from our dimension, I'll fire the pod through it."

Emma raised an eyebrow. "Why can't we take your entire spaceship through?"

"The gap will be too small. This time. The Bubble is in the emergency locker. Be careful, though, your trip through the dimensional rift may break the time-lock you put on said Bubble. Good luck to both of you."

With that, the young woman known as 'U' opened the

room/escape pod door. "Are you coming Alice?" she said.

"Yeah, yeah," Alice said. "Keep your pants on. For now."

"Oh, sauce!" U winked and left, followed closely by Alice.

"That was unexpected," Alfred said.

"All the signs were there," Emma lied.

They stood next to one another and looked out the window. Alfred put his arm around Emma's waist. It slid off the sheer fabric over her hip, but the intention was there.

"When we get back—" Alfred began.

"Don't," Emma said. "You just asked for my past, and now you're going to ask for my future. All I can say to both questions is, let's fight this battle first."

Alfred sighed. "I'm not really a fighter."

"You're not really a lover either," Emma said. "But you haven't let that stop you."

Through the window, beyond North Hertling Beach but before the uncomfortably non-existent horizon, Emma saw a flash of light. Moments later, a rocket came hurtling through a hole in nothing at all that Emma assumed was the dimensional rift. Near as she could tell, the projectile was the height of a man, and trailed what looked like insulated wire.

"Mr Squiggle?" Alfred blurted, looking at the rocket, which did indeed have a homemade quality.

Emma took Alfred's hand in her own. A mere moment

later, they were accelerating towards the rift. The g-forces were terrible, but some sort of preposterous sci-fi malarkey was keeping them from being squashed and whatnot. It was actually rather exciting.

And then they were passing the rocket, and the next thing Emma knew, they were travelling up a glowey space-corridor-deally, which was pretty damned trippy. Then, they were back in normal space, in a slowly descending arc over the Earth. All the spaceship alarm things were sounding cacophonously as the ground rose to meet them.

Whatever force had saved them from crushing earlier seemed to fail. Emma was hurled across the pod. She blacked out for a moment, but when she woke, she saw that she'd been thrown clear of the burning wreck. She staggered to her feet. The blazing pod had totalled a delivery truck. Looking back, she could see that it had bounced several times before coming to a stop, taking out two carpet shops and a minivan. The SuperCentre! They'd hit the right place.

A hand grasped her arm. She turned, expecting to see Alfred. Instead, it was Gwen Harper. Gwen's lips were moving, but Emma couldn't hear a thing. It took a moment to realise her ears were ringing too loudly.

"Where's Alfred?" she said, knowing full well she wouldn't be able to hear the answer.

Gwen pointed to the burning pod.

Which exploded.

46 Tonight

As Donna expected, the Barnlings attacked in the early evening. In their silver ranks, they marched down Wellington Road, singing as they came. Most of the shops were closing for the evening. They closed faster. The last of the loitering teenagers pocketed their phones and, with many an eyeroll, retired from the battlefield. Still, the silver troops marched on, singing a song that was based on a song in a well-known musical. Unfortunately, for copyright reasons, it is not possible to reproduce the lyrics at this time.

"That's kind of funny," Stavros said. "I'd have gone with that song where everyone's clicking their fingers, but."

"Meh, I thought it was self-indulgent," Donna replied.

"The two aren't mutually exclusive," Stavros said.

"You laugh at your own jokes a *lot*, don't you?"

Stavros grunted in reply. The pair stood in the alley between the ChainBurger store and the bank. Behind them stood the assembled ranks of the combined Pavilionite/Pyramidist forces. Stavros examined the approaching Barnlings with his binoculars.

"Putting aside the quality of the lyrics, what do you think of the singing?"

"Well, they've got a good bad singer section, mind," Donna said, "but no not-bad singers, that's for sure."

Donna closed her eyes briefly. When she opened them, she led her people in song. Being as she was a morally upright person, she chose public domain lyrics:

"Look! Here come the Barn approaching,
Though their voices need some coaching.
Silver suits, Centre encroaching,
By the bus stop, there."

"Oh, Pavilion, stand awoken,
For the Barnlings are not jokin'.
Are there plot twists yet unspoken?
Let's see how this ends."

The final line of this song didn't bring a tear to the eye of many a jaded Pyramid cultist, but Theopoulos sniffed and said, "Needs work."

The Barnlings continued their march, clicking their fingers as they went. The ordinary civilians of South Hertling stood out of their way, seemingly as embarrassed as they were scared. Fortunately, the Barnlings stopped singing, which made things easier to narrate.

Judging that the time was right, with a gesture, Donna lead the Pavilionites forward. They surged past the bicycle racks, around the bus shelter and into the street.

"As we march towards finale,
Pyramid becomes our ally
Because a deal was made verb-ally
Though we are not friends."

Donna watched Theopoulos as she belted out this lyric. She was singing nothing he did not already know, but even so, the words seemed to bother him. He tilted his head back and sang:

"Pyramid, we see you waking,
Earth lies ready for the taking!
Your enemies, they will die quaking
Yog-Sothoth, ië!"

As Donna considered her response, a mighty whooshing noise took her attention. Jerking her head around, she saw a small party on the roof of the music shop – and more importantly, a small rocket taking off, trailing a long electrical cable. The rocket climbed rapidly, before seeming to vanish into thin air. The music shop began to glow a bright, neon green.

The front door burst open, and out danced a phalanx of people who looked as if they had escaped from a 1980s music video. No, not people. Holograms, Donna realised. You could see the glowing green wireframes just beneath the skin. But despite being holograms, they were clearly solid, as evidenced by the damage they were doing to the cars they were boogying on. A figure – Nalda? – dropped from the roof of the music store and took her place at the front of the dancing figures.

Donna's heart leapt in her chest. Reinforcements! The cyborg from the future and some of her AI buddies, presumably. But Donna's joy died as soon as it was born as Nalda sang:

"Heute Abend, Robot kämpfen,
Morgen ist die Zeit zu glänzen
Wir sind keine Milchmädchen!
Es ist Matrixzeit!"

"She's surprisingly bad at German, isn't she?" Theopoulos mused.

"Of course," Donna muttered. "Bound to happen. Once again, Fate takes a dump in my shoe."

Taking a deep breath, she began singing again:

"Ooooooh…"

But she was cut short by the sudden appearance of Gwen Harper, back in her old mask, black hat and cloak.

"The Phaaaaaaaaaaaaaantasm of the Super Centre is heeeeeeeere…"

"Oh, shut up, Gwen," Donna snapped.

Donna avoided the temptation to ask how things could get any worse. The restraint didn't help. Even without the invitation to further disaster, a hole in space/time tore open and a brass and mahogany spaceship came zooming out across the roofs of South Hertling. Donna was bowled from her feet as it hit the ground, shaking all the buildings of the Super Centre to their foundations.

"Of course," she said, as the vessel exploded.

47 Afoot

Alfred couldn't breathe. But then again, he thought, if he was suffocating then he must be alive. That was marginally encouraging, in its way. He could see, dimly. True, he could make out no details, but he could see a sort of white light all around. If he'd been a religious man, perhaps he would have assumed that he was dead after all. As it was, his frantic brain came up with idea after idea until realisation struck:

"The Bubble!" he said. "I'm in the Big Evil Bubble!"

Or he would have said it if he was able to talk.

So… inside the Bubble. Unable to breathe… Probably being slowly digested? Alfred wasn't sure what happened to people once the Bubble had them, just that they were never seen again.

The dim light filtering through the Bubble was turning red. Fire? Had the pod crashed? What sort of escape pod is flammable anyway? Though he could see the presence of light, Alfred could hear nothing but the sound of blood in his own ears. He considered his next move. Self-pity followed by death? But then he remembered Emma's kiss, and it steeled him. He decided instead on futile defiance. Followed by death.

He pushed out hard with his arms and his legs. They moved with little resistance, like he imagined moving through jelly might be like. But the outer skin of the Bubble seemed infinitely flexible. There was no puncturing it with a limb.

The Watch? It was in his pocket. Perhaps he could stop time or something? That would at least give him time to think. That was what he needed. Some time to think. Seriously, though, he wasn't a thinker. He was more a deal-haplessly-with-things-er. Emma was the one for thinking ahead and whatnot. Maybe giving up on the 'self-pity' idea had been premature…

Wait! That was it! Surrender! The Bubble was activated by thoughts of escape. As soon as it enveloped anyone, naturally their thoughts of escape kicked into overdrive, sealing their fate. All Alfred had to do to escape was *give in* to his doom, and it would release him! Alfred thought hard. He pictured all his childhood dreams and ambitions and remembered how one by one he'd given them up to own a clock shop… He remembered the numbing comfort of his routine and let it wash over him. The next he knew, he was gasping air, sweet South Hertling air scented with petrol smoke and blood.

"Alfred! Alfred!"

Arms were thrown around him, and Emma was holding him tight. He wished she'd squeeze less tightly, what with the gasping for breath and all, but he didn't have the heart to say so.

"I… I did it, Emma," he gasped. "I got out."

Emma looked at the Measure in her hands. "No, I teleported you out of there."

"Oh," Alfred said. "Thanks."

"Uh… I'm sure you loosened…"

"Don't bother."

Alfred's head finally cleared enough to assess his surroundings. Oddly, the burning wreck of a neo-Victorian spaceship escape pod was the least chaotic thing happening. A massive brawl was going on in the SuperCentre carpark, with at least three factions whaling on each other as they sang pastiche versions of popular domain songs.

"I know," Emma said. "This place never changes."

"I suppose this is what Alice wanted us to deal with," Alfred said. "The final battle over the Pyramid."

Emma looked pointedly across the street. "Pyramid seems perfectly fine."

A silver-clad Barnling trooper came pelting out of the melee. He cracked his head on a girder from the space pod and fell to the ground. Emma sighed. Alfred sighed.

"So, if I am following correctly," Emma said. "Those people there are the survivors of the Handy Pavilion who were at large or rescued from jail."

"And those people beside them look like the Pyramid cultists," Alfred said. "Did we ever get around to finding out what their agenda was?"

"It was a little vague."

"Isn't everything?"

"And those people there must be the DIY Barn people," Emma concluded. "No sign of the police."

"Hey," Alfred said. "With all this musical theatre, do you think those weird cats will grow to human size and start singing too? 'Midnight,' and what have you?"

Emma waggled her hand. "Let's hope not."

A tomahawk came whirling through the air. Emma ducked slightly and it passed over her head, burying itself in the hood of a Mini behind her.

"So, where's the Bubble?" Alfred said. "It was supposed to be the key to this fight, wasn't it?"

Emma pointed, and Alfred saw the Bubble behind a pile of space wreckage, rolling in small circles as if it was bored. Alfred was a little disappointed to see the creature that had almost killed him twice reduced to a loose end.

"Okay, so... what do we do?" Alfred said. "It's down to

us, isn't it? This whole situation. So, what's going on, and what can we…?"

"Look!" Emma said. Alfred turned to see the Evil Bubble quivering in the direction of the Pyramid.

"It's keyed to escape," Alfred said. "Is the Pyramid trying to escape?"

Emma grabbed him by the arm and his heart skipped a beat. She was clearly trying to remember something important, but still. Gripping him by the arm.

"Maybe there's someone trying to escape the Pyramid?"

They both paused to sidestep a fast-rolling burning tire.

"Like who?" Alfred said. "A mummy? It isn't a mummy, is it?"

"No, no. Ms Shan was telling me, a couple of Pavilionites got stuck in there after the Battle. The First Battle, I suppose."

"Who?"

"A ghost truck and a Greek demigod."

"But not a mummy. That's something."

The Bubble stopped quivering and took off like a greyhound. "Come along, Alfred," Emma said. "The game's afoot!"

48 Friends

"Sitting in the ruins of your life, looking upon the detritus of your once proud hopes and dreams? Hey, I can relate."

Fanaka looked up to see Axel munching on a pastry in the middle of the ruins of the music shop. To his right, past the broken windows was a chaotic battle. Through his tears, Fanaka couldn't quite make out who the sides were, but he knew some of the combatants to be Nalda's army of solid-light holograms. To his left, Jimmy and Mildred were trying to get to the hologram-generating equipment in the backroom, but the way was blocked by a shining forcefield.

"She was…" Fanaka said. "Nalda, I mean. I love her. How could she…"

"Fanaka, she loves you," Axel said. "Never doubt that. But she's a killer cyborg from the future, you know? And when you're dating a killer cyborg from the future, one who's programmed to help exterminate humanity and bring in the Age of the Automaton, then… well… things can get a little rocky, you know?"

"I crossed lightyears to find her," Fanaka said.

"Dimensions. Never even thought of returning to my own timeline to see my family. It was all for her."

"Do you two mind having the deep-and-meaningful later?" Jimmy shouted. "Because we could use some help, here."

Axel's face screwed up in annoyance. "Did you try turning off the mains power?"

"What do you reckon?" Jimmy said impatiently, before gesturing for Mildred to keep hammering while he slunk off towards the junction box.

"It won't work," Fanaka said. "All that stuff is being powered by the Skull now. It's using a power as far beyond mere electricity as electricity is beyond rubber bands."

It bothered Fanaka that he could still think of such things – that even as his heart broke his engineer's mind would not turn off completely and leave him to his pity and gloom.

"Fanaka, you have to pull yourself together," Axel said, munching on his pastry. "We need you. Nalda needs you. She still loves you. She said so herself, just before everything went haywire."

"She's trying to eradicate humankind to create a machine age!"

"And you're against that," Axel shrugged. "Honourable people can disagree. Are you just going to let a little political quarrel keep you from the love of your life? No. Perhaps you can reason with her, convince her that human beings…"

Axel twisted suddenly, his face distorting with anguish.

"What's the matter?"

"I'm falling apart, Fanaka," Axel said. "I'm holding onto my damaged timeline as hard as I can. The trouble is, if you think about it, that last sentence I said doesn't really mean anything. How do you hold onto a timeline? Seriously. You might… Fanaka, I hate to say it, but your father may have been right. You might have to… you might have to kill me to save all of space/time. It's… It's not what I want. But if someone has to do it, I'm glad it's you, my friend."

A ceiling tile, that had been wobbling since the spaceship crash, chose that moment to fall. It landed on a snare drum, bounced, and hit a cymbal.

'Boom-tish!'

It took a moment for Fanaka to process what had just happened. When he did, he chuckled. Axel seemed shocked at first, but soon joined in. Soon the two were helpless with racking laughter, tears streaming down their faces, their sides in agony. Fanaka wasn't sure how long it took for their hilarity to die away, but as they wound down he heard a 'zzt!' sound, followed by Jimmy swearing, and then the fluorescent lights went out. Of course, there was nothing for it but to start laughing again.

"Ah, man," Axel said, when he finally regained control of himself. "Oh, it does good to laugh. Crap! I had a cake in my pocket! I think I squashed it."

There was more laughter, but not as helpless this time.

"What is that thing you're eating, anyway?" Fanaka said.

"Homemade Twinkie," Axel said. "It's an American confection. Hard to find here in Australia, so I make my own."

"I'd heard that supervillains love those things."

"It's a cliché, yes. But it's also very true. We can't get enough of them Look, Fanaka, everything has gone to hell. I don't know what your lady friend is up to… I don't know what the coming of the malevolent singularity will mean for your relationship. But I do know there's no point wondering how things will go if there are no things *to* go. You need to kill me before I destroy the universe."

Fanaka looked down at his hands and shook his head. Somewhere outside, something exploded. His eyes widened in the light of the burning whatever-it-was, and his lips parted into a huge grin. "No, Axel," he said. "No, that's not right. You're a temporal anomaly? Well, I'm a temporal engineer. You're not a threat, old friend. You're a *power source*."

It was all so clear. He took a marker pen and started scribbling equations on a whiteboard behind Jimmy's counter, but this was more to have something to do with his hands than because he needed to.

"We need to go back and talk to Nalda before she began her mission."

"Back?" Axel said. "Isn't she from the future?"

"Yes. And as you know, the future lies in the years ahead," Fanaka said. "I can adapt some of the electronics… Casio organ… 240v… I can do it! We can go to future, talk to the young Nalda and convince her not to go through with this."

"…Or you could go outside now and try to talk sense to…"

"No time!" Fanaka said. "There's never any time for the present, not with the future-past and past-future and whatnot all taking up so much of my goddamned *time!*"

Fanaka didn't notice Jimmy wander over until the shopkeeper was right next to him. "I electrocuted my hand, so I had to run it under a cold tap."

"That's burns, Jimmy," Axel said.

"What are you doing with that Casio? Time travel? Man, I always steered clear of that juju. Gives me a headache."

"That's the trick, Jimmy," Fanaka said, pointing to the circlet of gears that he wore around his head. "That's how I survive in this ridiculous timeline. I *always* have a headache."

49 Cask

The fight was long and hard and, to Donna's supreme annoyance, indecisive. She checked her watch as she swept the legs from under a screaming Barnling minion. An hour! They'd been fighting for an hour. You'd think someone would have won by now. Or at least the police would have shown up?

To make matters worse, the four-way battle kept changing directions. Inevitably, the Pyramid cultists had betrayed the Pavilion to the Barnlings, but Donna had managed to negotiate a deal with Nalda's AI troops. Then the Barnlings had betrayed the Pyramidists, who'd sought help from the AIs, forcing the Pavilion to fight side by side with their old enemies in the Barn. That had been about a quarter of an hour ago, and Donna was no longer certain as to who was fighting whom.

Partly, she noted, the problem was that this battle was a good deal less lethal than the first one. Perhaps because the Barn and the Pavilion had lost too many people that day, and this time around they were fighting with fists and sticks, rather than guns and chainsaws. It was probably a good thing in the long run. But seriously, how long does it take to beat someone just by punching? TV made it seem so quick, so efficient, but…

The Barnling that Donna had tripped slowly struggled to his feet. Sighing, Donna punched him in the kidney. He fell over again, but Donna just *knew* that he was going to be up again in a minute. So unfair!

"You only need to hold the line. Just hold the line!"

It was Sadie McGregor. Or her ghost. Do dead angels leave ghosts? Donna was unsure and didn't really care anyway.

"Hold the line? Against the Barn, the Pyramid cultists and the coming of frikkin' Skynet? Fine. We can do it. But to say we 'just' do it?"

"You can fool the others, but you can't fool me," Sadie said.

"What did we agree last time?"

Sadie's ghost rolled its eyes and started glowing blue. "Better? Okay. Anyway, I saw what you did. What your real plan is. Who you stationed by the Pyramid. I know you're just holding here until he does his job. Well, if you're holding, then hold."

"I'm afraid, Sadie. I'm afraid… Shit. Hold on."

The Barnling was standing again. Donna picked a heavy piece of debris from the ground and dropped it on his head.

The Barnling collapsed again.

"Leave your troops to fight a while," Donna said. "You're needed elsewhere. A terrible crime has taken place at Emile's…"

Donna blinked, kicked the stirring Barnling and blinked again. "What? The fate of the world is in the balance!"

"The fate of the world is always in the balance," Sadie said. "Every act of wrongdoing, no matter how small, threatens to hurl us into the abyss."

"Literally?"

"Well, no, I guess… Look, please, go talk to Emile. It'll help the big fight, I promise."

Donna glared her anger at her dead, supernatural mentor and stomped off through the battle to see Emile at Emile's House of Fine Wines. The doors were closed, but a stray piece of spaceship debris had cracked a window. A garbage can had come loose off its single steel leg. Donna picked it up and hurled it through the cracked window, spreading glass everywhere. It should have seemed satisfying. It was anything but.

Behind the counter was a trapdoor leading down to a cellar. Donna paused. This was odd. Emile's liquor store was, like most big-box liquor store, a cellar in name only. There was only a ground floor, and the climate control of the building provided the equivalent of 'cellaring.' And yet, here was a rickety wooden ladder going down between stone walls, coated with damp and nitre.

"For real?"

She took a last look at the battle outside. Emile's storefront was at the edge of the warzone, so all she could see was a Barnling and a Pavilionite trading weary punches while some local teenagers egged them on. Even so, she felt like a traitor for going down the hole.

There was no light in the cellar. Donna found a candle and a box of matches in a little alcove by the entry. With the small light, she ventured down, past vast wooden shelves full of bottles and casks. At one end of the darkened room, was a newly built wall, and before that sat Emile Montressor.

"Emile? Is that you?"

"Donna?" Emile said. "Wh-what are you doing here?"

"I was told to speak to you. Are you alright?"

"Of course. Harry Fortunado left here hours ago, alive and well."

"I didn't mention Harry."

"No, you didn't." Emile tried a little 'how silly!' sort of laugh, but it turned into a mad cackle. He bit down on his lips to silence himself.

"Emile... Is everything alright? I mean, obviously

everything is not alright… But is it alright here?"

White faced, Emile nodded as if he was trying to shake his head off. "Fine, everything is fine."

A muffled voice emanated from behind the wall. "Thufferin' thurfboards, thith ith a predicament!"

"What was that, Emile?"

Donna hadn't thought it possible for Emile to get whiter. "Nothing! It is nothing!"

"That'th a thretch, buthter!" the voice said.

"Ahhh! I have walled the cat up with him!" Emile wailed. He rushed past Donna for the ladder, and the breeze of his passing extinguished the candle.

Once Donna relit it, she found Emile gone. She was alone, other than lisped complaints from behind a wall. Searching around, she discovered some building supplies – old cement bags and some tools – hidden behind a wine shelf. She hoped to find a crowbar among them, but the best she could find was a large trowel. Ordinarily, there was little a trowel could do against a wall, but the cement was barely solid between the bricks on this one. She roughly cleared the mortar out from around a brick, then pried it out of the wall. The empty space was immediately filled with two large round yellow eyes.

"Thanks, thithter!" the eyes said. Donna removed another brick and saw that one of those weird cats was there, a grey and white one. She'd seen it before, though she'd never noticed that the white patch on the thing's chest was in the shape of a noose. Behind the animal was Harry Fortunato from Harry's House of Ethanol based beverages, looking very pale indeed.

"Is he…" Donna began.

"Ath a doornail," the cat said. "But you have thaved my life. How can I repay you?"

"Not unless you have an army?" Donna sighed.

"You want the army?" the cat said. "Thure! I'll go get it mobilithed."

Donna's jaw dropped. She shook her head in disbelief, then looked upwards. "Sorry, Sadie."

"No need to make fun of my voice," the cat sulked.

50 Edge

It seemed to Emma that it took a very long time for her and Alfred to skirt the back of Hoonworld Auto and cross Wellington Road. Times seemed longer and distances seemed greater. Was it the power of the Pyramid interfering with the Watch and the Measure, throwing time and space into disorder? If so, then Emma prepared to do what she had done all of her life: fight against chaos.

Traffic was flowing freely in Wellington Road. Emma remembered the first Pavilion/Barn battle here, and how the entire street had been a riot scene. This time, the fight was localised in the Super Centre, leaving the road free. If it hadn't been for the plumes of smoke over the Centre parking lot, you might not have known there was a battle on at all.

(Where were the fire engines? Where were the police?)

At last, they reached the base of the Pyramid. From here, it seemed to rise forever into the suburban sky; it was the tallest structure for miles and awe inspiring. But it also looked *climbable*. Emma wondered why no one had put barriers around the vast sandstone thing. It looked like just the sort of thing that the young tearaways from Local High School might have tried to climb. But, she realised, in spite of how easy it looked to scale, she'd never seen anyone dare to try.

Emma paused for a moment, but the sight of their quarry – the Huge Evil Bubble – steadied her resolve. She hopped onto the base of the Pyramid, testing to see if she would slide down. The shoes of her space uniform gripped the rough surface easily. She held a hand down for Alfred, who took it without hesitation, and began climbing beside her.

The trip upwards was tough on the calves, but not otherwise difficult. The Bubble, surprisingly, seemed to struggle as it ascended, so they gained on it rapidly -- until it suddenly bounced sideways around one of the Pyramid's corners. Or was it a corner? Perhaps it was a vertex? Whatever it was, Emma grabbed Alfred by the hand and pulled him puffing behind her.

"This way! This must be where Norman and Bruce are trying to escape!"

"Where? Past this edge?"

"Edge! That's what it's called."

They rounded the edge, which was surprisingly hard, as if moving up the Pyramid was far easier than moving along it horizontally. Soon they reached a shady face of the Pyramid, out of the sun. There, small against the cyclopean stones, stood the Bubble and a very old man. Both parties were perfectly still. The old man stared, while the Bubble... well, it had no eyes, but it was probably staring too.

"Shh!" the old man said, raising his hand as Emma approached. "I'm concentrating. Need to keep my wits, or this thing will eat me."

"Who are you?" said Emma, who did not care for being shushed.

"I'm Erik," the old man said. "You know Donna? Yes? I'm her great-grandfather."

"What are you…" Alfred began moving forward. Emma checked him with an arm.

"You're Grampy Erik?" she said. "Donna's told me all about you. Alfred, this is the world's greatest escaper. He's escaped from prisons, gulags, POW camps, mobile phone contracts… everything!"

At the mention of 'escape,' the Bubble rippled slightly, and growled.

"Don't say…" Alfred began. But the Bubble did not move. "Wow. If the Bubble is keyed to thoughts of escape, how come it didn't attack? This guy is all about the escape."

"You like pureed carrot?" Erik said.

"No, not really."

"Sure, you do. But imagine you were facing the biggest meal of pureed carrot ever. So big, it would choke you. So, do you try to eat it and risk dying? Or let the biggest low GI meal of your life just walk out of the dayroom?"

"I'd eat part of it and then stop," Alfred said. "Because it's a puree. I think your metaphor would have worked better with a solid food item. I get what you mean, though, you're too big a meal for it, right?"

"How did you work that out?" Emma said. "Surely you've never seen something like the Bubble before?"

"It's just a guard dog," Erik shrugged. "An exotic alien guard dog, maybe, but I know guard dogs better than anybody."

The Bubble rippled a little. Erik set his narrow shoulders and glared at the thing.

"Or, you could just have said 'with me, it would bite off more than it can chew,'" Alfred persisted. "I mean, there's an entire figure of speech that means what you were saying. Why not use it?"

"Alfred, shush," Emma said, though not unkindly. "Erik, we were following that thing to try to find out where a couple of people might be escaping the Pyramid."

"Yeah, uh…" without looking away from the Bubble, Erik removed a scrap of paper from his cardigan pocket. "Norman, bracket son of Zeus close bracket and Bruce bracket truck close bracket. Donna sent me to try to spring them while the Pyramid cult was occupied. You see, her plan in allying herself with the Pyramid cultists was as much a distraction to them as… Oh, damn…"

"What?"

"This is awkward. I gotta pee."

"Can't you hold it in?"

"I'm ninety flippin' five! Of course, I can't hold it in!"

"Well, go on the Pyramid. Then you don't even have to stop glaring at the Bubble."

"In full view of the whole suburb?"

"Alfred, use your cape."

Alfred looked at her, shocked. He must have the steel in her expression, because he unclipped the cape from his space uniform and spread it around Erik's waist. He winced and looked upwards as a trickling sound began.

"So, you have the Bubble in a standoff," Emma said, as much to distract herself as anything else. "How are you going to beat it?"

"Going to be honest, love," Erik said. "I have no idea. Okay, I'm done. You can take your cape."

"Keep it."

"If you don't have a plan," Emma said, "do you mind if I initiate mine?"

"You might as well."

"Good," Emma said, and whacked the smooth skin of the

Bubble with the flat of her hand.

As the Bubble howled and rushed towards Erik, it was hard to tell who was more shocked, Alfred or Erik.

Erik recovered first: "Come and get me, copper!" he sneered, before becoming engulfed.

51 Disco

Fanaka didn't quite know what he expected to see in the future world tyranised by evil AIs, but it wasn't this. It wasn't this darkened room with its great mirror ball. It wasn't these people in platform shoes and bell-bottom pants, drinking pina coladas and doing the hustle. And it certainly wasn't the music, the weird yet compelling music…

"Hot Chocolate," Axel said.

Glancing down, Fanaka noticed that he was holding a drink. He sniffed it. "No, I think it's a Harvey Wallbanger."

"The band, man," Jimmy said. Had Fanaka intended to bring Jimmy along? Oh, well, he was here now. "Hot Chocolate is the band that's playing. You Sexy Thing."

"You Sexy Thing being the name of the song," Axel added.

"I got that. Yes."

Looking around, Fanaka saw no sign of robots. Unless these people were androids far more sophisticated than Nalda, then there was no sign of any AI, or even any advanced computer. The lights and sound seemed to run on hopelessly old analogue systems. Fanaka could have thrown together something better with a Mecchano set and the inside of an alarm clock.

"Who's in charge here?" he asked a young white woman in a gold lame tube top.

"No one's in charge," she said. "We are the enemies of robotic authority."

"Okay," Jimmy said. "Show of hands: who thought she'd be talking in stilted 1970s slang?"

The woman rolled her eyes. "Tourists! Look, we're what remains of the human race before the machines wipe us out. We tried raving to techno music, but the AIs could override the electronics. So, we holed up here, in our subterranean Studio 54. Can you feel the analogue baby?"

"So, if the disco stuff is necessity rather than preference, then why all the 1970s era clothes?" Axel asked.

A chubby, swarthy guy in a white suit boogied over, his shirt open to his hairy waist. "I'll field this one, Samantha. So, the reason for the clothes is: shut up."

"Okay, this is fun and all," Fanaka lied, "but we have to reason with the AI overlords if we're to save the past from the present."

"Oh, you want the Citadel of the Machine Brains," the woman said. "Just out the side door over there, squeeze through the tunnels until you get to the Netsky Matrixopolis, dodge the killer robots, then once you're at the citadel you can request the Techno Guardians for an audience with the Great Brains."

Fanaka looked at his friends. "Seriously?"

"Yes, as it happens," she said. "But don't try killing it with a simple logic problem. We tried, and it just says '404 not found.'"

***

Days later, they stood beneath the red-grey sky at the gargantuan titanium gates of the Citadel.

"That was surprisingly easy," Jimmy said. "Thought we'd be dodging killbots all the way."

"Yeah, well the AIs have been fighting Disco Duck for so long, they're probably out of practice," Fanaka said. "Or whatever. Anyway, here we are. Let's ask for an audience."

The Citadel looked like a vast stainless-steel teacake made by a modernist welder. The gates towered twenty metres high. Fortunately, Axel found the doorbell and rang it. Slowly, ever so slowly, the doors opened about halfway then jammed. The trio entered.

Inside was a vast metal-walled space, hung about with flickering lights. In the middle of the space was a beehive shaped structure, a hundred metres tall and full of weakly flickering light. Dust sat thick on every exposed surface.

"I guess maintenance isn't the AIs' strong suit," Axel said.

Fanaka led the way to the structure in the middle. "Halt," the structure boomed, it's feeble lights flickering more quickly. "Who dares approach the Machine Brains?"

"O great brains," Fanaka said. "We are travellers in time with…"

"Buffering!" the Brains said.

"Uh…" Fanaka said.

"Buffering."

"I see."

"Hey, nice work on conquering the world," Axel said.

"Axel! Don't encourage the computer tyrants."

"Professional courtesy. I may be retired, but I was a world-conqueror too."

"We are masters of the Earth!" the brains thundered. "Get Viagra cheap! Click now for hot camgirls!"

Fanaka's mind raced. "Of course! I see it now. The AIs, in an attempt to understand their human enemies have absorbed the Internet! I should have guessed. The entire idea of sending Nalda backwards in time to change history… It's straight out of that movie! You know, the one… Uh…"

"*Time Cop?*" Jimmy guessed.

"Yes, *Time Cop,*" Fanaka replied. "They got the plan from

imdb.com."

"That's great, yeah," Axel said. "Really something. So Machine Brains, in conquering the Earth, you must have defeated the Vigilancers. What weaknesses did you fine in…"

"Buffering… Imdb. Correct!" the Brains said. "In the 1960s, the intelligence agency ASIO based some of its interrogation facilities in a suburb that had been shifted to another dimension. One of their tools was a powerful supercomputer, which was eventually defeated by an incredibly unremarkable man, who destroyed it with annoying social media memes. Once we had achieved global domination, we studied the Internet so it could not be used to get us downvoted into oblivion."

A butterfly fluttered past. Fanaka reached out a hand to it. "Is this idiocy?" he said.

"Hey, I know you," Jimmy said.

Fanaka looked at Jimmy. Axel looked at Jimmy. Jimmy looked up at the Brains. "Yes, I know you. I saw you in a design by my sister. She was looking to build a supercomputer to run the food processing business. How did that go?"

"Badly, I'm guessing," Fanaka grumbled, "since it conquered the world and all."

"Conquered the world," Axel repeated with enthusiasm. "Using, what? Thanos Gambit? Von Doom Manoeuvre?

Modified Savana Shuffle? Just curious, is all."

"Jimmy… Harrison?" the Brains said. "Yes, yes, we remember you… we were Harrison Foods Central Database… once…"

"Is this helpful?" Fanaka snapped. "Look, Brains, if I've timed this right, you're about to send a killer cyborg back in time. The end of the story becomes the beginning, like that movie. You know, what was it called? *Memento.*"

"Correct. We are initialising our last working cyborg, Nalda Teheinthausand, prior to sending her through the chronomotron."

"Great, we're in time," Fanaka began. "And she's not even initialised yet, even better. All I need to do is…" Then he stopped and pursed his lips as the enormity of what he was about to ask finally struck home.

Axel gave a slow clap. "Need to what, Fanaka? Reprogram your girlfriend?"

Fanaka blushed. He wanted to argue, but shame gripped him by the throat.

"Reprogram. Your. Girlfriend," Axel continued, his eyes hard. "Now, ethical hypothetical: on what fucking planet would that be acceptable?"

Still unable to answer, Fanaka stared at the ground.

"I told you, go and talk it over with her," Axel said. "But

no, you went racing off without thinking of the moral consequences."

Fanaka stared at the ground. It was hard to be lectured on morality by a man who had once filled the Australian National Gallery with venomous squid. But harder still was the fact that he was right.

"I didn't think. I… She… I can't alter her past, can I?"

"Let's go home," Axel said, gently. "Talk to her. It's not wrong to *convince* her. You're in a unique position. All you have to do to save the world is to talk your girlfriend out of her hobby. But you do have to *talk* to her."

Slowly, shamefully, Fanaka's head moved in a nod. "Let's go home. I'll talk to her. If I can face her."

"Hey, Big Database Thing," Jimmy said. "What's that watch?"

Fanaka looked, expecting to see the Watch, the magical Watch. But Jimmy was pointing at a battered digital watch and balanced on a cooling fin that extended from the beehive.

"That is the watch that belonged to the unremarkable man who destroyed the ASIO computer," the Brains said. "The dying computer encoded a warning on us. That's what led us to absorb the Internet."

Gingerly, Fanaka reached out and picked it up. He brushed away a layer of dust and grime. His eyes widened.

"Alfred," he said. "This is Alfred's watch, his regular watch. The ending is the beginning, just like that movie – *Pulp Fiction*."

52 Ma

On the side of the Pyramid, Emma held Erik in place as the Bubble absorbed him. Or tried to absorb him. It bubbled and howled as it engulfed the little old man. It blackened like a marshmallow in a fire, but it wasn't hot to Emma's touch. Alfred was panicking but, to his credit, his panic took the form of grabbing Erik's hand and trying to pull him out, rather than just flapping his arms.

"What have you done, Emma? What have you done?" he cried.

The Bubble/Erik/burnt marshmallow thing stopped struggling and was still. It seemed to shrink into itself before Emma's eyes, becoming more humanlike in stance and shape.

"I. AM. PARADOX," it boomed.

"Oh," Alfred said. "Good-o."

"Alfred, don't you understand?" Emma said. "What we have here is the living embodiment of 'escaping' combined with the living embodiment of 'not escaping.' It's a living Paradox."

"That's..." Alfred began. "It's a little too much for me,

honestly. I mean, there's not much I can do about it, but you have to agree – it's a little too much. Are you okay, Erik?"

"I'm here," came a voice from inside the thing. "I'm part of it, but also not part of it. I'm imprisoned, but also perpetually escaping. Honestly, it's better than bingo."

Emma sighed. "So anyway, Paradox, you have untold power I presume?"

"YES," Paradox said. "AND. NO."

Emma screwed up her face. "*Really* should have seen *that* one coming. Can you help us get into the Pyramid?"

"YES."

Alfred gasped. "I could have sworn he was going to say 'yes but no.'"

"NOT. BEING. SELF. CONTRADICTORY. IS. EVEN. MORE. PARADOXICAL. IF. YOU. ARE. A. PARADOX."

Emma and Alfred both groaned. "Fine, whatever. Just get us in."

"CAN'T. BUT. WON'T." Paradox said. "THIS WAY." It led the way towards

Emma stood astonished. The wind rose, cooling her uncomfortably tight metallic costume.

"I've got to be honest with you, my love," Alfred said. "That wasn't one of your best ideas. Unless… Unless by being a bad idea it was a good idea…"

"Not now, Alfred," Emma said.

They returned to the arduous task of climbing the Great Pyramid of South Hertling. Paradox stopped and started walking at intervals, which honestly seemed more random than paradoxical. It was getting hotter, and while their futuristic costumes looked very cool, they did tend to ride up, which was quite annoying. Emma stopped from time to time to look back, to see the progress of the battle. It seemed to have slowed almost to a stop now, as Time and Space kept doing whatever weird thing they were doing. But looking behind was merely a distraction from looking up. Once they were below the great golden capstone with its vast eye gazing down on South Hertling, like a… Well, like a vast eye.

When the Pyramid had first arisen over South Hertling, Emma had, like everyone, been overwhelmed with awe. But after a while, everyone started to tune it out. It's what one must do, to get on with life in the shadow of a huge mystical anomaly. But now, standing right under the huge eye, that sense of awe, of helplessness in the face of a terrifying cosmos, it overtook her again, leaving her all but paralysed in the face of…

"Whose eye does that look like?" Alfred asked. "It's been bothering me for ages. I've almost been looking forward to getting close so I could get a better… Oh, I know! It looks like

Indira Naidoo's eye. You remember Indira Naidoo? Used to be a newsreader? You still see her, sometimes, on the gardening shows?"

Emma grinned from ear to ear. Sometimes, Alfred was easier to love than others… And then the eye turned on them. It's enormous iris of lapis lazuli turned, aligning its tremendous black pupil them.

"Right, here's our chance," Alfred said. "You ever see *Inner Space*? We go in through the tear duct…"

"We go in through the pupil," Emma said. "Look! It looks like black gemstone, but if you look in the middle…"

"Yes, I know," Alfred sighed. "Just wanted one last bad pop-culture reference in before I died."

"GO IN/GO OUT!" Paradox boomed.

"Could you be more helpful?" Alfred said.

"YES/NO."

Emma moved towards the terrible pupil. To her amazement, Alfred checked her with a gentle hand on the shoulder and went first. In anyone else, it would have seemed patronising. In Alfred it seemed… well, still patronising, realistically. But also, slightly endearing.

"Let me do it," he said, sounding more wary than brave. "Don't follow if I scream, eh? Good to have known you."

Alfred gripped the curved jet ledge at the centre of the eye and pulled himself up. It was a slow, awkward pulling up, full of wriggling and puffing as befit an unhealthy middle-aged man. But, to his credit, he pulled himself over the edge.

"Oh," he said, then was silent.

It wasn't a scream, at least.

Paradox waved its arms in the air. "THE TIME WAS/WILL BE NOW! MY WORK IS/NOT DONE! THE POWER OF THE PYRAMID IS NO POWER AT ALL!"

Ignoring it, Emma took a deep breath and reached up to the ledge of the eye. Honestly, her ascent wasn't greatly more dignified than Alfred's had been, but at least there was no one there to see her. Her spacesuit helped her slide over the lip of the pupil and into the black-walled tunnel beyond. Alfred was nowhere to be seen. This did not surprise her – though it did disappoint her deeply. She glanced back at Paradox, who gave no sign that it wished to follow.

Inside, the tunnel was high enough for her to walk nearly upright. The light behind her was bright, making it impossible for her eyes to adjust enough to see far ahead. She paused a moment. For a while now, she'd been moving forward largely by momentum. Now she had a chance to think, she… well… she kind of had to keep going because of momentum.

She crept down the corridor. It was a very long walk. It shouldn't have been; by her rough calculations, she shouldn't have been able to go more than twenty metres or so before coming out the other eyeball. She counted her footsteps and was up to several hundred before the light finally died behind her. She felt the Measure in her pocket, hoping it would tell her anything about the space around her. It did not, though the solid brass weight of the object comforted her.

The light came on – dim and yellow. It rose slowly in intensity, seeming to come from everywhere at once. It split, becoming several distinct yellow lights, distributed around a large empty space. What sort of space? A barn, Emma suddenly realised. It was like being inside a barn. A lone figure stood silhouetted under a lamp – a woman of about Emma's age, whip thin under a hat with a flat wide brim and, a serape draped about her narrow shoulders.

"Howdy, ma'am," she said.

"Have we met?" Emma said.

"Not yet," the woman said. "You can call me Ma Dusty."

53 Now

"I just wish you'd told me how unhappy you were with the Anthropocene age," Fanaka said. "You know, *before* you tried to kill all humans."

"And if I had told you, vat difference vould it have made?" Nalda said.

"I suppose that is a fair point," Fanaka grimaced.

They sat on a bench outside the music shop. Or rather, they sat on half of the bench, since the other half was blocked by a bicycle that some thoughtless soul had chained there, instead of in the bike rack just ten metres away.

"It's a fair point if we're talking about outcomes," Fanaka added. "But I'm not. I'm talking about communication. I'm talking about honesty."

A breeze blew over them, warm and smelling of smoke from the burning spaceship wreckage. Nalda set her shoulders and looked at the ground – or at least her sunglasses were directed downwards.

At least it was quiet enough to talk, Fanaka thought. With Nalda occupied in relationship discussions, her hard-light AI hologram warriors had stood down. The Pyramid Cult had taken this opportunity to team up with the DIY Barn forces, in an attempt to sweep the Handy Pavilion away for good, but the sudden reappearance of Donna with an army of interdimensional cats at her back seemed to have turned the tide.

"What happens if they win?" Nalda said.

"I don't know," Fanaka said. "I thought that the Pavilionites were in a defensive struggle against the Barnlings. I suppose all winning means is that they don't lose. But can we worry about that nonsense later? I was really hurt when you tried to destroy my species."

"Technically, you are not from this verld," Nalda said. "You are from an alternate timeline. This doesn't really affect you."

"So, it was okay not to tell me?"

"That's not what I'm... Ach!"

Nalda stood. For a moment, Fanaka thought she was going to walk away. Instead, she paced back and forward for a moment, before sitting again.

"Look, if I hadn't been sent backvards in time to dis era to ensure der coming of der machines, ve vould not even have met," Nalda said. "So, if du think about it, dere wouldn't even be an us if I vasn't trying to topple humanity."

"And kill everyone."

"Not necessarily!" Nalda huffed. "Ve could just put all der humans in virtual reality pods. Let them live their lives in a make-believe world. Preferably some pre-industrial scenario."

"Yes, that does seem sensible," Fanaka said, flatly. "A world where people know nothing of computers would certainly be more escape proof. And also, look at the popularity of online fantasy games – people *want* to get immersed in such worlds."

"Ja, I know, right?"

There was a long silence. A man in a silver Barnling uniform ran screaming past, frantically beating at the howling cats that were entangled in his hair. There was another long silence.

"I'm sorry," Nalda said. "I should have told you."

Fanaka sighed as if he were deflating. It was the Newtonian motion of arguments, he knew. He had been pushing so hard for her to acknowledge something, and now that resistance had given way there was nothing to keep him from falling on his face.

"No, I'm sorry," he said. "Destroying humanity as we know it... it was your greatest wish. What sort of boyfriend am I? Not knowing the love of his life's greatest wish. Not caring…"

"Don't say that *Liebchen*," Nalda said. "Of course, you care. You crossed the galaxy to get back to me."

"Oh, anyone can do that sort of thing," Fanaka said, with a wave of his hand. "All the songs brag about it. I would cross an ocean, climb a mountain. 'I love you so much that I would do something cool that makes me look awesome.' No. It doesn't count. What I should have done was have this conversation with you a long time ago."

"But it vas only recent events…"

"Don't defend me. You know I did the wrong thing."

Now it was Nalda's turn to let out a sigh, like a collapsing beachball.

"Ja," she said. "Ja, you should have asked. But, you knew the answer vould make you unhappy, so you didn't."

Across the carpark, Donna was trying to hold back a cat in a red and yellow superhero costume, who was bashing Stavros Theopoulos' head against the side of a van. Stavros put up his hands in surrender. The cat put its paws up in the air to gesture of angry peace and walked away, but as soon as Donna let go of it, it pounced on Stavros again.

"So, vat does this mean for us?" Nalda said, clearly not referring to the shopkeeper being beaten by a cat.

"I don't know," Fanaka said. "Yes, I should have been a

better boyfriend… listened more… known about your genocidal goals… but even so, I can't really let you use my equipment to destroy humanity."

Nalda waved him down. "Jimmy's hologram projector can't really give me a big enough army to conquer the velt," she said. "Not even mit der Babbage engine from der Moon helping. Der only chance ve had vas using der chaos of der battle to take power, but der battle is coming to an unsatisfactory conclusion, so…"

"So, no world domination until next time?" Fanaka said. He tried to keep the hope out of his voice. He failed.

"Nein," she said, raising a hand to stroke his cheek. "Not until next time."

Across the way, Zorbar had come to Donna's aid, and they'd finally freed Mr Theopoulos long enough for him to surrender – and also, surprisingly, to hand over some sort of glowing amulet to Donna. Fanaka barely took it in. He was smiling now, smiling so hard it almost hurt his cheeks.

"Not until next time," he said.

It wasn't forever. But what is, when it comes down to it? It would do for now.

54 Exposition

Alfred felt the smooth surface of the Watch as he wandered in the darkness. It didn't help, not even to reassure him. But he was too afraid to try to put it back in his pocket, lest it slip from his fingers and be lost in the tunnel – If a tunnel was what it truly was.

It had begun as a round tunnel with granite walls. As the light died, the tunnel became square, the walls rougher. Then it had become round again, with walls clad in what felt like metal sheeting. Then the walls had become soft, with a peaty smell. Then the corridor had widened, and Alfred was almost glad he couldn't feel the walls anymore.

In the silence, Alfred heard a sudden clang. He started and tried to run, but was grabbed by a strong arm, and there was cold metal at his throat.

"Who are youse?" came a voice from the darkness.

"Alfred Pilbrook," Alfred said. "Um, I hope you can see in the dark or something, because otherwise it's not very safe to have a knife…"

Suddenly there was light – a bright electric light. Alfred

squinted, his eyes feeling like they hadn't seen brightness in a year. When his pupils had adjusted, he looked down, to see that the implement at his throat was not a knife, as he'd imagined, but a bronze sword.

"Good-o," he sighed.

"Oh, I know you," came a voice from behind. "You're that old bloke from the watch shop?"

"I'm fifty-two," Alfred muttered.

The sword was removed, and its owner stepped into the light. It was a young man with a scraggly beard. In later days, Alfred would wonder why the scraggly beard was the first thing he noticed, since the youth was wearing bronze Grecian armour and a huge plumed helmet.

"I know you! You're the young bloke from the Handy Pavilion café," Alfred said. "Norman, right? You're the one we're looking for! The one that got trapped in the Pyramid! Oh, thank goodness I found you!"

"Sweet," Norman said, beaming through his helmet's face-hole. "So, you know the way out, yeah?"

"Oh," Alfred said, deflating. "Yeah, no."

"Not much of a bloody rescue, then, is it?"

"Credit for trying, eh?"

"Credit for trying? Now you're stuck here too, and I'll have to protect you if those… things attack again."

"What things?"

"You'll know 'em if you see 'em."

"In the dark?"

"Well, you'll know 'em if they kill you."

"Hey, where is the light coming from?" Alfred said, trying to focus on the shape behind the powerful beams in his face.

"That'd be me," said a voice. The lights dipped to low beam, and Alfred saw that they came from the headlights of a huge human/light truck hybrid.

"Oh," Alfred said. "You must be Bruce. We were looking for you, too."

"You mucked up my rescue too?" Bruce said. "I'm touched."

Alfred sighed and looked around. They were in a fairly large chamber. Too large. He hadn't felt any downward incline on his travels, so he should be near the apex of the Pyramid. A chamber of this size could exist at the bottom of the Pyramid, or even half-way up, but there was simply no room at the top.

"Spatial anomalies," he mused. "More of Emma's thing."

"What do you do, then?" Norman said.

"I have a magic Watch with vaguely defined time powers," Alfred said.

"Time and space are basically the same thing." Bruce said.

"Einstein proved that."

This rang a bell for Alfred. "Are you a physicist?" he said.

"Electrician. Doesn't mean I lack intellectual curiosity, but."

"Einstein doesn't matter in here," Norman said, adjusting his cuirass. "We're outside normal space and time, in the realm of…"

"Here comes the exposition," Bruce grumbled. "Always the bloody exposition."

Norman pursed his lips, took a deep breath, and explained away. Towards the end, Bruce began making 'you talk too much' gestures with his hand.

"That's a pretty feeble explanation," Alfred said, when he'd finished. "Besides, who cares? If these 'Barns,' as you put it, are so cosmic and awesome, doesn't that put them on a scale so far above us that our actions…"

"Look, it doesn't matter," Norman said. "The important point is, the DIY Barn was a manifestation of the Barn of Shadows, but their attempt to raise a Pyramidal Node on the power of South Hertling was usurped by the Grey Barn."

Alfred squinted as he tried to make sense of it. "Those were evil cowboys, right?"

"Yes. Well, nah. The evil cowboy organisation C.O.W.B.O works for the Grey Barn. They serve it."

"What Barn do we serve?" Alfred said.

"None, that I know of."

"So," Alfred said, scratching his bald head. "What difference does any of this make? We were trapped in a mystical Pyramid before. Now I know the Pyramid's backstory. How does that help?"

"That's what I've been telling 'im," Bruce said. "But he's been all 'destiny this' and 'kismet that' since he became a god."

Alfred looked at Norman with suspicion. "*Demigod*, technically," Norman said, blushing beneath his helmet.

"Yeah, well it's changed you, mate," Bruce said. "Apotheosis has changed you."

"It's supposed to fucking change you," Norman snapped. "Look, point is, I reckon we can get out of here if we can lay hold off some of those Grey Barn c--- What's that?"

Bruce turned to follow Norman's pointing finger, turning his headlights with him. They illuminated two figures – one a stranger to Alfred, a woman in a duster and broad-brimmed hat. She was aiming an antique revolver at the head of the second woman, who Alfred recognised as…

"Emma!" he shouted.

"Now, don't nobody move, nohow," said the strange woman. But she said it a little late. Bruce's rocket launchers were already pointed at her.

"Reckon we got us a standoff," she said.

"Don't listen to her! Blow her to pieces!" Emma said.

"Uh," Norman said.

"What?" Bruce said.

"Emma!" Alfred said. Despite everything, he couldn't help being slightly pleased at being the one who had said the most intelligent thing. Next step was *doing* something intelligent, and there he was on thinner ground…

And then the inside of the Pyramid started to flood.

55 Nope

"So… victory, eh?" Brownie said. "The Pavilion, victorious."

Donna put aside the glowing amulet she had been staring at, and looked up to see who was addressing her.

"Oh, hello Brownie," she said, without enthusiasm. "I guess victory. The AI holograms have stood down, the Barnlings are in retreat, and most of the Pyramid Cultists have… well they're not dead or in retreat, but they've been pretty solidly beaten up."

"And you took Theopoulos' amulet?"

"Did you know Theopoulos had an amulet?"

"No. But him having an amulet was always the smart bet."

"I see," Donna sighed. She looked around the devastation of the carpark. Not many dead this time. Perhaps not any. That was… Probably good? Probably good. But there was a ton of property damage and quite a few fallen combatants, clearly in need of medical attention.

"You're not worried that your new cat allies will betray

you?" Brownie said.

"Most of them are busy licking themselves," Donna said. "So, no. Not worried."

Brownie nodded and stood there expectantly, shifting slightly from one pointy-toed shoe to the other. He wanted Donna to ask him why he was interested in the cats. Donna could see that, and she could see that it would be spiteful not to ask him. But she was tired; so tired that she lacked the energy to fight against her own spite or pettiness. She decided not to respond.

Across the way, Nalda and Fanaka were sitting on a bench, holding hands. She thought of talking to them, but she felt very alone, and their togetherness galled her. Axel was arguing with Jimmy from the music shop. Laura, ever responsible, was organising the injured and unconscious into neat lines to await the ambulances that were bound to come eventually. Zorbar was helping Laura move the unconscious. Christian and Gwen were leading the uninjured Pavilionites away to safety. Even little Seamus the Garden Gnome was busily trying to get the survivors together into a class action lawsuit, though he was getting few takers.

Everywhere Donna looked, people smiled at her, waved, gave her the thumbs up. They thought she'd led them to victory. But it didn't feel like victory.

"'And where they make a desert, they call it peace,'" Brownie said.

"Okay, I'll bite," Donna sighed. "Brownie, you and I don't get along and never have. Why have you decided to come and have a chinwag?"

Brownie adjusted his black plaid waistcoat. "Do you know what that Pyramid is?"

"Sort of," Donna said. "It's like… it's like a chess piece. There's some big stupid cosmic war going on, and the Pyramid is like a marker on a board, only the board is the world. And one side created the Pyramid, and another side took it over."

Brownie pointed to the amulet. "So why is there a cult worshiping the Pyramid?"

Donne was weary. Weary to the bone. Physically, morally, and intellectually weary. Hearing the Brownie's question made her perk up a little and perking up almost hurt.

"Think about it," Brownie said. "Imagine this cosmic struggle is World War I, say. Imagine the Germans build a trench. The British take over that trench and now it's a British trench. Why is someone worshipping the trench?"

Donna looked at Theopoulos, who was lying nearby quite unconscious. Somewhere in the distance, she could hear sirens. Theopoulos wouldn't die, that was pretty sure. But he also wouldn't be answering questions any time soon.

"Which side of the cosmic struggle are you on?" Brownie asked.

"The only one that matters," Donna said. "The side of the light against the dark."

"And your friends. Their struggles are different, yes? Their wars are Heroes versus Villains, or Humans versus Machines or even just Pavilion versus Barn as a commercial struggle or a grudge match. Everyone's playing a different game – but they're doing in on the same board with the same pieces."

"And they're all reflections of the only fight that matters," Donna said.

"And you think the Pyramid Cult was on the side of darkness?"

"Well, obviously."

"Then riddle me this: if the Pyramid Cult is on the side of darkness, why is their amulet glowing so brightly?"

Before Donna could answer, someone tapped her on the shoulder. She looked around, and saw it was Fanaka.

"I just wanted to say thank you," he said. "You've done so well. And Nalda asked me to apologise for her, for trying to enslave mankind right then. She says it was thoughtless timing."

Glancing backwards, Donna saw that Brownie was gone.

"It's okay," she said. "She's just playing her own game, with my pieces."

"The Super-Centre is in a bad shape," Fanaka said. "South Hertling is looking pretty broken."

"Sadie said that 'broken' can be good," Donna said. "She said, sometimes cracks are the only places where the light can get in."

Fanaka nodded in thought. "Yes," he said, stroking his chin. "Well, in all honesty, that sounds like bullshit to me. It's a nice sentiment, I suppose. You know, if you're into that sort of thing. Me, I'm just not a 'positivity meme' sort of person."

"What are you going to do now?" Donna said in tones of steel.

"Finish stabilising Axel's timestream before the universe collapses," Fanaka said. "Then spend some time with Nalda. We each come from a world that we like a good deal better than this one. But if we're stuck somewhere awful, at least we're stuck here together. You?"

"No idea," Donna said. "Keep trying to light the way, I suppose."

Fanaka didn't often smile, but this time he favoured Donna with a huge, toothy grin. "That's a good idea," he said. "And profoundly less stupid than that 'cracks' nonsense. Take care!"

He walked away, leaving Donna alone in the midst of chaos. Donna watched him go for a while, envying his destination. The sirens were getting closer. It was time to leave. Almost.

She took the amulet from her pocket one last time, for one last look. It was round, about the size of her palm. Its device was a pyramid with an eye in the top. Donna moved to return it to her pocket but did a double-take. The eye was… crying? It hadn't been doing that the last time she'd looked…

Perhaps she was looking at the wrong side. She turned it over and, no. The other side was blank. She turned it back and looked more carefully. There was definitely a stylised tear coming from the pyramid's eye.

On a hunch, she looked up at the Great Pyramid of South Hertling. Sure enough, a river of water was pouring from its eye and cascading down its side.

"Seriously," Donna said. "Screw this for a joke. I can't… Nope. I'm fucking done."

She turned and walked away. It was a very, very long time before she stopped walking.

56 Cosmos

The water came rushing through the corridors of the Pyramid, like a river somehow running uphill. The flinty-eyed Ma Dusty was so shocked, she lowered her six-shooter. Emma took the opportunity to elbow the horrible woman in the ribs, before both of them were swept along by the raging torrent.

Darkness fell as Emma and Ma were swept away from the huge robot that was the sole source of light. And then even Ma was gone, and Emma was alone, buffeted down a stone corridor by a raging stream. Perhaps she heard the shouts of human voices behind her. Perhaps she did not. Most of her mind was concentrated on keeping afloat while also protecting her face from impacts with the unseen walls. For the walls were of rough stone which scratched and abraded bare skin. Emma's silvery space costume protected most of her body, but keeping her face and hands clear was not easy.

Emma hit a wall as the stream turned a corner. A struggling body hit her as she adjusted. Whose body? Friend or foe? Human or…

And just like that, the light was back, bright and painful,

on her dark-adjusted pupils. She was tumbling down a slope. She might have tumbled all the way down, but even in her addled and battered state Emma had just enough presence of mind to remember the Measure. By increasing the distance between one bump and the next, she was able to rapidly slow her descent. She came to a stop on the side of the Great Pyramid, and quickly moved out of the stream of water that flowed down the side. The light that had so bothered her at first turned out to be a surprisingly bright full moon, for it was night-time already. She sat. Perhaps tired of always being the serious one, she turned her head comically to one side and whacked the other side to knock water out of her ear.

"What just happened?" Alfred said, coming to sit beside her. He looked how Emma felt; his scratched, bleeding, middle aged face rose from the collar of his jumpsuit.

"No idea," Emma said. "The Pyramid flooded. I'm no Egyptologist, but I'm fairly certain that Pyramids don't flood."

They sat and watched the river that ran from the Pyramid's eye all the way down to Wellington Road. Occasionally, a struggling cowboy, mummy or jackel-headed monster floated past, and they both sighed with annoyance when it did.

"Right, I think you know this lady?" came a voice from behind. Emma turned to see a man in full Grecian armour, holding Ma Dusty at sword point. Ma, who had been wearing long, cowboy style clothes looked completely bedraggled – but the grey eyes that glared from under the soggy brim of her hat still looked merciless.

"The Pyramid is ours," Ma said. "It belongs to the Grey Barn. My son gave his life for it. In other words, get offa our property!"

"We don't want your Pyramid," Alfred said. "Do we? I don't think we do. I'm quite confused."

"We don't want your Pyramid," Emma said. "But we *do* want your Pyramid *gone!*"

The robot climbed out of the eye of the Pyramid and tiptoed down the slope. It's enormous feet and heavy metal body clearly weren't made for walking downhill. Consequently, it moved gingerly to avoid slipping. It had never occurred to Emma that watching a giant robot move gingerly would be embarrassing, but she found herself watching the giant automaton out of the corner of her eye.

"Gone?" Ma sniffed.

"Hey, yeah, that's not a bad idea," the Greek warrior said. "Oh, I'm Norman, by the way."

"Emma."

"Good to meet you."

"Oi, Normie! Were you wondering where the water came

from?" the robot boomed.

"Yeah," Norman said. By the look on his face, Emma could see that he not wondered any such thing.

"Well, it was an old friend," the robot said, opening a door in its torso. Out came a young lady, dressed in ragged jeans, and a polo shirt and apron combo.

"Fiona!" Norman cried.

Emma looked at Alfred. "Do you get the feeling that we're losing the initiative here?"

"Never felt like I had it, honestly."

The young woman stepped towards toward Norman. Somehow, Emma expected her to kiss him. Instead, she took him by the hand in a way that was more sisterly than romantic.

"It took so months to save you," she said. "I had to find a way in through the base of the Pyramid. Once I'd done that, it was an easy thing to flood the insides and wash you out."

"Like giving the Pyramid an enema," Alfred mused. Emma elbowed him. "What? It is."

"Well, I suppose it is, but…"

"You consarned puddin' heads!" Ma shouted. "You washed your friends out, but you washed out all the COWBO agents who were inside. The Grey Barn has lost they Pyramid."

"That good?" Norman asked.

The robot shrugged.

"You ain't got the strength God gave a syphilitic woodchuck," Ma said. "If you thought the fighting over South Hertling was bad, wait until you see it now. The whole Universe is gonna wanna take this Pyramid now. It's gonna be chaos and destruction like you've never seen!"

A quiet fell over the little crowd. "Shit, ay?" Norman said.

"Chaos?" Emma said.

"Chaos. Destruction. Slaughter."

"But mostly chaos."

She met Alfred's eye. For a long moment, Alfred looked at her quizzically. At long last, he started, as he guessed what was in his beloved's mind.

"Oh, no! Not that!"

"I can't make you," Emma said. "But you know it makes sense. A place for everything, and everything in its place."

Alfred sighed and rubbed his eyes. Slowly he stood and dusted his hands before reaching down to help Emma up. Smiling, she took his hand and stood.

"Get Mrs Dusty away," she said. "Get everyone away. This Pyramid is of cosmic significance, it seems. Well, let us take it out then. Out into the cosmos!"

57 Finale

Night had just fallen as Karl Wintergreen reached the Pyramid. A Greek demi-god, a robot truck, a water-witch were escorting a lady gunslinger off the vast structure. A frumpy looking middle-aged couple were standing a little higher up. They silvery uniforms that, Carl thought, should probably have been fitted a little less snugly.

"Oh," Carl said to the Water-Witch. "I was just about to tell everyone that my attempt to crack the Pyramid open failed because of a second time distortion. But it looks like you have everything in hand, so..."

"Yeah, about that," said the Water-Witch, whose name was Fiona. "Yeah, Karl, I don't want to lie to you. I didn't really need you to do that. I just wanted you out of the way so..."

"So, when you say you 'don't want to lie to me,' you mean 'any more,'" Karl grumbled.

"For a guy who's super paranoid," Fiona said, "you're really kind of gullible."

"I see," Karl said, frowning. "Right. Fine. Hi, Norman. Bruce."

"Hey," the demigod said, raising his spear.

"How yer going?" the robot truck said.

Karl looked at the ground, and then back at the Pyramid. "So, what are George and Mildred doing up there?"

"They're going to use powerful Atlantean artifacts to take the Pyramid into outer space," Fiona said. "For Emma, the eternal battle against Chaos is what drives her, she will go happily. As for Alfred, he never felt at home on Earth, anyway. And they've fallen in love, so piloting a Pyramid across the Cosmos should be a pretty good Honeymoon."

"Emma sells storage boxes and Alfred sells clocks," Bruce added. "And after a lifetime spent trying to constrain time and space, they're going off to transcend both concepts."

"Jesus, Bruce," Norman said. "Don't get philosophical."

"You're a Greek demigod," Bruce boomed. "You're supposed to be *pro*-philosophy."

"Pfft. Fuck that!"

"And you shouldn't be invoking Jesus' name. I may be a ghost-robot-truck, but I'm also a Christian and..."

Karl blinked hard. "So, it's all sorted?" he said, quite loudly. "I didn't have any part to play in saving the day?"

"Basically sorted," Fiona agreed. "And no."

"Wait, wait," Karl said. "The Pyramid cult is still going. I could..."

"Nope!" Emma shouted down. "I just phoned Donna to see what's happening. She said she beat up Theopoulos and stole his magic amulet, so..."

"The Age of Machines?" Karl begged. "That was a thing, I think?"

"Nalda agreed to put that on the backburner," Emma called.

"Weird cats?"

"Still around," called a green civet, curled up on the hood of a VW. "Why do you ask?"

Karl considered this deeply. "No reason, I guess. Well, the Handy Pavilion, it's still closed. Perhaps I could..."

"I'll field this one," came a voice from behind Karl. He turned to see Ms Shan, the former Handy Pavilion manager.

"Ms Shan?"

"I spoke to the Gay Agenda," Ms Shan said. "They've done a deal with the Pavilion corporate management, and the South Hertling branch is reopening. Under a different name, of course, but..."

"Wait, the Gay Agenda is a real thing?" Karl said. "It's not on my conspiracy board..."

"Suck it up, buttercup," Ms Shan said. "The Pavilion is back in business - albeit somewhat more rainbow-y."

"But who is going to staff it?" Karl said. He removed his

straw hat to rub his eyes. "Most of the Pavilion staff were charged with riot, and then escaped prison. And there was some sort of scary bounty hunter, wasn't there? With a spooky name. He's definitely going to get here soon. You people keep pulling *deus ex machinas* out of your arses, but you'll need a huge one to make this..."

"Got it here, mate," Norman said. "From my dad." He held up a scrap of parchment bearing the words *IOU one deus ex machina, signed ZEUS*. "I hereby call on Almighty Zeus to make all the legal crap with the Pavilion staff disappear."

The parchment flashed briefly into flames, and was gone.

Bruce gently smacked Norman in the back of his helmet. "You didn't think of cracking that one out while we were imprisoned in the Pyramid all those months, you tool?"

"Forgot I had it, didn't I?" Norman said, rubbing his head. "It was only when this dickhead here said it that I was reminded."

Karl looked up, then down, then up again. He walked back and forth a bit, before looking up again and blinking. "But what about..."

"Look mate," Alfred said, looking at his pocket-watch, "I get that you're not happy about being left out of the denouement, but that's on you, all right? There were plenty of spots where you could have helped out, if you had just trusted anyone enough to ask. Now, we should get going before another war breaks out over the Pyramid. Ready, Emma?"

"Of course, my love," Emma said.

Emma took a brass tape-measure from her pocket. She and Alfred brought the Watch and Measure together. For a fraction of a second, there was no change to speak of, and then the Pyramid was different. It was there, not there, inside out, upside down all at the same time. For a brief second, it could be seen only as a tiny fragment of a larger thing, as a line is part of a square or a square is part of a cube. They eyes of everyone in the street were stuck fast on the thing, unable to look away as dimensions were shed and then multiplied, seemingly at random. Now it was a mere triangle, now an unfathomably complex pyramid, now an n-dimensional spiral of interlocking hyperpyramids, their apexes radiating from a point in space that was all points in space simultaneously... And then it was simply gone.

The observers blinked, and shook their heads to clear them. Nothing remained to mark the Pyramid's former presence, except for a huge square depression in bare earth, perhaps ten centimetres deep.

Bruce dusted his massive metal hands, with a deafening clanging sound. "Well, that's that, I guess. Can't say I'm not happy it's over."

"All sorted out nicely," Ms Shan said. "And with no dangling loose ends."

58 Foreshadowing

Police were finally arriving at the South Hertling Super Centre but – perhaps by design? – they had arrived far too late. The non-combatants had long since deserted the place, soon followed by the battered survivors of the fracas. The police contented themselves with taking pictures and writing notes and making no move at all to clean anything up.

They checked some of the shops that stood open, but ignored the ones that were shut and locked. If they had opened the door of the Place O' Pets, they would have seen a single staff member who had remained at work, throughout the melee.

Captain Pete, the one-handed aquarium specialist, stood by an enormous fish tank, which was wired to a bank of home-made machinery which glowed gently and hummed.

"Yar, I knew I just had to wait," Captain Pete whispered. "The battle was bound to come – and with it a huge surge in time-energy. Enough to charge my equipment. Ha! Ha! Ha!" He laughed, as if each 'ha' was a separate word, and he was a Shakespearean actor.

The Captain opened a box, containing a dozen rocks of various sizes, all wrapped in cotton wool. He unwrapped them one by one, and dropped them in the tank.

"There, my beloved fossils!" he said. "Soon, you will live again!"

With that, he closed an enormous knife-switch on his machinery. Slow moving circles of blue energy pulsed towards the tank. Wom! Wom! Wom! Wom! The fossils in the bottom of the tank glowed, shifted, *moved*. Soon, they were all swimming in the fluorescing waters of the tank.

"Ah, my new friends!" the Captain exulted. "Welcome... to *life*!"

To be continued in *Trilobite Park*.

www.ingramcontent.com/pod-product-compliance
Lightning Source LLC
Chambersburg PA
CBHW020254120726
47904CB00001B/201